T0208977

Limbo, Mississippi

A Ghost Story

Douglas J. McGregor

iUniverse, Inc.
New York   Bloomington

Limbo, Mississippi
A Ghost Story

This is a work of fiction. All of the characters, names, incidents, organizations, and dialogue in this novel are either the products of the author's imagination or are used fictitiously.

iUniverse books may be ordered through booksellers or by contacting:

iUniverse
1663 Liberty Drive
Bloomington, IN 47403
www.iuniverse.com
1-800-Authors (1-800-288-4677)

ISBN: 978-1-4401-7925-9 (sc)
ISBN: 978-1-4401-7926-6 (ebk)

Printed in the United States of America

iUniverse rev. date: 9/25/2009

FOR STU

Gone but not forgotten

ACKNOWLEDGEMENTS

I would like to thank Dani Brassard for creating the cool cover; my son Travis, for appearing on the cover (not that I gave him much of a choice); my daughter, Ashley, for her help and support; and my wife and best friend, Barbara Botham, for her support, perceptive comments and editorial prowess.

PROLOGUE—2005

"Ya know Grandpa, attics are prime locations for ghosts."

I can't say exactly what I expected to talk about with my grandson that afternoon, but certainly I never dreamed we'd be discussing whether or not there were ghosts haunting my attic. Thus proving, I suppose, that you just never know what's dancing around in someone's noggin.

"Attics, graveyards and crossroads are where you're most likely to find them," he continued on as though he was an authority on the subject, pausing midway up the attic stairs. "And I've seen them too. I've seen the fightin' ghosts at the Squirrel Flats Cemetery. Grandma says ya knew those two ghosts in real life."

"Grandma talks too much."

"I'd like to hear the story about those two killers."

"Maybe next Halloween when I'm in the mood for a ghost story," I said, and with a flick of my hand, gestured for him to start climbing.

Ben didn't move. "Did anyone ever die in this house?"

Awe geez. I knew the answer cuz my Pa had built this farmhouse in the early 1920's and I had been born here and had lived here most of my life. But my grandson was a bit of a 'Nervous Norman' so telling him the truth might make him leap over me and run from the house, screaming.

"Well? Did anyone ever die here?"

"Why the heck are you so interested in ghosts anyway?"

"I told ya about my friend, right?"

"Which friend?"

"The one that died."

I nodded, and to make sure we were talking about the same friend, asked, "He was in the minors with you, right?"

ix

"That's him," Ben returned. "His nickname was Bogey. We played together for years. Me at shortstop, him at second base. We did 'hard time' together as he liked to say, ridin' the bus, goin' from one hick town to the other. Then in 04 we both got traded to different teams. And soon afterwards—"

"Can we discuss this once we're off these damn stairs?"

He turned abruptly and climbed the rickety old stairs to the attic hatch. I followed closely behind and heard him curse softy as he fiddled with the toggle bar holding the hatch in place.

"Ya believe me, don'tcha, Grandpa?" he asked suddenly, looking down at me. "About seein' the fightin' ghosts at Squirrel Flats? What were their names again?"

"Cole Conklin," I said. "Cole Conklin and Snake Richards."

"Snake? Really?"

"It's a nickname," I explained. "And yeah Ben, I believe you."

The tension in his cheeks relaxed some. "It was weeks after Bogey's funeral. I went back to the graveyard to lay some flowers at his grave. It was dusk, and that's when I saw them wrastlin' each other." He shrugged. "Why would they be fightin'?"

I knew the answer but stayed quiet cuz telling him would only make him ask further questions and the last thing I wanted to do was egg him on.

"I never ran so fast in my life," he continued. "Ya seen them, ain't ya?"

"Never in their ghostly form," I replied, realizing I was stretching the truth a tad. I had seen them after they had died. Heck, I had even spoken with them. But Ben didn't need to know that story cuz recanting that horrific tale to him would surely make him leap over me and run from the house, screaming.

The toggle bar holding the hatch in place squeaked hellishly as he worked it back. The lid popped gently up a quarter inch. He swung up the hatch, the hinges squealing like an excited five-year-old on the playground, making me wonder how long it had been since I was last up here. A year? Two years? Who knows? That's the problem with getting old, your memory fades—at least about some things.

Ben coughed, and with his free hand, waved away the dust cloud hovering in front of his face. Using his other hand, he unhooked the flashlight from his belt, turned it on and shone the beam up through the opening. A blizzard of snowflake size dust particles danced in the beam of light. I waited for him to climb up; instead he looked down at me.

"I knew something was wrong with Bogey before he died, Grandpa," he said sadly. "And I've seen him since his death. I've seen his ghost." He paused, allowing me to absorb that info, and then added, "Ya do believe me, don'tcha, Grandpa?"

"Yeah, I believe you. Cuz I've seen my share of ghosts." Which was the truth. "Now move."

He poked his head up through the opening and I half expected him to start screaming. Not cuz of seeing a ghost. No, I suspected we were ghost free. Yet, there might be something else waiting for him up there in the darkness. After all, a hot, closed up environment was a perfect recipe for an infestation of something creepy crawly.

Ben climbed up inside the attic and wrapped his knuckles on a crossbeam. "Ghosts? Ghosts? If there are any ghosts up here, don't fret, it's just me and my Grandpa."

"Thanks for announcing us," I muttered, and climbed up through the opening. He reached down, grabbed my arm and helped me up. I could have done it on my own, but hey, if he was willing to help, I was willing to let him. My eighty-five-year-old knees sure appreciated the gesture.

The attic was as hot as the beach at noon and as dark as a cave. It was stuffy with dust and stale air, making my old lungs work hard.

I unhooked the flashlight hanging from my belt, switched it on, and pointed the beam of light on the crossbeam directly above the hatch. The light switch was right where I remembered it was. Guess my memory hadn't faded as much as I'd thought it had. I reached over and flicked up the switch. The lone, dusty sixty-watt bare bulb came to life directly over our heads.

Right then, for the briefest of moments, I remembered a time back in the 1940's when I came up here and read by that dim light. I wondered if the book I had looked at was still up here. Probably. Unlessing Sally or one of our eight kids took it.

I glanced about at our attic treasures—or as I like to think of them, our garage sale fodder. Simply put, most of the stuff was junk. And the junk stretched off into the darkness in all directions from the hatch. It was a storeroom of old dusty furniture, stacked boxes, racks of clothes, tied up plastic bags, footlockers and spider webs.

"Eh, Grandpa," Ben muttered, looking as serious as a funeral director. "Is that all the light there is?"

"What were you expecting? Chandeliers?" I held up the flashlight. "We've got enough light."

"Yeah, but it ain't safe."

I assumed he was worried about the dangers of maneuvering around all the obstacles up here in such dim light. I assumed wrong.

"These shadows are no good." He pointed at the sixty-watt bulb. "This light throws harsh shadows. And I read all about harsh shadows."

I couldn't imagine a reason why anyone would read up about shadows, harsh or otherwise. A shadow, after all, is nothing more than a patch of shade. So what's there to read up about?

"Since Bogey's death I've been studyin' up on the supernatural and in one of the books I read there's a chapter on shadows. Like did ya know that if ya injure yer shadow ya could have problems?"

"I know I'm having problems with my grandson right now," I said with a raised brow and smile.

"No, really. It's true. Oh, and never stand where yer shadow falls on a coffin. If it does, it could get buried with the deceased."

My wife Sally and I had attended some old coot's funeral just last week and for the life of me I couldn't remember if my shadow had fallen on the lout's casket. I sure hoped not. If only I'd learned of this earlier.

"Oh, also, whenever yer around a campfire, if anyone's shadow appears to be headless, they'll surely die by the end of the year."

"Headless, huh? Well, that makes sense."

He looked at the floor. "Ya think I'm crazy, don'tcha?"

"Not at all," I said, feeling a might disappointed in myself for my flippant talk. "Why don't you tell me about your dead friend."

He groaned with reluctance, making it clear his feelings were still smarting.

I sat on the arm of an old sofa and motioned for him to speak. "I really wanna hear it. Sides, I need a moment to rest my weary bones before we start looking through stuff. So please—tell me."

"Well, like I was tellin' ya, we had gotten traded to different teams at the end of 04 and, like the old sayin', 'outta sight, outta mind'. Weeks went by without me thinkin' about him, and then, one day, I was at a bookstore, and reached for a book but pulled another book by accident off the shelf. And do ya know what the book was on?"

Since I wasn't psychic, I shrugged.

"It was a book on how to deliver a eulogy."

"It's a coincidence."

"I don't know," he muttered skeptically. "Maybe. But there's more weird stuff. See, the next day I was buyin' groceries and suddenly, outta nowhere, Bogey popped into my head. I couldn't think of anythin' else but him. The thought of him was burnin' in my head like a fever. So I raced home and called him. I didn't know what to expect, but he answered the phone as though nothin' was wrong. We talked for about a half hour. Nothing important, just regular stuff. Then he told me he'd call durin' the week and we'd go out. And do ya know somethin'? I knew as I hung up that I'd never talk to him again. I just knew it. And sure enough, couple days later his girlfriend called and said he had dropped dead."

"I've heard that the soul gives off a different vibration when the body is coming to a close. I guess you were sensitive enough to pick up on it."

"But I didn't even see him."

"I think we're all connected through the universe somehow," I said. "And the connection with him was too strong to ignore."

"What about the book on eulogies? Why did it just pop into my hand?"

"I don't rightly know, Ben. But I think you should chalk it up to coincidence." I motioned with the flashlight. "C'mon, let's find that baseball equipment you want."

He nodded glumly and started forward, weaving around old furniture. I followed closely, making sure to stay outta his shadow.

"After the funeral, I was watchin' TV and heard a noise on the patio," he went on. "So I looked out and there, sittin' on the picnic table was Bogey."

"You say anything to him?"

"Yeah, I spoke to him," he admitted. "After I got my nerves under control, that is. I opened the patio door and stood there. He was my friend so I knew he wouldn't harm me. Still, I didn't leave the house."

"He say anything?"

"He asked me if he was dead. I said 'yeah'. He looked sad. Then he waved and disappeared. I ain't seen him since." He turned to me. "Think he'll return?"

"Hard to say. But if I had to bet, I'd bet no. He just wanted to confirm he had passed over."

He nodded, walked forward and, resigned to leave the 'ghost' conversation at that, asked, "So what are we all a lookin' for? A box? A bag?"

"The equipment should be in a trunk with a gold handle…I think."

"I sure appreciate this, Grandpa. We ain't got funds at the Mission for baseball equipment and the kids sure wanna play."

"Anything to further the game," I said.

He cleared cobwebs away with the flashlight, moved aside a stack of cardboard boxes and crept forward. "I don't know how ya can find anythin' up here."

"Did your Grandma tell you to say that?"

He laughed, and for just an instant, the way the harsh light caught the side of his face, I thought he looked exactly like my Pa, who many people had said looked a lot like me. Ben had my red hair, blue eyes and freckles. He also had a bit of my baseball skills. He never made it to the majors like I had. He toiled in the minors for years, making an okay 'buck' for a man in his twenties, but once you reach your thirties you have to give up the dream of playing in the pros cuz there are just too many younger kids with blossoming talent to choose from. If you ain't made it by then, you ain't gonna make it. Youth is all the rage, right? So now he was working for the city of Goonberry Gulch, helping out the poor. It didn't pay much, but damn, it was honorable work.

He suddenly shushed me. "Did ya hear that?"

"Hear what?"

"I thought I heard a whisper."

"Just me breathing."

"I don't think so," he went on in a hush. "This was a whisper…a whisper with a groan. A voice callin' out to us."

We waited in silence but heard nothing. He was my grandson so I couldn't say anything too bad, but I was thinking it. "You're all on edge cuz of the stories we've been talking about."

"Naw." He shook his head. "It's cold up here. Do you feel it?"

He was right. We had walked into a cold section, though I didn't think there were any sinister overtones attached to it. No doubt we were in a draft. Probably if we looked hard enough we'd find a vent blowing in cold air.

"I feel a presence."

I didn't feel anything but the cold air.

"I think there's a spirit up here," he whispered. "A ghost."

"You're imaging things."

He turned in a slow circle, shinning his flashlight beam over everything. "Maybe this ghost has come to warn us, or tell us somethin'. Do ya have a Ouija board so we can ask it questions?"

"A Ouija board? Is that one of them boards where you push around some triangle to spell out words?"

He brightened up. "Yeah, do ya have one?"

"Are you kidding? Don't be talking about that around your Grandma. She thinks those things are the Devil's tools. Me too, for that matter."

"We need one, cuz I feel there's a spirit tryin' to communicate with us."

"If that's the case, the spirit is doing a lousy job."

As Ben went to refute that, a loud thud behind us made us jump. I nearly messed my pants as well, though I didn't tell him that.

He brushed by me, his flashlight beam shone on the floor.

"It's a book," he said suspiciously, walking toward it. "It's fallen open." He crouched beside it. "This must be the message."

"The book fell cuz we moved the box it was in. Gravity did the work—not a ghost."

He looked up at me. "All the boxes around here are taped, Grandpa."

"Must have been sitting on top."

He didn't argue the point but he rolled his eyes, making it clear he thought I was wrong. He shone the light on the book. "It's a book on the Confederacy."

My heart skipped a beat and I squeaked out a long "Ohhhhhhhhh."

"Does that mean anything to ya?"

"No," I lied, thinking back to that time in the 40's when I'd come up here to read. It seemed that same book was still here after all. It also seemed that same book wanted to be reread.

He shone the light on the page it had fallen open at. "It's a biography on a Major Breckinridge." He looked at me, slightly puzzled. "Isn't that the name of the hikin' trail in the woods?"

I swallowed hard. "Yeah, the trail is named after him."

"Does this Major Breckinridge mean anything to ya?"

"No…well, kinda." I heaved a sigh. "It's just a coincidence."

"What kind of coincidence?"

"The kind you don't talk about. Now do you want that equipment or not?"

"Grandpa, what does Major Breckinridge want with ya?"

"Nothing," I said, laughing nervously.

"I can tell it means somethin'."

"Listen," I said, thinking over how I should explain it to him. "A long time ago, I came up here, found the book you're now holding and read Breckinridge's bio."

"Wow, that freaky."

"It's just a coincidence, that's all. In fact, the book probably fell open to that page cuz I had pressed the book's spine at that spot as I was reading."

He thought about it for a moment. "Yeah…I guess."

"C'mon, let's find the equipment and get outta here."

He nodded, stepped over a long rectangular box that held an artificial Christmas tree, skirted around an old armchair covered with a white sheet and stopped beside a footlocker with a gold handle.

"Think this is it?"

I motioned for him to open it.

He crouched down and lifted the lid. Dust particles swirled about like snow in the wind, and waving them away, he leaned over and looked inside.

"Naw," he muttered a second later. "Nothin' in here but an old paintin'."

"It's probably one of your Grandma's masterpieces." Sally had gone through a painting phase in the mid nineties, and though I love the woman dearly, most of her artwork looked like it had been painted by the dog.

Ben laid his flashlight atop an old TV and lifted out the painting. I couldn't see the painting clearly cuz he was in the way but it looked like it was an 18 X 24 inch canvas.

"I don't think it's one of Grandma's," he informed. "It's a one-room schoolhouse in an empty field. There's a woman standin' by the door wavin' at children."

I suddenly felt weak in the knees.

"It's by a Betty Zuckerman." He turned to me. "I've heard that name before."

I cleared my throat. "Yeah, Betty was a legend in these parts when I was growing up. She won a gold medal for swimming in the 1924 Olympic games in Paris."

"Oh yeah? She sure had talent with the paintbrush." He stood and turned to me. "Is she still alive?"

I shook my head.

"How did ya end up with this?"

"She gave it to me. The woman in the painting is my Ma, your Great Grandma."

"Ya don't say." He paused then, shining the light on me. "Are ya okay?"

"Listen Ben, I think I know what's going on. I think I have to tell you my story...before it's too late."

He said nothing, staring at me, looking scared.

"The only person I ever told this story to is your Grandma, but I think you need to know it. So let's forget about the equipment for now and go downstairs."

"What story?"

"It happened a long time ago. When I was fifteen. It was summer time, and the year was 1944..."

PART ONE—1944

(1)

"I'm afraid."

Her Mississippi 'speak' was as thick as bog mud, and though I was a native son of the region I missed what she said and asked her to repeat it.

"Lord a-mercy, Johnny, I'm afraid," Nurse Bilodeau continued in a voice barely above a whisper. "Scared about what may happen to our town. And I'm scared about who I should tell. I don't want folks thinkin' I'm plum crazy. I don't wanna end up in the third floor nut-bin, strapped to a bed. That's why I wanted to sit in the last booth. Cuz here we can talk in private."

We could a sat pretty near anywhere in the diner and shouted at each other and still not have been heard cuz the diner was near empty. Aside from us tucked away in the last booth along the wall, there were only three others in the room, and two of them—the chain-smoking old gents sitting at a table by the door—probably couldn't hear well anyway. And as for Emma-Lou our waitress? Well, she was perched on a stool behind the counter listening to the war news pouring out from the Zenith radio. If the worry lines creased into her chubby cheeks and forehead was any indication, the news was plum bad. Like me, she had a vested interest in the war, and had confided in us when we arrived that she hadn't slept well in weeks cuz her brother, Rick, was fighting in the Pacific and hadn't written in a long while. She feared the worst. I knew how she felt.

"I hope I can confide in yuh, Johnny?" Nurse Bilodeau went on, her voice dark and gloomy like a doctor about to deliver bad news.

I shrugged. "I guess."

"And will yuh keep this to yourself?"

"I guess," I muttered, wondering who the heck she thought I might blab to. I only had one close friend, Sally. And she lived five miles from where I was staying at the hospital and her phone was broken so unless I came across a carrier pigeon, getting word to her would be quite a chore.

She sighed with relief. "Thank yuh. Talkin' to yuh is like talkin' to an adult cuz yer as smart as a whip cuz yuh got so much larnin on account of yer Ma's teachings. Yuh even talk like a big city slicker from up north. So I'm blessed to have yuh in my company. And if I don't tell someone about this I reckon my head may pop."

The thought of that made me grin cuz her head was the size of a peanut. In fact, she was a small woman, maybe a hundred pounds soaking wet, and no more than five feet tall. Though I ain't no judge of ages, I figured she was pushing sixty cuz her hair was as gray as a Rebel uniform and her face was heavily lined like the inside of a catcher's mitt.

"Now I don't mean to scare yuh none—"

"No offense, Nurse Bilodeau," I cut in sharply. "But there is nothing you can say that'll scare me. Cuz I'm already plum scared outta my head as it is. My Ma is dying, my Pa is missing in Europe and the bank is gonna take back our farm at the end of the summer. So I don't think I can be any more scared than I already am."

"I understand," she said with a nod, and picked up her coffee mug. Emma-Lou had filled the mug to the brim and a huge drop sloshed over the side and hit the paper placemat in front of Nurse Bilodeau, partially blotting out the smiling Goonberry Gulch Gopher in the center. The gopher was the diner's logo initially, but the town of Goonberry Gulch had adopted the gopher as its symbol and images of smiling gophers with huge teeth were plastered up all over town. Even my church-league baseball team was called The Gophers.

"I ain't been able to sleep well of late," she informed.

I knew how she felt cuz I was sleeping in a chair beside Ma's bed in a stuffy hospital room that smelled of sickness.

"And I've been havin' bad dreams. Real bad dreams."

"Maybe it's cuz of the war."

"I don't think that's it."

I waited for her to elaborate, but her pause ensued long, making the moment awkward, and forcing me to add, "Ma always got me a glass of warm milk whenever I had a nightmare."

"I don't think warm milk will do the trick this time," she revealed. "See Johnny, things are outta kilter. I keep seein' a town being destroyed." She shook her head at the thought. "I don't even know if it's Goonberry Gulch. It could be Possum Hollow or Squirrel Flats. But it's a town, and it gets totally flattened. And you're in the dream, Johnny."

"Me?"

She nodded. "Yer standin' next to a man dressed in black."

I cared little for the direction the conversation had suddenly taken and looked out the window. The western sky was orange and yellow; the streetlight across the street was glowing. No one was in sight.

"Maybe yer in my dreams cuz we've become so close over the last few weeks."

"Yeah, maybe," I muttered, wishing she would leave me outta her dreams.

"I know I shouldn't fret—they're just bad dreams, after all. Nightmares. But they seem so real. I wake up screamin'. And now I'm worried they may come true?"

"Do you have the 'gift'?"

"Of foresight?" she asked, and shook her head. "Not that I know of. At least I've never had it before."

"Then I wouldn't worry." I shrugged. "It's just like you said, they're bad dreams."

"What if I'm a-getting the 'gift'?"

I'd never heard of anyone acquiring the 'gift' so late in life, but I suppose there were exceptions.

"There's more," she went on. "Do yuh know what happened to Doc Rose?"

Everyone in town knew what happened to Doc Rose, and I nodded, cringing at the horror the poor man must have endured before dying. I wouldn't have wished the method of his demise on my worse enemy.

"I'll be truthful with yuh, Johnny, I'm afraid to use the outhouse at home. I try to wait until I get to work so I can use the indoor plumbin'. Cuz I don't wanna die like the Doc. Can yuh imagine? Goin' out to use the toilet, sittin' down with the newspaper and suddenly—crack! Yer fallin', fallin' into blackness, into a stink that is simply unimaginable. And then 'whoosh', yuh plunge into a sea of warm waste and start to sink." She shook her head at the thought. "And I'm like the Doc. I can't swim. Can yuh imagine drownin' in a sea of waste?" She shook her head. "Lord a-mercy."

Lord a-mercy, indeed. Though it was over ninety degrees in the diner, the thought made me shiver. It also killed my appetite. I gently placed my knife and fork on the table and pushed my plate aside. I'd eaten most of the meatloaf, but not the double scoop of mash potatoes or corn kernels. Maybe Emma-Lou would have a 'go' at the leftovers once we left.

"After the funeral last week I went and visited Doc Rose's widow. Now she's a bit of an odd one"—she twirled a horizontal finger beside her head to indicate the woman was nuts—"but she told me that when the Doc didn't return from the outhouse, she looked out the window and saw somethin' take him."

"Something? What do you mean? An animal?"

"Naw, weren't no animal. It was tall, gray creatures—monsters she called them. They walked away from the outhouse with him—or rather with his soul."

I grinned. "She's seeing things."

"That's what I thought at first," she returned. "But it awoke a memory in me—an awful memory."

"You don't believe in these gray monsters, do you?"

"I ain't sure. See, Doc Rose's widow ain't the first person to ever claim seein' these things."

"Oh?"

"My Pa—God rest his soul—seen them once too. He never told me about it, though, but at my Ma's funeral—heck, I was only a youngin of five or six at the time—I overheard him tellin' my uncle that he'd seen these gray things with Ma while he was out in the field. At first he thought he was seein' things, but it bothered him so much he went and checked on her and found her dead at the bottom of the stairs. She had tripped on the carpet, fell, and broke her neck." She shrugged. "I had plum forgotten about Pa's story until I spoke with Doc Rose's widow."

"There has to be an explanation. What could these creatures be?"

"Soul catchers," she returned at once. "When the body dies, they come and take the soul."

An unwanted smile spread across my face and, not wanting to bruise the woman's feelings, I casually looked out the window so she couldn't see it. The street had been empty before, but not now. A man in a white sailor's uniform stood under the streetlight, and though it had been awhile since I'd seen him, it looked a heckuva lot like Rick, Emma-Lou's brother. It appeared all her worrying was for naught, and I glanced at Emma-Lou for the briefest of moments, happy for her good fortune. When I turned back to the street, Rick was gone. But that was impossible. No one could disappear so quickly, and I inched up outta my seat, my face close to the window, craning my neck from side to side to see.

"What's wrong?" Nurse Bilodeau asked.

"I thought I saw someone."

"Who?" and she looked out the window as well.

I was afraid to speak openly incase I was wrong. The last thing I wanted to do was give Emma-Lou false hope. "Uh...I guess I'm seeing things."

"It's dusk," she said as though that explained everything. "It's harder to see at dusk."

It was as good an explanation as any and I settled back in the seat.

"Anyway Johnny, as I was a-saying, there is more to Goonberry Gulch than meets the eye."

"More? What do you mean?"

"My Pa always referred to the Gulch as the center of all weirdness."

"Really? I don't think the Gulch is any weirder than Possum Hollow or Squirrel Flats."

"Pa claimed there was a ghost town a-yonder in our woods. He weren't specific, mind you, at least not around me, but he said this place gave off an evil vibration, and cuz of this vibration, weird things were happenin' in town and people were goin' loco." She gestured with a hand in the general direction of the hospital. "I think that's why there are so many crazy people locked up in the third floor nut-bin."

I wanted to talk about something else but since she seemed so committed to the subject at hand I threw in my two cents. "Nurse Bilodeau, some folks just ain't born with a good head on their shoulders."

"Yer right," she said. "Some folks are born that way and some folks turn that way cuz of moonshine or disease, but I think it's more than

(2)

I awoke with a start and sat up in the chair, a stabbing pain in my back from sleeping in such an awkward position. The pain, I knew, would go away once I walked around and warmed up the muscles. The challenge now, though, was getting outta the chair. Luckily, I was fifteen, not fifty.

I stood, stretched, gritting my teeth at the sharp, stabbing pain in my back and thought about last night's visit to the Goonberry Gulch Diner. The meatloaf was sub par; the conversation was, if nothing else, entertaining to the point of being comical. Gray things stealing souls? Evil vibrations? A ghost town in the woods? Oh please. It was downright fiction. Something you'd read in a Washington Irving novel. What happened as we left, however, was anything but fiction, or comical. In fact, it was downright gut-wrenching and sad enough to make the most coldhearted person weep.

As we had stood at the counter paying the check and chatting with Emma-Lou, the door opened and a telegraph deliveryman entered holding an envelope. Emma-Lou's face went ashen.

"Is the telegraph for me?" she managed over trembling lips.

It was indeed for her and, to quote Nurse Bilodeau, "Lord a-mercy". The message (read aloud by Emma-Lou) had all the warmth and sympathy as a punch in the stomach. It simply stated that her brother had been killed in combat. Too bad, so sad. Thanks for helping out the war effort. End of story.

As for the whys and wherefores of Rick's demise? Uncle Sam failed to include any details, leaving Emma-Lou with a head full a questions to go along with sorrow.

I had never seen someone cry so hard, and as Nurse Bilodeau hugged the poor, crying woman, I stared out the window at the empty street and wondered who I had seen standing under the streetlight.

Obviously, it had not been Rick. Still, if I had been in open court I would have sworn on a stack of Bibles it was him. Of course, for that to be true it meant I had seen…

"I don't believe in ghosts?" I whispered. "Ghosts aren't real."

Course, just cuz I didn't believe in ghosts didn't mean they didn't exist. Luckily, I had a whole lotta other problems this morning to occupy my thoughts.

I approached the bed, stepping around the metal stand on wheels holding a bottle of clear liquid which dripped through a rubber tube into Ma's arm, and stared down at her. She was curled up in the fetus position, shriveled as a prune and comatose as a drunk on a Sunday morning. She hadn't opened her eyes in about a week, and though I had built up a great deal of denial over the last few months, even I suspected I'd never see her open her eyes again.

Her breathing sputtered now like a fuel-starved engine and Nurse Bilodeau had warned me that when this happened the end was near.

Well, if nothing else, at least I wouldn't be left wondering how she had died.

I leaned over and pulled the bed sheet up to Ma's chin. The skin on her face had shrunk like a sponge in the sun, making her eyes bulge like those of a gold fish. Her eyelids were parted ever so slightly and encrusted with yellow sleep. Her lips, ridged with dry spit, were drawn back tautly, exposing teeth caked in a dull film. Death, in this case, was ugly—as ugly as ugly gets.

Every morning I would kiss her cheek and as I bent over to do so now I caught a nose full of vile, sick rot. I gagged, my stomach twisting in a knot. Sweat broke out on my forehead and my gore rose. I backed away, silently praying that last night's meatloaf would not end up all over the floor.

But it was coming—chewed and half digested, it moved with the force of a run-a-way locomotive. In other words: unstoppable.

I ran to the room's lone window, pressed my nose against the rusted screen and sucked up the early morning air, still praying my meatloaf would not make an encore. My stomach did a slow somersault and I bent over and retched. I waited for the steaming mess to shoot out, but—thank God—nothing came up. How's that for a small miracle?

Eventually my stomach settled and the sweat on my forehead cooled and dried up. Before long, I straightened up and looked through the screen at the world beyond this hospital room. The sun peaked over the horizon, throwing a soft glow over the crushed-stone parking lot one floor below where I stood. The lot was near empty cuz the graveyard shift was small and the dayshift was still an hour off.

I saw a car shrouded in a whirlwind of dust approaching. The road should have been blacktop by now. If not for the Germans and Japanese I suppose it would have been. But thanks to those two dastardly countries, manpower and provisions were in short supply.

A black Ford coupe entered the parking lot and came to a stop beside Nurse Bilodeau's hailstone dented station wagon. Sheriff Nibbs sat behind the wheel with a tanned elbow cocked out the window. I could see a toothpick clamped tightly between his teeth. He never went anywhere without one. It was his security blanket; either that or he was part beaver.

He rolled out from behind the wheel, his saddlebags of good living jiggling like Ma's chocolate pudding and paused by the open door, an odd look on his face. Then he broke wind so loud I heard it on the second floor. It came out in two loud, long, trumpet blasts, and his face relaxed as the wet sounding rips drew to a close. He sighed, sniffed the air like a hound dog and flapped the seat of his britches to bang out the foul air. I smiled in spite of my troubles.

I watched him waddle across the parking lot, his belly swaying like a cow's udder, and disappear inside. His early arrival was routine, for his brother-in-law worked in the kitchen and fed him free food and coffee.

He had paid us a visit shortly after Ma was admitted to the hospital. She had been in her right mind then and had expressed her concern over what would happen to me if she died. Sheriff Nibbs had turned on his southern charm and assured her all would be fine.

"Don't fret none," he had said, his voice smooth as a baby's behind. "I'll call the army base in Biloxi. Sure, there's a heckuva lot of confusion over there in Europe now with our boys landing in France last month. But surely somebody must know where Billy is at. Once they hear of yer hardship, they'll discharge him at once. After all, somebody has to take care of the boy. So leave it to me. I'll get back to yuh."

So far he hadn't gotten back to us.

"Johnny…"

I turned from the window and damn near fainted. Ma was sitting up and her eyes were open.

"Johnny, come 'ere dear."

I hurried to her, making a conscious effort to breathe through my mouth, and took hold of her cold, weak hand. "Ma…are you okay?"

With a hollow sigh, she settled her head back down onto the pillow. "Have you heard from your father?"

I considered lying. But how could I lie to Ma?

"No," I returned sadly.

She closed her eyes, and small crumbs of yellow sleep rolled down her cheeks. "Okay," she said quietly. "When he does get home, tell him I love him."

I felt the sting of hot tears at the back of my eyes.

"Oh, and Johnny, use your talent."

"My talent?"

"You're gonna have to use your talent before this is over."

"Before what is over?"

She opened her eyes, and in the volume of a mouse's squeak, managed, "I love you." She then closed her eyes and was still.

"Ma…Ma…Ma…"

I stared into her still face, my thoughts frozen in shock. Tears welled up in my eyes. This can't be happening. It just can't. Right? She's just asleep. She ain't dead. She can't be dead. I refuse to believe that she's gone.

With tears rolling down my face, I groped for her wrist and felt for a pulse. I found no trace of a throb, weak or otherwise. It was as though I was holding a cold, lifeless fish. Surely I was doing this wrong. Surely she still had a pulse. I just couldn't find it. Nurse Bilodeau would find it. And if not her, then some smart doctor would find it and assure me Ma was still alive. Cuz she had to be alive. She just had to be, right?

As that question floated in my head, my denial fell apart like a sandcastle in the wind and I cried so hard all I could see was a mishmash of runny colors. I backed away from the bed and hid my face in the corner of the room, wondering what I would do now.

Sally came to mind at once. She lived across the road from us, and we'd been friends for as long as I could remember, and right then, I needed her more than anything in the world. I wanted to call her but the telephone at her grandfather's house was out of service cuz of last week's storm, and would probably stay that way for quite sometime cuz most of the telephone company's employees were off fighting Hitler or the Japanese equivalent. So if I wanted to talk to her, I was gonna have to go to her.

Suddenly that seemed like a real good idea. I could use the exercise and fresh air.

But before I went anywhere I had to find Nurse Bilodeau and tell her what had happened. And as I turned to leave, I saw something move out the corner of my eye. I turned back, and though my vision was blurry with tears, I saw something that stopped my train of thought dead in its tracks.

"I'm seeing things," I muttered, and blinked rapidly to clear my vision.

The blinking worked. In fact, it worked too well. I saw them clearly now—too damn clearly. They were gray, hairless, stick-figure thin and tall. They were as naked as a new born babe but were void of gender parts—in other words, they were doll-like in the crotch. Their eyes were large and pink and their mouths were bitter, straight lines. There were four of them, all gathered around Ma's bed, staring down at her like worried doctors.

"W-what do you want?" I said, forcing the words out over a constricted throat.

They ignored me.

I thought of Nurse Bilodeau's dead father then, and of Doc Rose's widow. I thought of Emma-Lou. Had these gray things come for Rick?

They reached down then and pulled on Ma's body as though it was taffy.

I tried to scream, but all that came out was a long sighing "Uhhhhhhhhhh."

Finally, I managed, "Leave her alone. Leave her—" Before I could finish the sentence the room began to spin and I spun with it, and then everything went black. Maybe it was for the best.

(3)

I jerked awake, my eyes snapping open like a runaway window blind, and sat up as bolts of terror zapped me. Escape was all I could think about and I was already crawling toward the door when I realized those gray creatures were gone, gone as if they were never there. Unfortunately, the memory of them had stained my brain like Indian ink. Still, thankfully, a small (mighty small) measure of denial assured me I had imagined them. It was the only explanation that made sense.

With my heart still pounding, I climbed to my feet and crept toward Ma's bed. Ma was still there—well, at least her body—and if a Bible had been handy, I would a laid my right hand on it and swore the position of her body hadn't moved since I'd checked her pulse.

And how long ago had I done that? A better question might have been: how long did my fainting spell last?

I couldn't say for sure, but it felt like time hadn't skipped that far ahead. Perhaps only a couple of minutes, maybe less, which made me wonder how long does it take to steal a soul?

As the question danced around in my head like an ugly troll with two left feet, my denial swelled. Along with assuring me I had imagined the whole thing, it also provided a reasonable explanation for what I had imagined. See, it stood to reason that the shock of seeing Ma die had given my brain a good old kick, and cuz Nurse Bilodeau had talked last night about gray creatures stealing souls, it only made sense that I would imagine seeing them. If she had said unicorns were stealing souls, I would have imagined seeing them beside Ma's bed instead.

What I had to do now was accept that Ma was gone and move on and forget all about these gray soul-stealing creatures. It was that simple, and thinking on it, thinking that better times surely lay ahead, gave me a small measure of relief.

The feeling, though, was short lived. Mighty short lived, for a few seconds later my brain got mighty crowded.

We all have an inner voice, of course, and my inner voice was working just fine. The problem was, along with my own inner voice was the sound of buzzing of flies. It was a soft, consistent sound, and though I knew the buzzing was coming from inside my head, I looked about the room for the flies I knew weren't there.

Then, suddenly, along with the buzzing, a voice weaved its way into the mix. *"Time to leave, Southpaw."*

The voice didn't belong to me. The voice was old and as smooth as velvet; the timbre loose like watery oatmeal with just a hint of Mississippi speak. The voice knew my nickname, which was almost as scary as hearing a voice to start with.

"C'mon Southpaw, get a hold of yuh-self. Make for the woods."

"This can't be happening," I said aloud.

"It is, Southpaw—now git."

Had I gone plum crazy? And for a few seconds I pictured myself wearing a straightjacket and being led up to the nut-bin on the third floor.

"If yuh don't leave now, Sheriff Nibbs is gonna get yuh. Do yuh wanna stay in an orphanage?"

The part about the 'orphanage' scared me right down to my toes. Of course Sheriff Nibbs would have to put me in an orphanage. I was a minor with no relatives, and why hadn't I thought of this earlier? My damn denial was to blame, I suppose. Now that it was out in the open, I was plum terrified. Like the voice said, I had to get outta this hospital and make for the woods.

I darted to the door, and as I reached for the doorknob, it started to turn. A bolt of fear burned through me. Was it Sheriff Nibbs? Had he come for me already?

The door opened and Nurse Bilodeau stood on the threshold. "Johnny, my shift is about done so I'll be heading home now. Is there—" She held up abruptly. "Johnny? Is yer Ma…"

I swallowed hard. "I think she's gone."

"Oh, Lord a-mercy," She muttered, and skirted by me and over to the bed. She checked Ma's pulse, first the wrist, than the neck. Then she turned to me, tears rolling down her cheeks. "I'm so sorry," she managed, choking up. "I'm sorry for yer loss. I thought the world of yer mother." She hurried over and hugged me hard. Then she stepped back, sizing me up, her red-faced grief subsiding slowly. "Yuh should sit. Yuh don't look well."

"I'm okay," I said, which was the truth. Physically, I felt fine. Mentally? Well, that was another story. Are you suppose to see gray creatures and hear voices after a love one dies?

"Is there anybody yuh want me to call?"

"My Pa."

Her cheeks puckered sourly and she lowered her gaze. "Yes, I'm sorry about that." She gave my hand a reassuring squeeze. "What about Sally? Do yuh want me to call her? Maybe the Pastor can drive her over. He should be alerted anyways. Yer Ma, after all, was part of his flock."

I shrugged grimly. "The Dickerson's phone ain't working since the storm."

"That's right," she said, nodding. "Yuh mentioned that last night at dinner." She glanced at the clock above the door. "I saw Sheriff Nibbs a few minutes ago. I'm sure he's still here. I'll ask him to drive yuh over to the Dickerson's."

"I'd rather walk."

Concern swallowed up the last of her grief. "Uh, I think I'll find the Sheriff and the three of us should sit a spell."

Since I didn't plan to be here, I simply nodded.

"Oh good," she said with relief, and unclipped the chart hanging at the foot of Ma's bed. She pulled a pencil out from behind her ear, and after glancing at the clock again, scribbled on the chart.

"What are you writing?"

"The particulars. Time. Date. Yuh know, so the doctor can fill out a death certificate." She finished scribbling, clipped the chart back on the bed frame and turned to me. "Johnny, it's warm as yuh know. So we're gonna hafta move her to the basement as soon as possible."

"Can I have a minute to say goodbye?"

She nodded, and with fresh tears spilling down her face, hurried from the room.

The voice and the sound of buzzing flies returned at once. *"Yuh gotta get outta there—Now!"*

Ignoring the voice, I unclipped the chart and read what was written:

Time of death: 6:47 am. August 1st, 1944

Nurse Bilodeau's name was signed at the bottom. It was all a might neat and tidy for something as messy as a cancer death. I decided if she could write something, I could write something too. Since I had no pencil, I dragged Ma's purse from beneath the bed and, finding no fountain pen or pencil, plucked up a tube of lipstick. I drew a large heart on the chart, and inside the heart, wrote:

Love You Ma. Johnny. XOXOXO

With tears streaming down my face, I dropped the lipstick back in Ma's purse and hurried to the door.

Use my talent, huh? I thought. *Okay Ma, whatever you say.*

(4)

At the bottom of the stairs, sunshine slanted in through the rectangular slab of glass in the door, highlighting the way to freedom. In a few steps I'd be outside and home free. Nothing could stop me now.

"Ease up there, boy," Sheriff Nibbs boomed.

I stopped and looked up at him, trying to work up the nerve to run. Before I could though, he lumbered down the stairs like a charging bull and clamped his bear-like hand on my shoulder.

"Where do yuh think yer a goin', boy?" he asked, his Mississippi speak thick as molasses.

His fat face was sweaty and nicked in several spots from shaving. The nick beneath his nose was partly concealed by a tangled mass of nose hair. He was a tall brute, way taller than me, and way heavier too. Three hundred pounds at least. Fat men sweat heavily in the heat, and the underarms of his beige sheriff shirt was stained wet with rank smelling BO.

"Are yuh deaf, boy? I asked yuh a question."

"I wanted to get some fresh air," I explained. "My Ma just passed and—"

"I know about yer Ma," he said with a hint of sympathy. "But yer fresh air can wait cuz we gotta jaw. So yuh come up here."

He pointed up the stairs and, seeing no way to escape, I walked beside him to the second floor corridor. Once there, he thrust a chubby digit at an empty bench by the wall. I sat beside an armrest; Nibbs plunked his massive bulk down beside me. The bench's wooden slates groaned under his weight but remained intact—the result, no doubt, of superior workmanship.

"I'm sorry about yer Ma," he began. "She was a good woman. Taught both my kids. And I like yer Pa a lot too. We grew up together. But he's a missin' and…"

"He ain't dead," I yelped.

"Didn't say he was, boy. I just said he was a missin.'"

"Did you hear anything?" I asked. "You told Ma and I that you were gonna call the army base at Biloxi."

"I called," he returned, chewing nervously on his toothpick. "And they ain't got back to me." He sighed as though talking to me was a strain; I suppose, in a way, it was. "See, it's a damn mess in France. Lots of our boys are dead and they're in so many pieces it's gonna take a while to figure out who's who."

"He ain't dead."

"I hope yer right, boy. But dead or alive, he ain't here to take care of yuh. And since yuh ain't got no kin—"

"I can take care of myself. I've been doing it since Ma got sick."

"Listen boy, yer underage. So yuh ain't got a choice." He shook his head. "Hells bells, even if I wanted to look the other way, Mayor Valentine would have my badge if he found out I let a minor stay by himself. Sorry boy, I ain't got a choice, I gotta take yuh to the orphanage in Vicksburg."

"Please. Just let me stay at home until you hear from the army base."

"Can't," he returned gruffly. "Sides, in thirty days the bank is gonna foreclose on yer family's spread. I've already got the eviction notice on my desk."

"Let me stay there till then. Maybe Pa will be back by then."

"Yer a dreamin', boy," he said, shaking his head. "Sorry. Yer next stop is the orphanage."

Clutching at ideas, I said, "What about Sally? Her grandfather, the Pastor, will let me stay at his place. He owes us. We gave him all our livestock." Actually, there hadn't been all that much livestock to give cuz the farm had gone downhill since Pa went off to war. Still, I figured we'd given him enough so he could keep me for awhile.

Nibbs shifted uncomfortably on the bench. "Uh, here's the thing, boy. I spoke to the Pastor Dickerson yesterday. See, Nurse Bilodeau has been updatin' me on yer Ma's condition and told me the other day that yer Ma would most likely be gone this week. So I asked the Pastor if he would take yuh in." He paused, cleared his throat, and sighing, looked at the floor in shame. "Sorry. He told me he couldn't keep yuh. Or wouldn't. I can't say why exactly, but I got the impression he don't give a dried-apple damn for yuh." He shrugged. "I know he never cared much for yer Pa, and I know he ain't so happy about yuh being cozy with his granddaughter. So maybe that's why he don't wanna keep yuh."

A heavy weight of desperation settled over me like a thick, wet blanket and I felt the sting of tears again. Then the flies buzzing in my head returned and the voice of the old man spoke up, *Bide yer time, Southpaw. Bide yer time.*

"It ain't a bad place where yer a goin'," Nibbs went on. "I hear the orphanage has a ball field. Yuh'll be able to play baseball again. Yuh sure liked doin' that."

"I don't wanna play anymore. I just wanna go home."

He shook his head and chewed on his toothpick. "I'm actually doin' yuh a favor, boy," he continued. "Maybe I'm savin' yer life. Cuz the Conklin Gang has been spotted in these parts. Yuh know about the Conklin Gang, right?"

"I know Cole Conklin. Ma taught him. And I know he wouldn't hurt me."

Nibbs snorted out a laugh. "Yuh don't think so, huh? He's turned into a rabid-dog killer. He's killed over twenty people with his straight razor."

"I can't believe he's in these parts," I said, more to myself than the sheriff. "Why would he come back here? Everybody knows him. He'd be recognized for sure."

"Hard to say, boy," Nibbs said. "The G-men figure he's got a friend or two in these parts that's willin' to hide him and his gang."

He went to say more, but Nurse Bilodeau leaned over the nurse's station wooden counter and held out the telephone receiver to him. "It's for yuh, Sheriff. Deputy Mumbles needs yuh."

Nibbs sighed. "Hells bells, Mumbles probably can't find his gol darn car keys again." He struggled to his feet, his knees cracking under his weight. "As for yuh boy, don't move a muscle. I'll be back."

As Nibbs waddled off to the nurse's station, I climbed to my feet, ready to run. Then, the voice in my head returned. *Not yet. Soon. But not yet.*

I sat back down an instant before Nibbs turned and looked at me. Seeing me still seated on the bench, he faced Nurse Bilodeau, took the receiver from her and, leaning his massive girth on the counter, put the phone to his ear.

"Hells bells, Mumbles, I'm a might busy now. What's the problem?" He fell silent, listening. A moment later, he said, "Ah hell, those no'count Valentine boys ain't our problem. They're the Army's problem." He paused. "Yeah, yeah, I'll talk to the Mayor about it." He listened some more and then said, "I gotta run the McGrath boy over to the Vicksburg Orphanage so yer gonna have to hold off goin' to Squirrel Flats. I know yuh wanna help search, but I need yuh to be here till I get back."

He was talking about the Squirrel Flats ammunition explosion. I had heard a welding torch had set off a bomb destined for Hitler. The resulting blast had set off other bombs and the entire structure had come down in a fireball. Hundreds were dead. Hundreds were injured. Hundreds were still missing beneath the rubble.

"Yeah," Nibbs went on. "The poor woman passed this mornin'. Damn shame."

"*Now Southpaw,*" the voice spoke up. "*Time to run.*"

As Nibbs continued to yammer on to Deputy Mumbles, I rose to my feet. Nurse Bilodeau and I locked eyes. Her face was ridged with concern, but then, after a few seconds, she smiled, nodded and motioned with a flick of her hand for me to get going.

I smiled at her and took off running.

(5)

I took the stairs two at a time, sprinted across the bottom landing and, with as much force as I could muster, slammed shoulder first into the door. It flew open as though a bomb had been set off next to it, and I ran outside. It was hot and sunny and about as beautiful as a summer morning can get.

Without looking back, I raced across the gravel parking lot, darting between parked cars, my Keds making loud crunching sounds like pigs chewing on feed. I spotted a beaten-down path in the narrow patch of scrub grass that ran between the parking lot and the forest and headed to it. As I hit the path, Sheriff Nibbs made it outside.

"STOP! STOP MCGRATH! STOP OR I'LL SHOOT!"

I stopped and turned. Sure enough, Sheriff Nibbs stood in the parking lot about fifty yards away holding his pistol at his side. I heaved a sigh, resigned to give up, and was about to start back when I realized how laughable his threat was. He couldn't shoot me. At least he couldn't shoot me and get away with it. I was an innocent, lily-white boy, who had just lost his Ma. Even Nibbs was smart enough to know his pistol was nothing more now than a noise maker.

I yelled out, "I'll be back", and then darted down the path. Nibbs let out a blood curdling scream and threatened once again to shoot me.

I figured he would fire off a warning shot, but it never happened; probably cuz there were plenty of witnesses watching from the windows of the hospital, and people tend to frown at gunplay involving innocent, unarmed fifteen-year-olds. He did, however, continue to make idle threats in a murderous tone—not that I listened, or cared.

I ran, and kept running straight into the woods. The path was narrow and crooked as a drunk's walk and froth with rocks, thick roots, and low hanging branches. Overhead, the canopy was lush green, so thick in spots it blocked out a good portion of the sun, casting the area in deep, gray shadows. It was hot enough to fry eggs on a rock and the humidity was thick enough to cut, but it seemed cooler here cuz of the overhead shade. The smell of pine and moist soil and green vegetation was a welcome change from the medical odors assaulting my senses in the hospital.

I kept up a relatively fast pace cuz I was worried Nibbs might follow me into the woods. But after about ten minutes of pushing myself hard, I slowed to a walk. Fat men like Nibbs generally can't run for long, especially in the heat, so I felt I was safe. For now anyway.

I played often in these woods, but this section was foreign to me. So I was in virgin territory, but not worried in the least cuz Pa had taught me a lot about how to tell direction in the woods by the position of the sun. Sides, I knew I had come from the east, and knowing that was half the battle. So even though the path was crooked, I felt I was still heading in a westerly direction. I needed to find a path that ran north, cuz north would take me home. North would take me to Sally.

As I walked I thought, and as many of you know, thinking too much can lead to trouble and before long my emotions got the better of me. I cried for Ma and Pa. I cried cuz the bank was gonna take our farm. I cried cuz Nibbs wanted to put me in an orphanage. And I cried even worse cuz the Pastor didn't want me to live in his house. That stung worst of all, and though I wasn't the vengeful type, I tilled vengeful soil over in my head. I just couldn't help myself. And as these wicked thoughts of revenge swirled about, I realized something—something real important. I couldn't go home. Not yet anyway.

Nibbs would most likely be waiting there for me. And if he was busy, no doubt the Pastor would be keeping an eye out for me. Granted, the Pastor's phone was outta order, but he had plenty of Mexican farmhands working for him that he could easily send to find the Sheriff. So for now anyway, I couldn't go home, and if I couldn't go home, where could I go?

The answer suddenly floated to the top of my thoughts like a dead fish: *Biloxi. I could go to Biloxi. I could go to the army base in Biloxi and ask if they knew where my Pa was at.*

Sheriff Nibbs claimed to have called the base, but what if he hadn't? What if it had slipped his mind? Sure, I knew he liked Ma and Pa a lot, and would do everything in his power to help them, but I always thought he was a bit of a bumbling buffoon and maybe he got busy and had forgotten to call. It happens.

Sides, even if he had called and was waiting to hear back from them like he claimed, I felt that something as important as this deserved a personal visit. Ma and Pa always taught me that if you want something done right, do it yourself. After all, it's easy to ignore a phone call, but a might hard to ignore a person, especially if that person is a teenager and standing in plain view, crying.

So I had a plan. I would go to Biloxi. But how would I get there?

I figured I was about two hundred miles as the crow flies to Biloxi. If I walked there, it would take a week. A lot of folks were hopping freight trains these days, so why not me? The problem was the train to Biloxi ran through Squirrel Flats, which was about twenty miles from where I was. It was an option, but not much of one cuz it still meant a day's walk. Then I thought about thumbing. Surely some motorist would find it in their heart to give a young man a lift on such a hot day, and if I got lucky, I might get a ride right to the front gate of the army base. The down side to thumbing, of course, was I'd have to stand out in the open on the side of the road, and thus, would be easy prey if Nibbs or Deputy Mumbles came along.

Still, I figured it was worth the risk. After all, I had no where else to go.

So I would thumb to Biloxi.

Yahoo. I had a plan and a place to go. Things were looking up.

Sort of.

(6)

Job number one was to find a way outta these woods.

I picked up the pace, hoping to find a path that led south. South would lead me to the town of Goonberry Gulch. Once I got there, I planned to make my way across town to the highway that ran to Biloxi. Once there, I'd be home free—at least I hoped.

As I walked, I daydreamed about Ma and Pa, about all the good times we shared. It made me sad, but not enough to cry. Who knows? Maybe I was all cried out by this point.

Time wore on and I eventually came to where the path split. Though both routes still meandered in a basic westerly direction, I followed the path that meandered more to the south. A short time later, the path came to an abrupt end at a rusted wire fence. Beyond the fence was a dirt field. I had obviously come to a farm, and where there was a farm there would surely be a road. My luck was improving…maybe.

At the fence, I looked out at acre after acre of dirt and weeds that stretched off to the horizon. The place had an abandoned feel to it. I had never visited a ghost town, but figured it would give off the same sort a feeling. Not that I believed in ghosts. I didn't. It was just that this place made me think of them.

And as I was thinking about that, another thought popped into my head, making me wonder if I should hop the fence—and not cuz I feared about running into ghosts. It was getting an ass-full of buckshot that concerned me.

See, this was Goonberry Gulch, Mississippi, and folks around here take a dim view of two things in particular: Yankees and trespassers. I didn't have to worry about the former. I was a southern gentleman, born and raised in these parts. But if a farmer caught me on his property without an invite, it wouldn't matter if I was carrying a Confederate flag and whistling 'Dixie'. I'd most likely get an ass-full of teeth from his hound or buckshot from his rifle. And if the farmer had a working phone, I might have a three hundred pound problem with a badge to contend with too.

Still, I couldn't just stand here all day.

So I hopped the fence and started walking, hoping I'd find a public road before the farmer found me. The sun-baked dirt was hard as cement so walking was easy. Except now I was out in the open and had no hat. Back in '44—though we didn't know it at the time—we had ozone. Still, within minutes, the top of my head was oven-hot, and being a redhead, I was prone to 'sun-stroke'. So I slid off the straps on my overalls, took off my t-shirt and fashioned the shirt into a hat, slipping it onto my head. I suppose I looked stupid. Thankfully no one was around to laugh.

It was right about then that I noticed something mighty peculiar. See, the sun was damn near overhead which meant it was close to noon. But that couldn't be. Ma had died between six-thirty and seven. I had spoken to Sheriff Nibbs shortly after that, a conversation that lasted maybe five minutes. Then I had fled into the woods and had walked for maybe an hour, an hour and a half at most. So it should have been no later than nine o'clock. Maybe nine-thirty. So where the heck had the last three hours gone?

It was a question I really didn't wanna think about but thought about anyways and grew more scared with each passing minute.

One thing for sure, whoever owned this field owned one heckuva large spread cuz it just kept stretching off to the horizon. From what I understood, the Pastor, Sally's grandfather, owned the largest spread in this area, but as I trudged along in this wasteland of a field, I was starting to have my doubts.

I kept checking the position of the sun. It didn't look like it was moving, which, of course, was impossible. Still, I'd swear on a stack of Bibles the sun was stuck in position.

Soon a feeling of bone deep isolation settled over me. I stopped and turned in a slow circle. The dirt field stretched out to the horizon in every direction. It was as if I was lost in an ocean of dirt. Though the idea was laughable, I felt I was no longer in Mississippi. I didn't think I was in Louisiana either, or anywhere in the good old US of A.

25

The thought was crazy, sure, but still I thought it.

Time ticked on and I kept walking. My desperation grew. I was on the verge of tears now. No matter what I told myself, I was convinced I had stumbled into an endless no-man's land. Such things weren't possible, but I couldn't convince myself of it. My paranoia ran amuck. And so I ran with it. And I ran and ran and kept running until I was completely winded and so soaked in sweat it was as though I had just come outta the Goonberry River. I finally fell to my knees, totally exhausted and breathing hard. And that's when I saw it—a barn. It was far off in the distance, on the edge of the horizon, but there it was.

Relief washed over me, and I climbed to my feet, feeling silly for the way I had thought and acted. But I wouldn't feel silly for long.

(7)

By the time I reached the barn, I was bone-weary and thirsty as a desert snake. Water was the only thing I could think of…well, that who's property I was on. An ass-full of buckshot takes priority over a drink of water any day.

I came up behind the barn, stepped over a mound of dirt that looked a lot like a grave, crept to the corner and took a look around. Twenty feet ahead, a tractor without tires sat up on wooden blocks, its rims flecked with rust. If I had to guess, I'd guess the tractor hadn't done any plowing in quite sometime. Beyond the tractor, a rusted-out potato planter lay on its side in a bed of weeds. Again, if I had to guess, I'd guess no one had planted potatoes with it in quite sometime. In fact, if I had to guess, I'd guess no one had been around here in quite sometime.

Of course, looks can be deceiving, so I kept my guard up and dashed to the tractor, crouching down beside it. From here I could see a two-story, white clapboard farmhouse that needed a month worth of repairs and a good coat of paint. It was damn spooky looking and all I wanted to do was put as much distance between me and it as I could. But first I needed a drink.

The water pump and wooden trough sat between the barn and the farmhouse on the edge of a small patch of grass and weeds. The pump looked like the one at home except this pump was caked in rust. I didn't care. A little rust never hurt anyone.

As I straightened up to dash to the pump, a whisper of a breeze kicked up a cloud of swirling dirt in front of me and made the weeds sway, stretching my already taut nerves tighter. On the heels of the wind gust I heard a bump, and paused, looking about like a paranoid gazelle in a lion's den. I wanted to believe it was only the wind knocking something over, but I just couldn't convince myself of that. My dry throat and mouth got the better of me, though, and I raced to the pump.

The trough was empty except for some dried leaves and thick layers of abandoned spider webs. I pulled down on the pump handle. The squeaking protest of rusted metal rubbing on rusted metal hurt my ears. I kept priming though, working the handle up and down, praying the squeak would fade away. It didn't, and an eerie thought echoed through my head: *Loud enough to wake the dead.*

Common sense told me to stay put, to keep priming the pump, cuz there was no other water around for miles. Still, my nerves screamed at me to run. I fought the feeling best I could and my inner voice screamed, *C'mon, c'mon, work…*

Sure enough, a moment later, I heard a guttural moan that weakened my knees with fright. Before I could run, I realized the noise was coming from beneath the ground. The pump was priming up, and soon a trickle of dirty, rusty water dripped out the tap. I kept pumping on the handle, and sure enough, the stream got thicker and the water got clearer. I removed my t-shirt from my head and stuffed it in my pocket. Then I stuck my head under the cold water stream. I felt instant relief.

Cupping my hands together to catch the flow, I slurped up the cold water, and kept slurping until I could slurp no more. My head ached from the coldness; that, however, soon turned out to be the least of my problems.

As I ran my cold, wet hands through my hair, I caught movement of something black out the corner of my eye and whipped my head in its direction, my heart starting to thump louder.

It came from the barn—a dog, black as midnight and so thick in the shoulders and hindquarters I thought at first it was a large bear cub. It meandered toward me slowly, growling angrily. Thick saliva dripped off its barred-teeth and its black button eyes twinkled with a cold, sinister evil.

As it came closer, I realized this was not your typical barn yard dog. This beast carried with it a horde of buzzing flies. The black cloud swirled about its head as though it was a juicy hunk of rotting meat. I'd never seen anything like it before. On a carcass, sure, but never on anything that was alive.

With my heart pounding in my ears, I stepped away from the pump, and realized I stood in a no-man's land, half way between the barn and the house. Now I could run fast—even faster when something with large teeth was chasing me—but I knew I couldn't out run this thing. And so if I couldn't out run it, I had to stand my ground and fight.

I quickly searched the area for a rock. I had a strong arm and was an accurate pitcher. If I could find a rock—if—I felt pretty confident I could hit the dog in the face with it. It might not stop it, but it might slow it down long enough for me to get to the house. Whether or not I could get inside was another story, but it was the only plan I could think of.

But there was no rock around to throw. So I opted for plan B: dirt. There was plenty of that around, and I bent over and scooped up two handfuls. Now I had to be accurate and hit the animal square in the eyes, cuz if I didn't blind it long enough for me to get away, I was gonna get an ass full of teeth and maybe a whole lot more.

I took a step back, trying to stay calm.

"Nice doggie...nice dog...sit...sit boy..."

It continued to advance, growling with a purpose.

I stepped back again, and as I did, I felt something hard and pointy in my back. I yelped and spun about, a scream building in my throat. I half-expected to see those gray creatures staring down at me. Instead, I saw the silver tip of a black cane. And holding the cane was an old man. Like the dog, the old man's head was surrounded with buzzing flies. I gulped and nearly wet myself.

"Are yuh a plannin' to throw dirt in my dawg's eyes?"

That voice.

"Well? Are yuh?"

"Uh, I thought he was gonna attack me."

The old man whooped out a phlegmy laugh. "Old Snotnose is as gentle as a kitten." He looked at the animal. "Ain't that right, Snotnose?"

Snotnose yawned as though the question bored him and dropped on his belly in the dirt, laying his head down on his front, outstretched legs.

"See, yuh ain't got nothin' to worry about."

I supposed he was right. I didn't have to worry about the dog. As for the old man...well, I just didn't know.

29

He was dressed to the nines in a black suit and white shirt. He had a good half foot on me—six four at least. Skinny as a beanpole, he was as old as time itself, bald as a melon, his dome plate covered in peach fuzz and buzzing flies. The flies crawled all over his face, up his nose and in his mouth and eyes. He didn't seem to mind or take notice. He smelled, too. But not of B.O. It was a chemical smell, the same sort a smell I'd smelled coming off the town's undertaker.

"I'm Charles Haddes," he said with gusto, the chicken gobbler beneath his chin quivering with each word. He stuck out his hand to shake.

I didn't want to shake with him, but manners dictated that I do. So I dropped the dirt and shook his hand, cringing inwardly for the few seconds it took. His grip was weak, his skin was cold and felt as icky as a dead fish.

"Mr. Haddes, I heard your voice in my head. I even heard the flies buzzing."

"I know, Southpaw."

"How do you know me? How did you talk in my head?"

"I don't rightly know. I ain't sure on a lotta things right now." He sighed sadly. "I seem to be missin' time, Southpaw. Cuz I ain't rightly sure where I am or how I got here."

"This ain't your house? This ain't your spread?"

"I think it is. But my mind is hazy. And I can't remember why I'm dressed like this. Or what I've been a doing, and where I've been a doing it. And why are all these flies crawlin' over me? And all over Snotnose? I can't even reckon why Snotnose is here. He shouldn't be."

"Oh? Why?"

"Cuz I remember buryin' him behind the barn."

I swallowed hard.

"If I got flies like he does, I reckon I'm dead too."

I gulped. "I see."

He shrugged. "It would explain a lot, Southpaw."

It sure would, I thought, but refused to believe it. "Uh, you know, Mr. Haddes, maybe I should be going."

"Yer here for a reason, Southpaw. I think the two of us have to jaw. So maybe we outta go inside and sit a spell—talk."

"Uh, I'm sorry sir, but ain't I got the time."

'Oh? Where are yuh off to?"

"Biloxi," I said. "I'm gonna go to the army base there. Maybe they know where my Pa is at. Maybe they know if he's dead or alive."

"I see," he said, nodding slowly. "Yuh know, I can't blame yuh for wantin' to know about yer Pa, but goin' to Biloxi ain't the answer. If yuh wanna know if yer Pa is dead, yuh gotta go somewhere else. Yuh gotta go to Limbo."

"Limbo?"

"That's right. Yuh gotta go to Limbo. Yuh gotta go to Limbo, Mississippi."

(8)

"Git Snotnose. Go wait in the barn," Haddes instructed, pointing with his cane. "If yuh see Sheriff Nibbs a comin', bark like hell." He looked at me. "Sheriff Nibbs don't care for my still. Not that it's all his fault. He gets his orders from Mayor Valentine, who's doin' his own bootleggin' and wants to cut out the competition."

"Really? I had no idea."

"Oh, yuh gotta watch out for the Mayor. He's a slippery one. Though, I suppose I'd still have bootleggin' trouble on account of that uppity Baptist preacher Dickerson. He don't care for my still none either."

"I'm well acquainted with him," I grumbled, a burst of fresh anger coming to a boil cuz of what I learned today. "I live across the street from him and attend his church."

"Be careful of him, Southpaw, cuz he's a sinner like the rest of us. He's even worse—actin' all high and mighty up on his pulpit, tellin' folks to do this and don't do that. Meanwhile he's sinnin' away over in Possum Hollow makin' ill-legit babies."

At first I thought I had misunderstood him, and seeing my stunned look, he repeated it.

"Oh yeah, Southpaw, the Pastor has done some seed plantin' over in Possum Hollow. And it ain't summer squash he's been a plantin.'"

"I had no idea."

"Few do," he said. "But yup, he's been spreadin' his seed over in Possum Hollow like some horny northern debutante."

"I can't believe it."

"I'm sure his flock won't be able to believe it either if word of it ever got out."

"You're right about that."

I followed him up the porch stairs, keeping my distance so as not to attract his flies—I had enough problems as it was. He opened the door, the hinges creaking eerily, and led the way inside to a kitchen. The air was hot and stale and smelled of mold. A thick layer of dust coated the floor and dust bunnies swirled by our feet as we walked. Breadcrumbs, mouse droppings and grit littered the kitchen table and counter. Not even a magician would have been able to squeeze another dirty dish into the sink. The green curtains above the sink were so old and threadbare you could see through them. Thick cobwebs hung from the light fixture and in all four corners of the room like silk drapes. It was a maid's nightmare.

Haddes hobbled over to the Quaker Social cast-iron potbelly in the corner. He reached inside the potbelly and pulled out a brown jug, snickering. "Gotta be careful. Prohibition is still on the books in these parts." He placed the jug on the table, pulled out the cork and brought his nose down to the opening, savoring the aroma. "Ah, the subtle bouquet of white lightin' shine."

He sure made it sound appealing, which left me a tad confused cuz I thought it smelt like turpentine. It must have tasted like it too, cuz after a short guzzle, he snorted and gagged and his eyes watered. The flies didn't care much for it either, cuz most stayed away from his mouth and nose.

"Yuh wanna snort of the creature?"

"The what?" I asked.

"The creature," he returned. "It's what my Irish grand pappy called liquor."

"Uh, no, I don't drink." I shook my head to back up my words and added, "Uh, Mr. Haddes, I really should be going."

"I reckon yer gonna wanna hear this story, Southpaw," he said, dropping into a chair at the far end of the table. He motioned with his cane for me to sit. Since I didn't feel he was a threat, and since I needed sometime to rest my weary legs, I pulled out the closest chair and sat.

"So where is this Limbo, Mississippi, you're talking about?"

"Have yuh been up Breckinridge's trail?"

"Pa and I used to hunt up that trail."

"In case yuh don't know, the trail is named after Major Beauregard Q. Breckinridge. He was a local boy, born and raised in the Gulch."

I knew that, and well…didn't care.

"When the war between the states broke out, he put a company of badasses together and rode north to give the Yankees a good spankin'. Except it was Breckinridge and his men that got the spankin'. His whole company got wiped out at Gettysburg. He survived, though, his legs and arms all shot up. He limped back to the Gulch with his tail between his legs."

Not that I cared, but here was a chapter of the war I had been oblivious to.

"By the time Breckinridge was back on his feet, the war was near over. Yet Breckinridge was a hard-headed S.O.B. and wouldn't listen. He put together another company of men. Except there weren't no men of fightin' age left in the Gulch. So he rounded up boys and old men. He even took a boy whose noggin was all messed up."

By 'messed up', I assumed he meant retarded, but didn't ask.

"I was only eight at the time, but my brother Daniel was fifteen and strong as an ox. Breckinridge wanted him so my Pa gave Daniel an old squirrel rifle and sent him off. All he was missin' was shoes."

I cringed at the thought of walking that trail without proper footwear.

"Four or five days later, Abby, the man with the messed up noggin, stumbled outta the woods, barely able to stand. He ain't et in days and his face and arms were all scratched and his clothes were all fulla cockleburs. Ma and Pa took him inside and feed him at this here table. He told them that Breckinridge and his men all went missing in this town called Limbo—a two day walk up the trail."

"Mr. Haddes, I've been on that trail and I've never seen a town."

"I don't reckon yuh have. Cuz it lies at the end of an alternate route, mostly hidden with bushes. It's an old Yazoo Injun trail. Breckinridge led the men that way cuz he was looking for a faster way north. And once on that trail, Abby said they spotted a flashin' red light off in the distance."

"Flashing red light?" I echoed.

"I know what's goin' on inside yer noggin. There weren't no e-lectrical back then."

Actually, the fact that electricity had only been in Mississippi since the turn of the century had escaped me. I only echoed what he'd said cuz it sounded so odd to come across a light in the woods.

"Ma and Pa thought Abby was confused on account of his weak brain, but they listened anyway. He told them the men all felt evil comin' off the place. But not Abby, probably on account that he had half a mind."

I'm sure, I thought, wondering if it would seem rude if I excused myself midway through his story.

"The evil got into the men's head and they started fightin' with each other. Lots of cussin', fistfights. Even Breckinridge. When one of his men begged him to turn around, Breckinridge cut the man's head off with his saber."

"Ouch," I muttered light-heartedly, not believing a word of what was coming outta this man's pie-hole.

"Some think that the evil from that place bothers folks here in the Gulch."

My ears perked up then cuz Nurse Bilodeau had raised the same issue at the diner last night. "Go on."

"They soon came to a rock outcroppin' overlookin' the town," he pushed on, chewing on a fly that had crawled onto his lips. "Abby said it looked kinda like the Gulch, only bigger, much bigger. The buildings were made of wood, and the wood glowed like a dim bulb. The flashin' red light hung above the town-square. I know now that the town square boarders a train station."

"How could that be? The train runs through Squirrel Flats."

"I don't think these tracks run to any towns we're familiar with," he said, and paused to take a sip of the creature. He choked slightly, perhaps swallowing some flies.

"I don't understand. These tracks run to Louisiana?"

"Oh, it's worse than that," he returned. "I think they run to Hell. But that's only my opinion. I can't say for sure."

"To Hell, huh? Okay. You know Mr. Haddes, I really should be going."

"A small graveyard surrounded by a stone fence sits in front the town," he pushed on as though I hadn't spoken. "Yuh can go into the graveyard, Southpaw, but don't go any further. Cuz if yuh enter the town, yuh'll be trapped."

I had no intentions of going anywhere near this make believe town he was talking about. Not wanting to debate the issue with him, though, I merely nodded at his instructions.

"Breckinridge ordered his men into the town—all except Abby. He made him stand guard inside the graveyard. That's how come Abby survived."

"What happened to them?"

"Don't rightly know. Breckinridge was the only one to make it back to the cemetery's stone fence. He was talkin' crazy from what Abby said. And he couldn't get over the stone fence. There was an invisible barrier stoppin' him."

"Abby had mental problems, right?"

"I know what yer a thinkin', Southpaw. And yeah, he had half a noggin, but he weren't no liar."

I could tell by his tone I had offended him so I asked a question to make it appear I was believing his crazy yarn.

"What happened to Breckinridge?"

"He wandered off to find another way outta the place."

"And?"

"Abby never saw him again. But he saw other things."

"What other things?"

"Ghosts. Spirits. The walkin' dead. They appeared outta nothing and ambled through the town as though it was a Sunday afternoon. Abby saw relatives that had died years before."

Unable to help myself, I grinned. "Is that so?"

My mocking grin made him frown, but he pushed on anyway. "Then he saw tall, gray creatures herdin' em along as though they were cattle."

"Gray creatures? I—"

"Yuh saw them snatch yer Ma's spirit, didn't yuh?"

"I imagined that."

"Believe what yuh want, Southpaw. I know my Ma and Pa thought Abby was crazy too. Still, somethin' had happened to Daniel, so Pa hiked up there. He came back a changed man, so scared from his experience his hair had turned completely white. He wouldn't tell me what happened, but I heard him jawin' about it with Ma. He claimed to have found the head of the solider Breckinridge had killed, and that the head talked to him and told him to flee."

"Really?" I said and, unwilling to listen to anymore delusional talk, rose to my feet. "I should be going, Mr. Haddes."

Haddes, undaunted, continued his story. "Pa told Ma that Abby was right about everythin'. The evil, the graveyard. He saw it all, and realized he was at the gates of the land of the dead."

"Land of the dead, huh?"

"I don't blame yuh for feeling the way yuh do. If I were in yer shoes, I'd doubt too. Even after seein' what yuh saw this mornin'. But ask yourself this, Southpaw, would yuh rather hike up Breckinridge's trail or sit in an orphanage? Cuz those are yer choices."

"I was thinking about going to Biloxi."

"Waste your time if yuh like—it's yores to waste. But if yuh wanna know about yer Pa, yuh gotta go up to Limbo. Pray that he ain't there, but look anyways. If yuh don't see him, then yuh ain't no orphan. If yuh do see him, then at least yuh'll know for certain."

(9)

I led the way down the porch stairs and across the compound to the pump, fixing to get a drink before I headed out. As I neared the pump, I noticed something rather disturbing. The sun hadn't moved. It was still directly overhead, and though it was bordering on triple-digit-heat, a shiver went up my spine.

"Excuse me, Mr. Haddes, but do you have the time?"

He shook his head. "Never carried a timepiece. Always told time by the sun. But it ain't movin', is it?"

"It sure don't seem to be."

He shrugged. "I'm a-thinkin' that time don't exist here."

That was a tough bit of info to swallow, but as much as I hated to admit it, his explanation made sense. I didn't believe it, though, cuz I didn't want to believe it. Still, it was the only explanation that made sense.

I primed the pump and took my drink, and when I had my fill, I turned to Charles Haddes, ready to make my 'goodbyes'. But I held up cuz the man was obviously troubled. He was looking off toward the barn, his eyes misting over.

"I'm afraid old Snotnose has moved on," he muttered, tears spilling down his cheeks. "I don't wanna spend eternity alone, but it looks like I'm gonna."

"Do you wanna come with me?" I offered. "We can walk slow. I'll get you to a doctor. Maybe he can fix your fly problem."

He shook his head. "It ain't suppose to happen that way, Southpaw. Yuh gotta do this on yer own. Yuh gotta meet yer destiny and that don't include a tired old ghost."

"For a ghost, you look awful real to me," I pointed out.

"Thanks for sayin', but yuh gotta do this on yer own." Using his cane, he pointed down the dirt road that stretched off to the horizon. "Yuh get a move on, Southpaw. Yuh got a long walk ahead of yuh if yer gonna get home tonight."

"I'll send someone back for you."

He shook his head. "I doubt whoever yuh send back will find the place." He pointed off down the road again. "Straight down this road, and keep on a-goin'. It'll take yuh awhile to walk outta here, or it'll sure seem like it. But don't give up, keep walkin'. Before long, yuh'll get to the end, and the end will take yuh to the woods. I know yer still plannin' to go to Biloxi, but it'll be too late to head there today. So look for a path that'll lead yuh back home. And yuh be careful in those woods, yuh hear?"

"I'll be okay. I'm used to being in the woods."

"I gotta feelin' yer gonna run into trouble before yuh get home. Big trouble. So keep yer wits about yuh. All goin' well, yuh'll get home before sunset."

"Okay," I muttered, wondering how he knew all this.

"Oh, and yer gonna have to go in through a basement window. But don't fret, cuz one ain't locked. It'll pop right open."

Since all I wanted to do was leave, I didn't debate the issue with him, but I knew he was wrong cuz there was a spare set of keys buried in the garden. And as for a basement window popping open? Well, since Pa was worried about our safety, he and I had gone around before he shipped out and put new safety catches on all the windows so such a thing wouldn't happen. But if Haddes wanted to believe that—so be it.

Without talking, we walked across the compound to where the dirt road began.

"I know yuh think I'm as crazy as a loon, but there are others in the Gulch that have been up to Limbo. My old partner Sam Knight has the best story. He lives close to yuh but I don't recommend yuh talk to him on account that he's a no-good boozer that owes me money. Yer best bet is to talk to yer neighbor, Pastor Dickerson."

"The Pastor? The Pastor knows about this place?"

"A long time ago the Pastor hiked up to Limbo lookin' for a friend. I ain't sure how it turned out but go talk to him. He'll tell yuh I ain't fibbing."

"The Pastor doesn't wanna see me," I said sadly. "Sheriff Nibbs told me."

"Don't give him a choice, Southpaw," he returned bluntly. "The Pastor talks a good game but when push comes to shove, he'll back down. Guys like him always do. So yuh go talk to him. Ask him how his ill-legit son Clark is doing over in Possum Hollow. That should loosen his jaw a bit."

"You even know his son's name?"

He grinned away a line of flies hugging his upper lip. "Ask him who he named the child after. The actor or the superhero."

I couldn't imagine ever arriving at a point in a conversation with the Pastor where such a question could be asked. Still, if the opportunity ever presented itself, I suppose I'd like to know the answer.

"Time to go meet yer destiny."

Though I didn't want to, proper etiquette made me offer my hand out to shake. He took it, shook it quickly, and then let his hand fall to his side. He then wandered away as though he'd lost interest in me.

I heard him mumble. "Dead is dead and gone is gone…walk toward the shinnin' dawn."

I had no idea what that meant, nor did I care. It was time to leave, and I hurried off down the road, headed toward the horizon and, according to Charles Haddes, my destiny.

(10)

It took a while. An hour? Two hours? I'm not sure. But eventually, things started to bother me. And what bothered me the most, aside from the sun not moving, was the total lack of green. I was surrounded by sun-baked dirt—a barren desert. There wasn't a bush, weed, or flower in sight. Nothing. Not a speck of green anywhere and this was mid summer. Even if we'd been suffering through a drought (which we weren't), there should have been green someplace. But there wasn't.

And aside from the lack of vegetation, there wasn't a thing crawling, flying or buzzing about either. Nothing. Not even an ant. Far as I could tell, I was the only living thing out here, and that bone-deep feeling of isolation I'd felt before returned with a vengeance and my stomach hiccupped with fear.

I told myself I had nothing to fear, that it was all in my head, and pushed myself to walk even faster. But it was as though I was on a treadmill. I was walking, sure, but going nowhere.

My mind was a storm of crazy thoughts and notions which no sense of reason could quell. Like what if this dead place just kept on going? What if it stretched off forever? How long could I survive without water? And how long would it be before I'd go plum crazy?

I thought of Charles Haddes, of course. How could I not? I found a bit—a very small bit—of comfort in what he had said about the journey being long but eventually I find the woods. If only I knew what his definition of 'long' was.

I also thought about his story, his wild, crazy, unbelievable story. Was the land of the day really just a two day walk up Breckinridge's trail?

Common sense said 'no' and I wanted to believe that the old coot was as senile as an outhouse bug and belonged on the third floor of the hospital—him and his flies. But I couldn't completely scoff at his crazy yarn cuz of one thing: Major Beauregard Q. Breckinridge, the main character in his tale of woe, had indeed existed, a fact I knew long before bumping into Haddes.

Since that much of the story was true, I suppose it was not outta the realm of imagination to believe that the Major had thrown together a platoon of teenagers, old men and, for comic relief no doubt, a slow-minded dimwit to head north to fight the Yankees. So if it was true—and for the sake of argument let's say it was—what had happened to them? Had they—like Haddes had said—wandered into the land of the dead, never to be seen again? Or had they met their demise at the hands of the Yankees? Or had they survived and lived out their lives in good old Mississippi?

It was a good question and if ever I got outta this crazy place where the sun don't move I knew where I could look for the answer.

See, Ma owned a book on famous Confederate soldiers. It had caught my eye in December as I hunted in the attic for Christmas decorations. It had been sticking out of a box and I had sat on an old sofa and flipped through its pages. From what I remembered, there were over two hundred biographies on Confederate dignities. Was Breckinridge's bio included? I didn't know but figured it was worth the climb into the attic to find out. If his bio was in the book, it could go a long way toward disproving the old coot's crazy story. And once I proved his story was utter fiction, I could confidently go off to Biloxi tomorrow knowing I was doing the right thing.

As I thought about all this, I noticed—to my utter joy—that the sun was no longer overhead. Without even realizing it, the sun had dropped in the sky like a leaky balloon. Time had bolted ahead. If I had to guess, I'd guess it was close to four p.m. now.

Time was apparently moving again, and so relieved that it was, I found
the energy to jog. Before long, I saw a trace of green poking up outta the dirt. The weeds were sparse, stunted, and looked like they had been sprayed with chemicals, but they were there, and that was something.

I ran even faster now, and a few minutes later a fat, lazy bubble bee buzzed by my head. Life was retuning.

A few minutes after seeing the bee, I saw the tops of pine trees on the horizon.

I had found the woods.

I was so happy I almost wept. Almost.

(11)

The late afternoon sun lengthened my shadow and caused deep pockets of eerie darkness in the thick foliage. The gentle breeze tickled the leaves, vines and small branches enough to cause those shadow pools to sway, making me think that something was gonna jump out and attack me. Normally I liked walking in the woods. But not today.

I hated being afraid; then again, after all I'd been through today, who could blame me? It was a miracle I still had my sanity. And how long would it last if I was still wandering these woods when the sun set? I hated the dark. Actually, to be more precise, I feared it.

I didn't wanna think about it cuz thinking about it made me worry even more. Thankfully though, before I could think myself into a panic, I came to a four-way junction in the path. Cuz the sun was ahead of me, I knew I was walking west. So I turned right, headed north.

The path was typical for the area: bumpy, rock-laden, and crisscrossed with tree roots. It was wide enough to walk along without brushing against foliage and ran relatively straight. It was still unfamiliar territory for me, which kept my nerves on edge.

The feeling, thankfully, didn't last long, for a few minutes later I rounded a bend in the path and saw something that totally eased my worried mind.

A boulder, slate gray and covered with patches of brownish green moss, sat half buried in the ground on the edge of the path, and though it looked like any other boulder, I recognized it cuz of a sign painted in white on its smooth side. Surrounding the message was a huge heart; written inside the heart were the words:

SOUTHPAW LOVES SALLY. XOXO

How's that for a Valentine's Day message? Short, sweet, straight to the point and, for the most part anyway, alliterative.

I had pretty much forgotten about that Valentine's Day message I'd painted for her, but there it was, still looking relatively fresh after six months. More importantly, I knew where I was and, relieved, I hurried along the path knowing I would be home before dark.

Just like that old coot said, I thought.

I tired to push him outta my mind but couldn't. He had made other predictions as well, and if his first prediction had come true—and it sure looked like it had—could his other predictions come true?

I couldn't see how they could. Still...never say never, right?

As I thought about it, doing my best to discredit the old coot's words of wisdom, I caught a whiff of cigarette smoke. Someone was smoking and that someone was close by. There was no need to panic though. Most likely it was a hunter or someone out for a stroll, maybe walking a dog, and I didn't give it a second thought. Then I came over a slight incline in the path and—"Oh my God"—I saw someone standing no more than ten yards away, and the sight of that someone chilled my blood and made my knees weak. My mouth fell open and my heart rate soared like a launched rocket.

It looked like the old coot was right again. He said I would run into trouble, and boy, I had run into trouble, trouble that was roughly the size of Mount Everest.

For one crazy second I actually denied the killer was there. Then the late afternoon sun glinted off the razorblade in his hand and reality fell back in on me like a tidal wave. Oh, he was there all right. A cigarette in one hand; a straight razor in the other, and now my brain was screaming for me to run. Run and keep running as if the Devil was chasing me. But before I could move an inch someone came up behind me and punched me hard in the lower back. I squealed, more with fright than pain, and dropped to my knees. An instant later, I felt another hot, stinging punch, this one higher and in the center of my back. I flopped onto my belly, turned over at once and stared up at two angry killers.

"You sure picked a helluva bad time to go for a walk," Cole Conklin growled around his cigarette.

He looked pretty much as I remembered him, except now, instead of a notepad and pencil, he held a straight razor that looked large enough to shave King Kong. He was about my height, five foot ten, and skinny. His arms and legs seemed too long for his body. The brush cut he had always sported had grown down to his shoulders. He had a dusting of facial hair now too, so spotty and fair you had to look twice to see it. His dark brown eyes were cold and evil, sinister enough to stop an old man's heart.

He was dressed like a used car salesman on a tight budget. His white dress shirt, opened three buttons from the collar, needed a spin in a washer with a cup of bleach to dissolve the blood spatters up the front. His black suit jacket looked like it had been tailored by blind elves, for the stitching was loose at the seams and one sleeve looked longer than the other. The jacket was wrinkled, dirty and stained to a hard shell. His dry cleaner would have a stroke if he brought that in to be cleaned.

His partner, a man known simply as Snake, was shorter, a runt no taller than five foot five, and thin. He had a nasty, jackal-looking face crisscrossed with white scars easily seen beneath the carpet of beard stubble. His hair was long and fanned out like a drape over the shoulders of his light gray suit jacket. His jacket, button-shirt and pants were spotted with dried blood. He carried a Tommy-Gun slung over his shoulder and had a pistol tucked in his belt. He looked like he was itching for a fight.

"I think I know this guy, Snake," Cole said, puzzled. "But what's his name?"

"Dog meat," Snake hissed back. "You wanna do him? Or should I?"

Cole crouched over and eyed me closely through the twirling smoke off his cigarette. "What's your name?"

Though my brain was frozen with numb-terror, I recalled the old coot's words of wisdom: *Keep your wits about you.* "Uh, it's me Cole, Johnny McGrath. Remember? We used to go to school together. My Ma was our teacher."

His eyes lit up with recognition. "Well, I'll be damned." He straightened up at once, tossed away his smoke and closed up his razor, sliding it into his pant pocket. "C'mon, get on your feet, McGrath."

I stood at once and we shook hands. I felt dirty for doing it, but I had to build up a rapport with him again if I wanted to keep breathing.

"Snake, this here is Johnny McGrath," Cole introduced as though we were at a party. "We were schooled in the same one-room schoolhouse. His Ma was the teacher."

Snake shrugged indifferently and looked away, not offering his hand to shake. Just as well. I didn't wanna shake hands with this murderous northerner anyway.

"She's a darn good teacher," Cole went on. "A real stickler for grammar."

He was right, and I'm sure if Ma had been around she would have been pleased to hear Cole speaking—for the most part anyway—with proper grammar. I'm sure she would have been aghast (like I was) to hear that his Mississippi accent was gone, replaced with a Brooklyn timbre, that frankly, seemed as natural as a cow wearing pants.

"Yes sir, your Ma is the best."

Snake sighed with annoyance, fished out a straight razor from his pocket, and flicked out the blade with the professional ease of a barber. "We better do him off the trail," he told Cole, and grinned at me, showing the finger width gap between his snarly yellow teeth. "Don't fret kid, the blade is so sharp you won't feel a thing."

My bowels groaned with fear and I nearly messed my pants.

"Ease up, Snake. I ain't finished talking to him yet."

"We ain't got time for you to walk down memory lane, Cole," he snapped. "Let's do him and get outta here before it gets dark and these damn skitters eat us."

Cole's eyes narrowed to slits and the look he shot Snake was evil enough to make an old woman faint. "Don't give me orders, Snake. I ain't on no timetable." He turned to me, his smile growing pleasantly as though he was a businessman about to close a deal. "So McGrath, tell me, are you still sweet on the Pastor's granddaughter? I remember you two were always holding hands."

"Uh, yeah, we're still good friends."

"Ah, she's a fine looking gal." He shot Snake a cordial smile, their recent bitter exchange obviously forgotten. "You should see this gal, Snakey. She's one hot tomato." And he whistled in awe.

I suddenly realized something I had failed to see years ago when we all attended school together. Cole Conklin, five years my senior, held a secret appreciation for Sally, a notion that, frankly, made me near sick to my stomach.

Snake must a needed a visual image of Sally to truly appreciation the story cuz he merely shrugged with all the enthusiasm of a bored cat, his weasel face creasing with a constipated tension of indecision. It was obvious he wanted to leave. Cole was either blind to it or ignoring it cuz he kept on yapping.

"So tell me McGrath, why are you out here? You got no farming to do?"

"We didn't plant this year cuz Pa is off fighting the Germans."

"Those damn Nazi bastards," he muttered, shaking his head. "I'd like to kill a few of them myself."

I'm sure you'd be good at it, I thought, *except, those damn Nazi bastards shoot back, unlike the innocent bank tellers you've been butchering over the last few months.*

"So how's your Ma?"

"Uh…Ma died today." The words sounded hollow and, like the whole conversation, surreal.

Cole hesitated, his mouth partly open. "Are you joshing me?"

"Ma passed of the cancer this morning at the hospital."

"Oh no," he groaned, and genuinely looked sad. "I always liked your Ma. She was always nice to me."

Snake slapped at a skitter biting his cheek and lost his patience. "C'mon Cole," he grumbled. "We ain't got time to hang out with this kid. Now let's kill him and get outta these woods before we get eaten alive."

Cole ignored his partner. "I'm having trouble figuring all this out, McGrath" he went on. "If your Ma passed today, why the hell are you out here in the woods?"

"Hiding from Sheriff Nibbs," I told him. "I'm wanted. Nibbs wants to put me in an orphanage on account I ain't got no kin. So I ran off on him."

"Well, ain't that interesting," Cole muttered, and stroked his chin whiskers with a thumb and forefinger.

"I hope you ain't thinking about letting him go," Snake barked. "Cuz that would be stupid. He'll squeal for sure."

"Shut your face, Snake," he fired back, and turned to me. "Our gang has suffered a few losses of late. How would you like to throw in with us?"

Snake cut in at once. "Our numbers are fine."

"Our ranks are thin, Snake," he boomed. "It's only you and me now. We need at least one more. And McGrath is a smart kid. Plus he's the perfect choice cuz he ain't got no kin to hold him back." He turned to me. "So? What do you say? You wanna throw in with us?"

"Uhhhhh," I sputtered.

"C'mon McGrath? You want in? Equal share."

"Uhhhhh."

Snake laughed. "I think you got your answer, Cole."

Cole ignored him and said, "You know McGrath, if you ain't with us, then you're against us."

"I ain't against you, Cole. I need to bury my Ma."

"Let's save him the trouble," Snake piped up.

Cole heaved a terse sigh. "Yeah, I suppose you're right, Snakey." He looked at me sadly. "Sorry McGrath. It ain't personal. It's business, you understand."

I took a step back. "I won't tell, Cole. Honest. Sides, I ain't gonna be around. I'm thumbing to Biloxi. Gonna go to the army base to see if they know where my Pa is at. He's gotta know about Ma dying, and that the bank is gonna foreclose on the farm at the end of the month."

Cole sighed with distress. "Sorry McGrath. I gotta go along with Snakey on this one." He looked at his partner and pointed at me. "Make it quick."

Snake beamed with the enthusiasm of a kid on Christmas morning and struck like a cobra. He grabbed my wrist in a vice-like grip, and yanked me toward the bushes.

If I was gonna die, I decided, I was gonna die fighting, so I made a fist with my free hand and walloped Snake with all my might in the side of his head. He yelped with surprise, lost his grip on my wrist, and flew forward into the bushes. He recovered quickly, spun about and came at me, slashing the air in front of him with the straight razor. He was slow, and I easily stepped back from his slashing blade. His momentum carried the blade away from me and his head forward. His face became a perfect target, and I pounded him square in the nose with a screaming haymaker. He squealed out an 'UHG" and stumbled backwards. As he was stumbling, I socked him again in the face with every ounce of strength I had. That knocked him on his ass.

I figured Cole would step in then to help his partner, and turned, waiting for the attack. Cole, however, surprised me. He stood in place, arms folded across his chest, chuckling as though he was watching a Vaudeville act.

Snake scrambled to his feet, a steady stream of blood pouring out both nostrils. I raised both my fists like a boxer, waiting.

"You son-of-a-bitch," he cursed and threw the straight razor to the ground. His move shocked me. Was this man honorable enough to fight fairly? It seemed outta character for such a lowlife.

Sure enough, Snake's true character surfaced. For instead of making fists and fighting like an honorable man, he drew the pistol tucked in his waistband and pointed it at my head. My heart nearly stopped. I could fight, sure, but I couldn't dodge bullets. Even if I ran full out he could easily shoot me in the back before I had gone ten feet. Sure, it ain't sporting to shoot an unarmed opponent in the back, but I didn't think he cared about such etiquette.

"You're dead," he hissed, his eyebrows crinkled with venomous hatred.

Suddenly Cole stepped forward and batted away Snake's pistol. It flew into the bushes, and Snake, outraged, turned to Cole.

"What the hell?"

"Enough," Cole snapped.

"Son-of-a-bitch hit me," Snake fired back.

"Yeah I know. I nearly laughed my ass off watching him do it."

"Let me kill him. Let me kill the son-of-a-bitch."

"I said enough. Gunfire will attract attention, and since you can't kill him with your blade, he gets to walk."

"No," Snake yelped. "Let me—"

Cole silenced him with a look so vile it would have blistered paint. He turned to me then, a wily grin creasing his cheeks. "You got quite a punch on you, McGrath. It's a damn shame you don't wanna throw in with us cuz we could sure use someone like you." He shrugged his brows and chuckled. "Though, maybe it's for the best, cuz I'd always be afraid of you turning on me."

"Cole, we gotta kill him."

"Shut up," he said over his shoulder. "You had your chance and you blew it. So he gets to go."

"He'll squeal."

"No he won't," Cole said evenly. "Cuz he knows that if he does, I'll hunt down his girlfriend." He looked me in the eyes. "That's your warning, McGrath. If you mention you saw us, I'll find your gal and torture her for a month before killing her—do you understand?"

I nodded.

"Okay, good. Now get." He snapped his fingers and pointed down the path.

He didn't need to tell me twice and I turned and hurried along the path, resisting the urge to run.

Then, before I had gone no more than ten yards, he yelled out, "Hey, hang on a sec, McGrath. I gotta a question for you."

I didn't wanna stop, but feared that if I didn't he'd shoot me in the back. So I stopped and turned. "Yeah?"

"Do you know if old man Knight is still alive? You know, Sam Knight?"

"I think so. I ain't heard he died."

Cole nodded. "That's good to hear."

I went to turn but he yelled out again for me to wait.

"Hey, McGrath, one more thing. You've lived in these parts all your life, have you ever heard of a place called Limbo? Limbo, Mississippi?"

Well, I'll be damned.

"It's suppose to be up along Breckinridge's trail."

I shrugged. "Nothing much up there but woods."

"That's what I always thought, but when I lived with Knight he told me about this place called Limbo. He said it was a ghost town, a place where the dead lived."

"A ghost town, huh? Sorry, Cole, I've never heard of it."

"I know what you're a thinking," he said. "Cuz when he told me, I thought he was plum loco too. But I think it's true. I think the place exists cuz Knight showed me pictures of the place." He shrugged. "Knight is a boozer, and talks a lot, but how can you fake pictures? Right? So it's gotta be true, don'tcha think?"

"I guess." And before he could say anything else, I turned and ran down the path as though the whole German Army was chasing me.

(12)

I ran as fast as I could for as long as I could and when I could run no longer I walked, looking over my shoulder every few seconds expecting to see Cole and Snake charging up the path toward me. Every time I looked, though, the path was empty, and before long, thankfully, the woods thinned and the scrub grass that boarded Route 9 came into sight. Hallelujah. Nothing like two psycho killers to get a man to run fast, huh?

I scurried up the embankment and stood on Route 9, happy to be close to home. Thanks to the Pastor's Bible-pounding influence with the City Council, Route 9, unlike most roads in the area, was paved. The road ahead was so smooth you could have shoot pool on it, and I took advantage of the smooth surface and walked down the center white line.

Ahead to the west, the sun was a bright orange ball on the rim of the horizon. My elongated shadow slanted out behind me. To the east, over my shoulder, I saw a plump moon hanging in a near black sky. In ten or so minutes it would be nightfall. As Haddes predicted, I was right on schedule.

I soon reached the top of a small rise, and from here, I could see the last of the day's light twinkling off the tin shingled roof of our farmhouse. The place had never looked better. My emotions bubbled up and I started to cry. No one was around to see, so I let the tears flow and continued walking, so anxious to get home now my heart rate sped up. Then, something dreadful occurred to me. Though Haddes never mentioned it, it was possible that Nibbs was laying in wait for me, hiding somewhere on the property, which meant I couldn't just stroll up the driveway like I owned the place.

I stopped, thought about it for a second, and then cut off from the road about twenty yards from our driveway, running down into the ditch. I jumped the wooden slat fence—which was waist high and more decorative than anything—and snuck up behind the barn, peering around the corner into the open terrain beside the farmhouse.

I saw no sign of Nibbs and wondered if he had gone home for the night. Maybe the skitters had driven him off cuz there were thick, black clouds of them buzzing about, driving me damn crazy.

I had to get inside away from them while I still had blood, so I went straight to the flower garden behind the house. At this time of year the garden would normally be awash with brightly colored flowers that would leave a person gawking in awe. This year, however, things were different. Neglect had taken its toll, and now, here at the start of August, the garden was a wasteland of green vegetation so thick it completely hid every inch of the dirt.

It was almost dark now, and relying on moonlight to see, I walked into the garden, not caring about where I stepped. Here, beneath this mass of green vegetation was a red and yellow rock that I had painted and given to Ma for her birthday about five years ago. She had loved it so much she put it in her flowerbed, and beneath it, we hid the key. "Just in case you ever get locked out," she had said. Well, the 'just in case' was happening. Thank you Ma for the foresight.

As I smacked skitters into red paste, I noticed a small area of flattened stalks. Someone or something had been in the garden, and my heart sunk as the fly-laden image of Charles Haddes rose in my mind's eye. Could that crazy old coot be right? Was the key gone? Would I have to use the window to get inside like he predicted?

I crouched, pushed aside the flattened vegetation and picked up the rock. The key was gone. Big surprise, huh?

Only four people knew of the key's location: Ma was dead; Pa was in Europe, perhaps dead as well, and, unless I had taken the key and plum forgot about doing so—which weren't too likely—it narrowed the list of suspects to one.

So why would Sally take the key?

If not for the feeding frenzy of skitters, I might have pondered the question at length. But all things considered, I had to get inside as fast as possible.

Haddes had instructed me to go in through a basement window, and at this point who was I to question him? The old coot had been right about everything else so far, and though I hated that fact, I decided—with the help of the skitters—not to fight it.

There were two basement windows on each side of the house. For those not good in math, that totaled eight. Each window was securely locked with a simple spring-loaded catch, and each catch worked just fine cuz Pa, worried about his family's safety in his absence, had checked and oiled them before he had shipped out last year. To the best of my knowledge, no one had opened them since then. So it stood to reason that I shouldn't be able to just simply 'pop' open a window with a simple tap. Then again, reason seemed not to matter anymore. Reason seemed to have taken a holiday.

I marched through the flowerbed to the closest window. Though it was difficult to see in the darkness, the window looked vault-like sealed. Still, what the heck? At this point I was willing to try pretty near anything to get away from these bloodsuckers.

I crouched, made a fist, and hammered the frame right where the spring-loaded catch would be. I expected it to hold firm. But dammit, I heard a soft 'pop' and the window creaked, opening a half inch. Hallelujah.

Once again, Charles Haddes had been right. And cuz of this, I really started to wonder if his crazy story about Limbo was true.

It couldn't be, of course. Cuz such things were just not possible.

Or was it?

(13)

It was hot and stuffy inside cuz the windows were closed. Since I couldn't very well spend the night in such stifling misery, I decided to open a few upstairs windows in the back of the house. Hopefully, if Nibbs happened by he wouldn't look too closely.

Using moonlight to see by, I climbed the stairs to the second floor. It was even hotter and stuffier up here. I wanted to turn on a light or two but didn't dare for obvious reasons. As I've said before, I hate the dark, but felt only slightly panicked cuz I was in familiar surroundings.

I ducked into Ma's sewing room, felt my way through the darkness to the window, and pulled aside the drapes. Moonlight flooded in, which, I soon discovered, was a mixed blessing. I could see now, sure, but the angle and strength of the light made harsh shadows with the items in the room, and those shadows—I would swear to this day—moved as though they were alive.

I told myself to relax, that the fear was all in my head, and took deep breaths to calm myself. I then pushed up the lone window. A blast of night air blew through the room. The air was warm but cooler than the air in the house so I stayed by the open window for a few seconds to enjoy it. And that's when I noticed something odd.

My Goonberry Gulch Gophers baseball uniform was neatly folded on Ma's sewing table. The last time I had seen the uniform, it was hanging up in my closet. How it had gotten on Ma's sewing table was a mystery. I hadn't done it, and unless Ma had snuck outta the hospital without my knowledge, I was certain she hadn't done it either. The garden key was missing so maybe Sally had done it. Why? I couldn't say. The uniform didn't need mending and, even if it did, Sally wouldn't be doing the mending. I knew for a fact she wasn't handy with a needle and thread. If she ever needed sewing done, Ester, the Pastor's live-in maid, did it.

I stepped over to the table and picked up the white cap, tracing my finger over the large black G sewn into the crown above the red bill. Doing that brought back a flood of memories. In my mind's eye, I recalled a snippet of crystal clear images of my no-hit pitching performance.

I felt proud of the accomplishment, and put on the cap. It still fit perfectly and I decided to wear it to Biloxi (that's if I was actually going there). Not only would it protect me from the sun, I felt the cap was lucky. I suppose it was all in my mind. Still, at this point, I could use all the luck—imagined or real—as I could get.

I picked up the white jersey with the red piping on the sleeves, admired the large red number 9 sewn on the back and then turned it around. Suddenly my train of thought jackknifed. The words GOONBERRY GULCH GOPHERS should have been sewn across the front. But those words were gone, replaced with the word LIMBO.

I stared in terror at the word, frozen like a statue. Suddenly the jersey came to life in my hand. It felt as though a foot-high gnome was yanking on it. But if it was a gnome, he was invisible, for I saw nothing, and flung the jersey away. I backed outta the room as if it was on fire, slammed shut the door as I left and leaned against the hallway wall, shivering with fear in the heat, trying to come up with a plausible explanation for what had happened.

But there were no explanations. And I knew then that, like it or not, I was destined to go to Limbo.

Limbo, Mississippi.

The land of the dead.

(14)

Before I went anywhere though, my curiosity needed to be scratched. So, using the drawstring hanging from the ceiling, I pulled down the folding stairs, cringing with gritted teeth at the squealing creak of bone-dry hinges and springs. The stairs were as rickety as an old man on stilts and I climbed up carefully, clutching the hand railings as the whole structure swayed from side to side.

The attic was as hot and as stuffy as the rest of the house and as dark as the inside of my pocket. Since there were no windows up here, I turned on the lone bare bulb mounted on the crossbeam overhead. A mass of thick spider webs shrouded the bulb's glow and I swiped them away with my hand. It helped to brighten the area—a tiny bit anyway.

I had never been scared to come up here before, but now I was a tad nervous. I was alone and, to be honest, I didn't remember the place being so dark and creepy and laden with spider webs. If Boris Karloff happened by with a moving-pitcher-camera we could have filmed a horror movie. Also playing on my mind was what I thought had just happened in Ma's sewing room. I wanted to believe I had imagined the whole thing, but in my heart I knew different. Forces were at work here that I couldn't explain.

"It's only the attic," I told myself angrily. "So act like a man."

It was hardly the stirring words of Knute Rockne, but they helped—a bit. And after taking a deep breath, I mustered up my courage and skirted around the boxes of Christmas decorations at the entrance, heading deep into the attic.

The floorboards creaked under foot and thin strains of cobwebs caressed my face and arms. I walked through a maze of cardboard boxes, trunks, and dusty furniture to the red and white chintz-covered sofa with the wide-arms and high-back cushions. The sofa smelled of mold and dog pee, which I guess was the reason it had been brought up here in the first place.

And as for the book? It was right where I had left it, perched on the sofa's arm, collecting dust.

I sat on the sofa, blew dust of the book cover and then laid the book on my lap. It was as large as a school atlas, thick as a good dictionary and gray as a Confederate uniform. It was simply entitled: THE CONFEDERACY. Below the two inch high plain white letter script was a black and white photo of General Lee mounted atop his horse, Traveler. Beneath the photo, running across the bottom in fancy gold script was the preamble to the Confederate constitution: *We, the people of the Confederate States, each state acting in its sovereign and independent character... etc...etc...*

On the first page was a colored picture of the Confederate battle flag, the Southern Cross. Beneath the flag was the publisher's credit: Perry, Pendergrass & Punsley Publishing: 1899. Lots of P's, huh?

I flipped to the index, ran a finger along the listings and, hallelujah, came across a listing for a Major Beauregard Quigley Breckinridge. Well, if nothing else, at least I now knew what the Q stood for.

I turned to the appropriate page, suspense swirling in my gut, and on first sight, felt a tinge of disappointment cuz there was no picture of the Major. Perhaps he was camera shy. Of course in the 1860's cameras weren't as plentiful as they are today so maybe he never got a chance to sit for a photo. Not that it mattered. I didn't come up here to see what he looked like anyway.

He was born in Goonberry Gulch, Mississippi on July 4th, 1824, a son of a blacksmith. He learned his father's trade, but joined the military, where he first saw action during the Mexican-American War of 1846. His bravery under fire vaulted him from mere 'grunt' solider to an officer. Once the war ended in 1848, he returned home and faded into the woodwork. There was no mention of a wife or kids, no mention of anything until the Civil War.

Sure enough, like Haddes had said, Breckinridge led a Mississippi unit into battle at Gettysburg. Things went poorly for him, and his entire company was wiped out. He was severely wounded and returned home to the Gulch a broken man, both mentally and physically.

And here was where things got interesting.

The rest of his biography seemed to be nothing more than pure speculation. He returned to battle in the spring of 1865, though no specifics were documented. All it said was that he had returned to battle with another Mississippi unit. As for what happened to him and his unit? It seemed no one knew—at least no one at Perry, Pendergrass & Punsley Publishing. It was as though Breckinridge and his men had vanished into thin air.

Yet, a plausible theory with a definite southern slant was hinted at.

See, at the time, groups of southern boys like Quantrill's Raiders and Bloody Bill Anderson were conducting a guerrilla war against the Yankees and the Yankees—it was believed—sent their own rebel units to combat the problem, and perhaps—perhaps now—Breckinridge and his men died at the hands of these cutthroat Yankees. Their bodies were never found, however, and thus, the mystery of what happened to Breckinridge and his men remains just that—a mystery.

Though I was from the south, I immediately scoffed at this brow-raising explanation. Even at fifteen, I saw the major flaw in this sort of thinking. See, if the Yankees did have rebel units—and I'd never heard of any—then why didn't they leave the bodies in plain sight to be discovered? After all, what's the point in conducting a guerrilla campaign if you don't install fear in the inhabitants? It didn't make sense.

I closed up the book, feeling disappointed in what I had read—or rather, what I hadn't read—and wondered what I should do.

Biloxi or Limbo?

Haddes and my crazy baseball jersey definitely wanted me to go to Limbo. I wanted to go to Biloxi cuz I felt that was the sane thing to do. But I also didn't wanna waste my time, and I felt now that going to Biloxi might be just that. After all, if a well respected lawman like Sheriff Nibbs got no information about Pa's whereabouts from the army, what made me think that I could do any better? In fact, it was possible they'd throw me in a cell and call Nibbs to come and get me.

So if not Biloxi, then Limbo?

It was a two day hike away and, for the most part, familiar territory. I could do it standing on my head. Plus, I liked hiking. I would need provisions, though: my shotgun, a knapsack with food, a canteen, matches...

As I made a mental list of what I'd need for the trip, I heard a loud bang. My heart nearly jumped outta my chest and I sprang to my feet, listening.

It sounded as though the kitchen door had slammed shut, and I held my breath, hoping I had imagined it. Maybe the wind had knocked something over in Ma's sewing room. Heck, for that matter, maybe my damn jersey had come alive again and was dancing about, knocking stuff over.

Then I heard footfalls on the stairs.

It had to be Sheiff Nibbs or his trustworthy deputy, Mumbles.

So much for my planned trip to Limbo. It appeared now I was destined for the Vicksburg Orphanage.

Lucky me.

(15)

I had two choices: hide or give up. The latter seemed too cowardly. If Nibbs or Mumbles was gonna haul me off to the orphanage, I felt obliged to at least give them a bit of a chase. I'd have no respect for myself if I didn't.

The first thing I had to do was get outta the attic. Sure, it was the perfect place to hide, but all Nibbs or Mumbles had to do was fold up the stairs and I'd be locked in. So I flung the book onto the sofa and bolted to the stairs, not caring about how loud I was. A glimpse down the hatch revealed an encouraging sight: the lights on the second floor hallway remained off. If I could get down these stairs and hide—say under a bed or in a closet—before the lights got turned on, I had a chance. A slim chance, sure, but again, no matter what happened, at least I'd respect myself in the morning for giving them a bit of a chase.

I started down the stairs recklessly fast, and missed a step. Suddenly I was falling. It was a short fall, thankfully, and I landed on my back with a loud thud. I wasn't hurt, though, more embarrassed than anything, and as I climbed to my feet, setting my baseball cap back firmly on my head, I heard the click-clack of a well-oiled shotgun being cocked.

So much for giving them a chase, huh?

I raised my arms to surrender and turned, expecting to see Nibbs or Mumbles. Instead, I saw a beautiful round face ringed with long blonde hair illuminated by the moon's soft glow.

I sighed with relief. "You ain't gonna shoot me, are you?"

Sally squealed, "Johnny!"

I held my arms out to her. "C'mere."

She laid the shotgun on the floor and ran into my open arms, hugging me hard. "I can't believe it." She buried her face in my neck and started to cry. "I'm so sorry about your, Ma, Johnny," she sobbed. "So sorry."

I realized then that Sally was probably as grief-stricken about Ma's passing as I was. Sure, they weren't blood kin, but they spent a lot a time together. Not only was Ma Sally's teacher and neighbor, she was also her surrogate Ma cuz Sally's real Ma had died in a car accident a couple years back. So like me, Sally had lost a big part of her life and was hurting too.

"I was so worried about you," she went on, and before I could reply, she kissed me hard on the lips and squeezed me even tighter. Then she stepped back, looking me up and down to make sure I was okay. "I'm so happy I found you, and that you're okay."

She had a couple of inches on me and probably outweighed me by fifty pounds. You wouldn't have called her fat, hefty maybe, but not fat. She was a farm girl after all, and hard working farm girls, just like men, tend to buildup a lot of bulk.

But she was no man. She had the face of an angel. Large blue eyes, round cheeks, slender nose and lips as full as lips get. Her smile was bright enough to read by, and her teeth were straight and white as the piano keys she enjoyed playing so much.

She was a smart gal, too—straight A's. And thanks to my Ma and Sally's northern educated grandfather, she spoke with the elegance of a politician.

"I thought you were Cole Conklin," she admitted. "There's a rumor that he and his gang are in these parts."

For half a second I considered telling her that I could substantiate the rumor, for I had not only seen them, I had, among other things, spoken with them. But that would open a can of worms I was not up to dealing with. Sides, Conklin had promised to torture and murder Sally if I squealed, so why tempt fate? And as for my civic duty? Well, sorry gang. I was fresh outta civic duty ever since Sheriff Nibbs told me I was destined for the orphanage. Maybe next week I'd feel more civic pride and responsibility and let the authorities know about the encounter. Then again, maybe not.

"So where have you been? Sheriff Nibbs claims you ran off on him."

"He claims right. He ain't putting me in an orphanage—not without a fight."

"You can stay with us."

"Oh yeah?" I muttered, and raised a brow. "What about your grandfather? Nibbs said he didn't want me staying with you."

She lowered her eyes in shame. "Don't worry about the Pastor," she assured me, lovingly running an index finger along my cheek. "I spoke to him and convinced him to let you stay until at least after the funeral."

"What happens after that?"

She sighed. "I'm not sure, Johnny. I don't want to argue with the Pastor right now. He's upset about your Ma's passing. And he's also mighty preoccupied on account of that ammunition explosion over in Squirrel Flats. In case you don't know a lot of people got killed and he has to go there tomorrow and help with the funerals. So this isn't a time for arguing. It's a time for grieving. So I've said my prayers and have turned it over to God. So it's in His hands now."

Sally, always the voice of reason, calmed my barking ego. "Okay. Fair enough."

She looked up at the open attic hatch. "What were you doing up there?"

"Looking at a book."

She cocked a brow at me as though I'd lost my mind. Who knows? Maybe I had.

"It's a long story," I replied, wondering how much of the story I should tell her. Sally had an open mind, but I strongly doubted that her mind was open enough to believe the Limbo story. Heck, I'd heard the story firsthand and had been bombarded with evidence and I was still having a hard time believing it.

"C'mon," she said, holding my hand. "Let's go home. You must be starving."

She was right. I hadn't eaten all day, and though I barely noticed on account of all the grief hanging over me, I felt hunger pains now.

She crouched, went to pick up the shotgun, but paused. "Do you have a window open? I feel a draft from under that door."

"Oh yeah, that reminds me, Have you been in Ma's sewing room?"

She straightened up and shook her head. "We've got our own sewing machine. Sides, I don't sew. Ester does the sewing at home. Why?"

"I want you to see something." I opened the sewing room door, flicked on the light and pointed at the jersey on the floor. "Take a look at that?"

She sighed wearisomely, walked into the room and picked up the jersey, holding it at the shoulders as though she was about to pin it to a clothesline. "Yeah, okay? So?"

"Do you see anything weird about it? Like what's sewn on the front."

She looked where I directed, and after a few seconds, held the jersey up for me to see. "What's wrong with this?"

"Look what's sewn—" I held up abruptly cuz I saw that the word 'Limbo' was no longer sewn on the jersey. The words—GOONBERRY GULCH GOPHERS—had returned.

"Well? What's wrong? Do you need this mended?"

I shook my head slowly. "You never touched the uniform?"

"That's right. I didn't know where it was."

"Someone put the uniform in here?"

"It wasn't me, honest."

"What about the key? The key under the rock is missing. Did you take that?"

She nodded. "Sorry. Nibbs made me do it. He wanted all the weapons removed from the house in case Conklin broke in and took them. So I let him in." She shrugged. "I guess I forgot to put the key back under rock."

"Nibbs has my shotgun?"

"Don't worry," she said. "He'll give back. It's not like you're going to need it anytime soon."

"Actually, I am gonna need it."

"Huh? Why?"

"If I told you, you'd never believe me."

"Try me."

"I'll tell you later," I said. "But first I have to talk to the Pastor."

(16)

Sally shouldered her shotgun as though she was marching off to battle, and together, we crossed the street and walked up the Dickerson's driveway. At the time, it was the only paved driveway in the entire county; a 'thank you back scratch' from Mayor Valentine cuz the Pastor had endorsed Valentine's candidacy last election despite evidence of mounting corruption at City Hall and the criminal antics of the Mayor's nineteen-year-old twin sons, Clem and Clancy, both of whom were now proudly serving our country.

Though this was the 40's and rural Mississippi, the driveway looked in no way out of place cuz the Pastor owned what could only be described as a mansion. It was a three-story, redbrick palace with big windows, blue shutters, upstairs balconies and a decorative masonry porch complete with marble pillars—a nice touch, I suppose, if you lived on Mount Olympus. Here in the Gulch, the pillars looked a bit too gauche, I thought. But what did I know?

As we approached the front porch, I caught a whiff of stale cigarette smoke and immediately thought of Cole Conklin. The smoker, however, turned out to be a grizzled-looking Mexican with long, greasy black hair and a five o'clock shadow as dark as a bear's coat. He sat on the porch steps with a rifle cradled in his lap and shot us a nasty look as we filed past him up the stairs.

The Pastor, I knew, employed a dozen Mexicans for the growing season, but it was odd to see them near the house. They had their own quarters in the back near the barn and were rarely seen anywhere but out in the fields. So why was the hired help totting a rifle and sitting on the porch, smoking?

Sally must have read my mind cuz she quickly said, "The Pastor posted a guard in case the Conklin Gang showed up." She rolled her eyes to let me know she thought the likelihood of that happening was remote. If only she knew.

Once we were inside, she locked the front door, stowed her shotgun in the closet and led the way along the hallway toward the kitchen. The heavenly scent of fresh baking lit up my appetite like a blowtorch on dry wood, and as I told her how good it smelled, and how hungry I was, the kitchen door swung open and Ester, the Dickerson's live-in maid, stepped into the hallway.

Seeing me, she froze in place, her bottom lip beginning to quiver. Her dark eyes filed with tears and she waddled to me, her short, stubby arms extended out in front of her. "Master Johnny," she wailed, and threw her arms around me, hugging me hard. I hugged her back and felt the sting of tears behind my eyes.

Ester was a fireplug on legs, as wide as she was tall. Her hair was a whitish gray and her skin was as black as black gets and as smooth as glass. Her cheeks, wet with tears now, were chubby balls of dough and her two extra chins giggled when she talked.

"I'm a sorry for your loss," she sobbed, and dried her eyes on her flour-dusted apron. "Your Ma was a fine woman."

"Thank you for saying."

She stepped back, bowed her head, made the sign of the cross and whispered a short prayer that started with "Our Father' and ended with "Amen".

The 'Amen' was punctuated by the grunt of thick phlegm hawked back through a nose. Ester, Sally and I turned in the direction of the rude noise at once. We saw the Pastor at the top of the stairs, hands on hips, looking down his nose at us.

"Well, well, well," he began smugly, and slowly descended the stairs with the same calculating malice of a lion closing in on its injured prey. "I see that Mr. McGrath has graced us with his presence. How wonderful."

Sally frowned so hard I saw lines crease her cheeks that I didn't know existed. I guess she expected her grandfather to greet me with a measure of sympathy cuz of my loss. So much for expectations, huh?

He stepped off the bottom stair, and stopped before me, his hands back on his hips again, his eyes narrowed to stern slits. "Sheriff Nibbs is angry with you."

I truly wanted to say the feeling was mutual, but stayed quiet cuz this was surely not the time to start an argument. After all, I had to stay here. Sides, if I was going to Limbo, I would need his help.

"I'm less than pleased with you, too," he declared.

The feeling was mutual. But once again, I stayed quiet.

He fished his pipe from the pocket of his red cardigan sweater and added, "Members of my flock should not be so disrespectful."

I stayed quiet—and to this day I don't know how I did it.

He lit his pipe with a gold lighter, raising a good cloud of smoke around his head, and regarded me in thoughtful silence.

He was a tall man—six four easy—and bone-thin. Pushing eighty, he looked every bit his age. His hair, what was left of it, was snow white and his face was as wrinkled as a well circulated dollar bill. He still had his teeth, but time and his pipe smoking had turned them a dandelion yellow.

"I told Sheriff Nibbs I would call the station if you happened by, but I forgot my phone service is still out of order." He grinned around his pipe, making it clear he had an ulterior motive. "When I tell the good Sheriff this tomorrow, perhaps he'll put some pressure on the phone company to get someone out here to fix the problem."

"Pastor," Sally began tentatively. "Johnny hasn't eaten all day. So—"

"It's his own fault," he cut in abruptly.

"Please, Pastor," she went on. "Johnny really needs to eat."

"He'll eat when I finish speaking to him." He glared at me through a thin veil of smoke. "We need to discuss a few things, make funeral arrangements." He snapped his fingers. "Follow me. We'll talk in my office." And with that said, he walked away.

Sally reached out and gave my hand a gentle squeeze. "Good luck," she mouthed.

I grinned with confidence cuz I knew I had nothing to worry about. Cuz while he was chastising me I remembered something Charles Haddes had told me, and that something, I knew, was gonna wipe the smugness right off the good Pastor's face.

(17)

If you had a problem say, with your faith, or if you wanted to plan a wedding or, as in the case now, a funeral, then Pastor Dickerson would meet with you in his office at the church on Goonberry Lane. Only the privileged few—people like Mayor Valentine or Sheriff Nibbs—were ever allowed to meet with him in his private sanctuary at home. So I felt honored, somewhat anyway.

The room was long, narrow and bathed in a soft white light from globe fixtures spaced out evenly every few feet on the crossbeam that ran down the center of the room. The walls were white-sanded wood planks—tasteful, and no doubt, expensive. A Betty Zuckerman oil painting of the Pastor's church hung on the wall between two long windows. Both windows were open wide and bugs—some the size of quarters—buzzed at the screens. The wood floor, worn smooth from wear, groaned as we walked toward the Pastor's massive oak desk.

The desktop was cluttered. A picture of Jesus walking across water, a white glow around His face, sat on the right corner of the desk. Tucked in behind the picture was the Pastor's black-covered Bible, dog-eared from use, and a telephone, which, at the time, was nothing more than a paperweight. A blue appointment book and a clean ashtray sat on the left corner of the desk. Next to the ashtray was a pristine copy of the Goonberry Gulch Gazette. The paper was turned the other way but, surprisingly enough, I discovered I was good at reading words upside down. What I read boded-ill for the Mayor, for the headline read: MAYOR'S SONS GO AWOL. Beneath the headline was a photo of a shirtless Clem and Clancy Valentine showing off their many tattoos at last year's 4th of July picnic.

The telephone conversation between Sheriff Nibbs and Deputy Mumbles at the hospital this morning now made sense. Obviously the Mayor wanted the Sheriff to find the boys before the MPs did cuz Sheriff Nibbs would certainly treat the boys a heckuva lot better than the Army. I wondered if the Army was looking for them as hard as they were looking for my Pa.

The Pastor, seeing my attention focused on the paper, cleared his throat gruffly. I looked at him and grinned. He frowned as if he had just caught me with my hand in the collection plate. His frown deepened as he picked up a straight-backed wooden chair from against the wall and banged it down in front of his desk. Then, with theatrical distaste, he thrust a tobacco-stained finger at the chair, jabbing the air several times for me to sit. Since he had asked so politely, I sat at once.

With an annoying sigh, he walked behind his desk, up to a floor unit air fan in the corner and flicked a switch. The device squealed to life and resonated along in a low, bee-hive buzzing hum. Once satisfied with the direction of the airflow, he eased into a squeaky swivel-tit chair with black leather seat cushions and rolled up to his desk. The newspaper sat right in front of him, and after an exasperated sigh and a frown that would give a child nightmares, he folded up the paper and bitterly threw it in the garbage can beside his desk.

"Those boys should be horsewhipped," he muttered. "Running off like that. And they are not even in combat. What kind of harm could happen to them cleaning latrines at an army base in Biloxi?"

He had a point. If you had to fight a war, fighting it there was certainly safe.

He cleared phlegm from his throat and stared at me. "As I said earlier, you've been disrespectful to Sheriff Nibbs. And disrespect can't be tolerated. I don't want disrespectful people dating my granddaughter. Do you understand?"

I nodded.

"Now I told Sheriff Nibbs that he would have to forgive you on account of your Ma's passing. But that's it. It can't happen again. Understand?"

Again, I nodded.

Satisfied he had whipped me into line, he put his pipe in the ashtray and leaned back in his chair. "Now, you can stay with us in the guestroom until after the funeral. After that you'll have to go to the orphanage." He shrugged his white brows indifferently. "Who knows, now that our troops are in France the war may soon end and we'll hear what happened to your father. If he's still alive, you may not have to spend too much time there."

Easy for him to say, huh?

"It's too bad about your farm," he went on with a hint of glee. "That's gone for sure, which is good news for me. Because once the bank puts your farm up for sale next month, I plan to buy it. I wanted Sam Knight's property, but he won't sell to me because he hates my guts."

I can't imagine why, I thought.

"So I guess I'll expand across the street instead." He shrugged with an air of superiority, making me feel as small as a bug. "If there are any keepsakes you want, you better get them soon because I plan to knock down the house and barn."

It was all I could do to restrain myself from jumping outta the chair and punching him square in his face. He certainly deserved it. Of course I couldn't do it. I had to stay here. Still, my bruised ego jumped its chain and I bluntly returned. "That may not happen. You don't own our farm yet. Understand?"

His face hardened and his mouth became a harsh line. "I'd be careful what you say and how you say it. The only reason I'm allowing you to stay here is because of my granddaughter."

"I know. Sheriff Nibbs made it clear that you wanted nothing to do with me." I wanted to throw in *'that's not so Christian of you'* but decided judging his Christianity was not up to me.

He sighed sadly. "Sheriff Nibbs talks too much. But since it's out in the open, I won't pretend it wasn't said." He leaned forward, his chair creaking, and put his elbows on the desktop. "See McGrath, I care little for my granddaughter's choice in suitors. Frankly, I think she can do better."

I was so crushed by his bluntness my whole train of thought stopped. I wanted to respond, but found I couldn't speak.

"Don't get me wrong, McGrath," he pushed on. "It's not that I dislike you, it's just that I think she can do better. Besides, I really don't trust you. You're a lot like your father, and your father and I have had our differences over the years. You're also left-handed, and though I know attitudes are changing about that, I'm still of the mind that it's the sign of the Devil. And the Devil should be avoided at all costs."

Well, if nothing else, at least he was being honest.

"Anyway, enough talk about that," he continued on in a cheerier voice. "I truly liked your mother, and since the good woman has passed, we have to plan her funeral." He flipped open his blue-covered appointment book and began leafing through the pages. "Since I have to conduct funerals over in Squirrel Flats tomorrow for some of the victims of the ammunition factory explosion, we'll have to schedule her funeral for later in the week." He hummed to himself as he looked over the book's pages. "How about Friday? That'll give the funeral home plenty of time to prepare the body and me time to work on her eulogy. I plan to speak for a good half hour about your mother. She deserves it."

"That she does," I replied, happy to hear I could still speak, but fearful cuz I knew all the civility in the conversation was about to come to a close. "Uh, Pastor, you can take your time with the eulogy cuz the funeral is gonna have to wait until next week."

He looked overtop of his book at me. "Nonsense, McGrath, we'll do it Friday. I'll make the time, don't worry."

"Next week," I shot back forcefully.

His eyes narrowed. "Listen McGrath, I don't think you're getting it. I know you're distraught over your mother's passing but you're going to need to grow up and act like a man." He sighed bitterly and flipped through the appointment book. "The funeral will be Friday. That'll even give my farmhands time to cleanup the cemetery. It's a damn mess over there since Groundskeeper Noonan went off to fight the Japanese."

"Take your time with the cleanup as well cuz the funeral ain't gonna be till next week."

He slammed shut his appointment book and tossed it on his desk. "Listen McGrath, I've had enough of you."

"I've had enough of you, too," I returned with such cold bitterness his eyes filled with fright. "You ain't making decisions about my Ma— understand?"

He shot outta of his chair like a jack-in-the-box and leaned over his desk. "Listen you little brat," he barked. "Just because my phone is out of service doesn't mean I can't get word to Sheriff Nibbs. I'll send one of my

Mexicans to fetch him. I'll have you in the orphanage so fast your head will spin."

"If you do, you won't like what will happen."

"Oh no," he challenged. "Are you thinking my granddaughter will come to your rescue? Because if you think that, think again. She'll do what I say."

"I would prefer to leave Sally outta this, as I'm sure you would want as well." And since he was standing, I stood as well and looked him in the eyes. "You're missing the point, Pastor. See, it's a long drive to Vicksburg, and with nothing to do, I may get talkative. No telling what may come outta my mouth. And we both know Sheriff Nibbs likes to gossip."

He grinned. "Are you threatening me, McGrath?"

"Tell me Pastor, have you been to Possum Hollow lately?"

"Why would I go there?"

"To visit your illegitimate son, Clark."

His eyes popped so far outta his head if he'd been wearing glasses they would have knocked out the lenses. His breath got caught in his throat, and though he tried to talk, all that came out was a long, "Uhhhhhhhhhhh."

Since he was at a loss for words, and since he had spoken so poorly about me and Pa, I sprinkled a little salt in his wounds for good measure. "Did you name him after Superman or Clark Gable?"

"How dare you," he managed finally, sputtering with frustration. He stormed to the door, his cheeks as red as barn paint. "That's it. You've crossed the line. I'll have Nibbs here within the hour."

"Do what you want. But I mean what I say. I ain't bluffing."

He whirled about, his eyes flashing angrily. "I have no illegitimate children."

I mimicked his earlier gesture, shrugging with an air of superiority. "I don't care if you do or not, but I am gonna tell Sheriff Nibbs about your son in Possum Hollow. And you can be damned sure he's gonna tell everyone he meets." I grinned, amazed at myself for how cold I could be when pushed. "The Mayor will sure be happy. Cuz with you in the news, it'll take the heat off him and his two good-for-nothing kids."

He leaned against the door, breathing hard—almost gasping—and I noticed the redness had seeped outta his cheeks. His complexion had paled, and was getting whiter by the second. He was close to keeling over, and though I was angry with him for how he had bullied me, I didn't wanna be responsible for his death. He didn't deserve that and I didn't deserve living the rest of my life knowing I had provoked his demise.

"I'm sorry if I've upset you," I said mildly. "But as you said, I have to act like a man. You'd have no respect for me if I didn't. And you'd keep treating me like you have if I didn't stand up for myself. So why don't we talk this through like gentlemen and come to some sort of an understanding."

"What do you want?" he asked breathlessly. "Are you going to blackmail me?"

I shook my head. "I just want the funeral to be next week cuz I wanna be at it."

His cheeks bunched up quizzically. "Why? Where are you going to be on Friday?"

"I have some place to go."

"Go? Go where?"

"Limbo," I replied evenly. "I'm going to Limbo. Limbo, Mississippi."

His face froze with horror-stricken shock, his eyes narrowed to pinpricks, and his already ashen complexion, paled even further. I had struck a nerve worse than revealing his Possum Hollow secret. And cuz of his reaction, I knew it was all true. Everything Haddes had told me was true. Limbo did exist. The land of the dead was a mere two day walk from here. Wow, you just never know what's in your backyard, huh?

"I'm leaving tomorrow," I said, and sat, hoping he would do the same. "As you know, my Pa is missing. If I see him there, then I'll know he ain't coming back. But if I don't see him, then there's still a chance he's alive."

"I see," he said quietly, walking behind his desk. "I don't know who you've been talking to, McGrath. But let me assure you, you're wasting your time. Limbo is a myth. A fairytale. It doesn't exist."

I ignored his lie. "I'll need some provisions for the hike. Two days there; two days back."

"Are you listening?" he asked gruffly, and dropped into his chair. "The place you're talking about doesn't exist."

I shrugged. "I'm still going. The fresh air will do me good."

He sighed and picked up his Bible for comfort.

"You should be happy," I went on. "Cuz if I do see my Pa there, if I know for certain he's dead, then I most likely won't return to the Gulch.

See, I don't plan to spend the next three years in an orphanage. I hear California is nice this time of year. Who knows? Maybe I'll take up acting. But no matter where I end up, you'll be rid of me—just like you want. Sally will be sad. But she'll get over me."

"Listen McGrath, Limbo doesn't exist. I don't know what you've heard or who you've heard it from, but let me tell you, you're misinformed."

"You're not a good liar, Pastor."

"Think what you want, but the place doesn't exist."

"The fear I saw in your eyes when I mentioned Limbo confirmed it."

He looked away for a moment, his eyes focused in the general direction of Betty Zuckerman's oil painting. Then he muttered, "You don't know what you're getting into."

"You're probably right. That's why I need to hear your story. You've been there. So I need to know everything you know about the place."

He looked at me sharply. "You've been talking to Sam Knight?"

I shook my head.

"Who's lying now, McGrath?" he questioned bluntly.

"It matters little who told me, Pastor. I know—that's all that matters."

He was silent, slowly running his thumb over the pages of his Bible; I stayed silent as well, allowing him the time to think.

Finally, he shook his head. "Sorry, McGrath. I can't let you go up there. One of these days I'm going to die and when I stand before the good Lord, I don't want your blood on my hands. So I'm going to contact Nibbs. If you want to tell him about my son—then so be it. I'll be defrocked by my congregation, no doubt, but you know something? Maybe it's time I retire anyway."

"Do what you need to do, Pastor, but if I end up in the orphanage, I'll just escape. Cuz one way or another, I'm going to Limbo. I feel it's something I have to do. I guess you can't understand that. But I feel it's my destiny to go there."

"Don't believe everything you think," he shot back. "That's the problem with people. They get something in their head and can't get it out. They end up making self- fulfilling prophecies. Don't do that. Don't act on assumptions. Throw away your broken thoughts—cuz that's what they are—'broken'. Act on facts. So forget about Limbo. After all, does it really matter if you see your father up there? Just because you don't see him, doesn't me he hasn't passed on."

"You make a good argument, Pastor. But a man has to do what a man has to do. And I feel I have to do this."

He climbed to his feet. "I have to summon Nibbs. I hope you won't speak too ill of me to my granddaughter. Once word that I have an illegitimate child gets out, she'll think plenty of bad things about me anyway."

"Pastor, if you want a clear conscious when you meet your Maker, then help me. Cuz I stand a better chance of survival if you do."

As he went to speak, a knock on the door made him pause.

"Pastor, Pastor," Sally yelled beneath the door. "Sheriff Nibbs is here."

My heart skipped a beat. I looked at the Pastor, expecting to find him grinning. Instead, he shot me a reassuring look and walked out from behind his desk.

"Stay here," he said, and hurried from the room, locking the door behind him.

He had me where he wanted me, and I considered going out the window. It was a short drop to the ground and I could easily sneak away in the dark. But I was too tired to run. Sides, what would I do then anyway? I needed his help.

So I decided to stay put and see what would happen.

(18)

Each second seemed like a minute and each minute seemed like an hour and, well, you get the idea. Time dragged, my anticipation built, and I kept looking at the window, wondering if I should open it and run.

Running would be easy. But was it the right thing to do?

The question crawled around my brain like a busy ant until finally, unable to stand it any longer, I climbed to my feet and went to the window. As I reached over to open the screen, I heard the key strike the lock. I was too late, and I stepped away from the window and turned toward the door.

The door opened and the Pastor entered the room looking like he always looked—slightly annoyed. He locked the door behind him and walked behind his desk, barely looking in my direction. He sat, noticed I was standing and, clearing his throat irritably, motioned for me to sit.

I sat at once. "Did you tell him I was here?"

He nodded and lit his pipe, using his hand to clear the cloud of smoke from in front of his face.

My heart started to beat faster. "And...?"

"And what? You're here and you're safe. That's all the man cares about."

"What did you tell him?"

"I told him you were sleeping, which of course is a lie. That lie is on you, and when you say your prayers tonight, I expect you to ask for forgiveness."

"Thank you."

"Don't thank me. Because if you do what you're planning to do, you're going to wish I had handed you over to him. You're going to wish you were at the orphanage."

Hardly, I thought, but kept the sentiment to myself.

"Let me tell you something, McGrath," he went on, leaning both elbows on the desktop. "The world is swimming with evil. I suppose on some level there is always an underlining current of evil about, but nowadays that evil is stirred up. The last place you want to be is in Europe or Asia or anyplace where people are shooting each other or starving to death. But where you're planning to go is far worse. Because Limbo isn't part of this world. It's a place that shouldn't be—a place no living man should go to. So you have to ask yourself, McGrath, do you really want to hike up there and look for a dead man? Because I guarantee you, you are not going to like what you find."

"Well Pastor, I won't say you didn't warn me."

"That's the thing, McGrath, you won't have the chance to say that. Because if you go, you most likely won't return."

"I guess that'll be good for you. You'll get your wish—me away from your granddaughter."

He sighed as though I'd just asked him to help me move something heavy. "Okay," he breathed, "what do you want from me? Provisions? A shotgun? My blessing?"

"Yeah. All those things. But what I really need is to hear your story. You went up there. I need to know what happened? What to expect?"

He nodded. "Okay, I'll tell you, and I'll ask the good Lord tonight to forgive me for doing so. But I need to know something first. What do you plan on telling my granddaughter?"

Good question. "Uhhhh, I don't know. I guess I'll tell her the truth."

"Think she'll believe you?"

Another good question. I shrugged.

He blew smoke out his nostrils. "Okay, for the sake of my granddaughter, I'll explain it to her—well, as best as I can. It'll also give me a chance to tell her she has a young uncle in Possum Hollow."

"Uncle in Possum Hollow, huh?" I questioned, pretending not to know what he was talking about. "I remember we talked about something like that, but for the life of me, I can't remember. It's plum gone. Guess my memory ain't that good."

The tension lines around his eyes and mouth softened and his body language relaxed. He leaned back in his chair, puffed on his pipe, and actually grinned. I guess I had said the right thing.

"You know what's funny about all this, McGrath? I always knew this day would come, that one day someone would knock on my door and ask about Limbo. I figured it would be a lawman looking for someone or maybe a reporter who had heard a rumor and wanted to investigate it. Never in my wildest dreams did I think it would be you. A person I baptized, a neighbor who has eaten at my table, someone who is close friends with my granddaughter." He shook his head. "You just never know what the day has in store for you, huh?"

Thinking about the day I just had, I nodded.

He turned to the picture of his daughter—Sally's Ma—hanging on the wall behind his desk. "When my Abigail passed, when the accident took her and her husband and Sally's sister, Becky, two years ago, I hurt so bad I wanted to die myself. I yearned so badly to see them once more that I considered going back up there."

"Did you?"

He shook his head. "I didn't because it wasn't right. Because the place isn't right. It shouldn't be there. It's there, sure, but it shouldn't be. It's wrong. Plain wrong."

"Do you know how it came to be?"

"I've heard theories on the subject," he replied. "Sam Knight thinks there's a rip in the fabric of our world that lets Limbo bleed through. Course Knight is a no-good boozer so why believe him? Though, I suppose it's as good an explanation as any."

"You heard about Limbo from him?"

He shook his head. "Knight and I both heard about the place from Charles Haddes. His family has lived in the Gulch since the early 1800's. Haddes's brother was a teenager during the Civil War and joined up with Breckinridge's platoon. Do you know that part of the story?"

"Yeah. I heard they got trapped in Limbo except for a retarded man."

"That's right. A man named Abby was the only survivor."

"Did you know him?"

"No. He died before I came to the Gulch."

"When was that?"

"I was probably about your age, give or take a year when I came here. Grant was president, or maybe it was Rutherford Hays. It was a damn Yankee that's for sure. My Pa had made a fortune in the Mexican oil business, but got out when the getting was good and bought this huge parcel of land in the Gulch, hoping to make a go at farming. I soon met Sam Knight, who, like me, is still living in the same house today. And through Knight, I met Charles Haddes. Haddes was older than us, but we still all hung around together. We used to go hunting a lot, and one night around the campfire, Haddes told us about Limbo."

"You believe him?"

He grinned around his pipe. "Would you?"

"Not without proof. Not without others to backup his claims."

"I felt the same way—though I must admit, Haddes sure spoke with conviction. With a smooth tongue like his, he should have been a preacher or politician instead of a no-good bootlegging boozer."

"I'm surprised you two were friends."

"There weren't that many kids to hang around with back then. It was them or be alone. Not that it mattered, because before long, Pa sent me off to seminary school up north. I can't say I cared much for those Yankees, or the weather for that matter, but I learned the gospel and got a fine education. I also learned how to speak. No longer did I use words like 'ain't' or 'gonna' or 'wanna'. I spoke properly. I think that's one reason I liked your mother so much. She spoke with an air of sophistication rarely seen in these parts. To bad others didn't speak like her."

Like Pa, I thought, who spoke hayseed south like most did in these parts.

"Anyway, once I graduated from school, I returned to the Gulch and I started preaching."

"What about Knight and Haddes?"

"I nearly forgot all about them. I was busy with the church and had made a great deal of church friends. And it was one of these friends— Lester Merriweather—that eventually led me back to those sinners. See Lester and I worked together at the church, organizing church socials and potluck dinners. Over the years we grew to be best friends. Then, a woman named Sophie joined the church and her and Lester fell in love and got married. I performed their wedding ceremony. A year later, Sophie died of the cancer like your mother." He sighed heavily as the memory of that time tumbled through his thoughts. "Lester was heartbroken, of course, and just dropped out of society. This was before the telephone, remember, so I couldn't call him, and though I rode over to his house as often as I could, it wasn't often enough because I was just too damn busy at the church. We just sort of fell out of touch."

Tears welled up in his eyes, and he paused to relight his pipe—though it didn't need relighting. Then he cleared his throat and continued.

"Finally one day I found a spare moment and went over to see him. He didn't answer the door so I checked the barn and found him lying dead beside his horse."

"Really? What did he die of?"

"A broken heart, I suppose." He shrugged. "There was no autopsy done. Our sawbones at the time, Doc Rathbone, hardly had the skills to do such a thing. He did examine the body and said there were no signs of violence or foul play. He wrote on the death certificate that Lester had merely expired. That didn't sit too well with me and before long I started thinking of Haddes and that crazy story he told me.

"I think it was 08 then, and though I hadn't spoken with Haddes in a good ten years, I went over to see him. He and Knight were bootlegging together at this point, and since I'd been preaching hard about the sins of their 'shine', I wasn't welcomed and soon found myself looking down the business end of two shotguns. So I talked quickly, and proposed a deal. I told them that if they gave me the exact location of Limbo, I would stop talking against their 'shine' operation." He grinned around his pipe. "They were more than happy to oblige, and told me what I needed to know." He chuckled lightly. "I guess they hoped I'd crossover and get trapped there. But I remembered the story of Breckinridge's platoon and knew better. So the next day, I saddled up Betty-Lou and headed for Limbo. I made it; the horse didn't."

"The horse died?"

"No. She was smarter than me, and bolted for home before I even saw the flashing red light. The evil drove her off." He leaned forward then, staring me in the eyes. "Let me ask you something: do you know what schizophrenia is?"

I shook my head.

"It's a mental disorder."

"Craziness?"

"You could call it that," he replied. "Do you know that in this area we have the highest rate of schizophrenia in the country?"

"Really? I didn't know."

"I'm not surprised. It's not exactly something the Chamber of Commerce brags about. Nor do they brag about the fact that we also have the highest suicide rate in the country."

"I had no idea," I muttered, and thought of Nurse Bilodeau. She had said that the Gulch was the center of all weirdness. It appeared the Pastor thought the same way.

"When you were in the hospital with your mother, did you hear about the patients on the third floor?"

"Yeah."

"Well, I have no proof, but I think most of those mental problems are caused by Limbo. There's an evil wafting off the place. It's just too damn close to our town."

"Why does it bother some folks and not others?"

He shrugged. "I don't rightly know. I suppose it's like any illness. Some people get sick and some people don't. But be warned, the closer you get to Limbo, the worse the evil gets."

I thought about the times Pa and I went hunting up there. Had he acted oddly? I couldn't say for sure. Maybe. I do know we never walked the entire length of the trail. We always turned back or took another route.

"I should have followed Betty-Lou," the Pastor went on. "But I was determined to see this through. So I kept going, and the evil got as thick as molasses. It made me think bad thoughts. I knew it was wrong. I'm a preacher, after all. I'm a man of God. I'm not suppose to think thoughts like that. Still, the thoughts were there. Every ounce of evil I had in me came out like sweat on a hot day. So if you go, McGrath, if you follow this through, be mindful of that. You are not going to like what you think."

My ego assured me that wouldn't happen. I could control my thoughts. "So what happened next?"

"I kept going, walking through thick, knee-high mist that just came out of nowhere. Soon I came to the top of a gully. The grass was long here and wild and I looked down and saw a graveyard. I was nervous, as nervous as I'd ever been, but I sucked up my courage and went down the hill into the graveyard anyway. It was a small place, maybe the size of my front yard, surrounded by a stone fence. There were only five or six tombstones and they were all inscribed with just single names. Jonathan, Michael, Daniel, Joshua." He shrugged. "Good strong Biblical names for sure. But that was all. There were no other words on the stones. No date of birth or death, no epitaph of any kind. Just the Christian names."

"Do you think it's a family plot? So no last names are necessary?"

"Even family plot headstones include the last name."

He was right.

"And I have never seen a headstone without some sort of epitaph."

Again, he was right.

"It was weird, McGrath. Weird and downright scary. For I would swear to this day that I heard banging coming from beneath the ground."

"Huh? Seriously? From the graves?"

He nodded. "At the time I thought it was my imagination. You know, because I was so scared. But I've thought about it often over the years and well"—he shrugged—"I really don't know for sure. Those buried there might still be alive."

"How is that possible?"

"It's Limbo, McGrath. As I said before, the place is just plain wrong."

"I'll say," I muttered. "So what did you do then?"

"I moved on to the cemetery's outer fence—the stone fence that borders Limbo. I could see a road leading to the buildings, and a crudely written sign that warned folks not to go any further. I wanted to go on, though, despite the warning, but didn't dare for fear of getting trapped on the other side. So I stayed put, watching. But I didn't stay for long."

"You saw them? You saw the ghosts? Your friend?"

He shook his head. "I never saw one ghost—but I heard them." Tears welled up in his eyes again. "I heard the souls of the dead crying out in pain. It's a sound I'll never forget. And then I heard a train whistle."

"A train? Out in the woods? Where does it go?"

"Hell," he answered abruptly. "It goes to Hell. And I know who the conductor is. Because after the train whistle, I heard the voice of a man I knew years before, a local man, a former member of my congregation who I liked a lot. A big, gentle man, who would sit in the back pew and laugh above everyone at my corny jokes. But all the laughing died when he turned into a cold-blooded murderer."

"Lou Purdy?" I asked breathlessly.

The Pastor nodded. "The most famous killer in these parts." He paused and puffed on his pipe. Then he added, "Maybe the evil wafting off Limbo made him do it. Or maybe he just turned into a killer on his own like Cole Conklin. I don't really know. But when I knew him, he was one of the nicest people I ever met. Loved life. And get this—he's responsible for starting the church baseball league you played in."

"Really?"

He nodded. "He loved the game so much he organized the whole thing."

"I had no idea," I said, truly amazed. "I only knew about him cuz he was a killer. And I've been to his cabin on the trail."

"That's where he did all his killing," the Pastor informed, shaking his head slightly in dismay. "He fled up Breckinridge's trail just ahead of the posse and crossed over into Limbo. People were angry they couldn't get retribution, but at least we were rid of him. He was the Devil's problem now. And it seemed the Devil put him to work as a train conductor. Because I heard him yell 'all aboard'. Then I heard him laugh—that familiar whooping, horse laugh of his. It sent a shiver down my back. " He shook his head at the memory. "It's a laugh I'll never forget. And then, just before the train pulled out, I heard him yell, 'Dead Time.'"

"Dead Time? What does that mean?"

"I'm not sure. But as soon as he said it, the ground shook. It shook so hard I could barely stand."

"Cuz of the train pulling out?"

"It was an earthquake," he said at once. "I saw it as an earthquake caused by the Lord. Divine intervention. The Lord wanted me to leave. And that's exactly what I did. I ran. And I kept running until I couldn't run no more."

"I see."

"So that's my story, McGrath. And now that you've heard it, I'm asking you not to go. Because if you go, you might not come back. And though we have our differences, I don't want anything to happen to you."

"I understand. And thank you for the warning, and the story. It was helpful."

He opened the desk's top drawer, and fished out a shiny object that he placed on the desktop in front of him. "This is Lester Merriweather's crucifix."

It was a gold cross on a gold chain, delicate, yet masculine.

"I gave the crucifix to him for his birthday one year and I inherited it when he passed. In his will, he stipulated I give it to someone I thought would need it most. I never met anyone I thought needed it...until now." He gestured for me to pick it up. "Take it, McGrath. Because I guarantee you, you're going to need it."

PART TWO—THE WALK

"The secret to getting from one place to another is rather simple:
You stand, put one foot in front of the other, and you keep doing
that until you arrive."

Source unknown.

(1)

I opened the door to the parlor, stepped out into the hallway and walked smack into the Pastor. He growled and stepped back.

He was showered, shaved and dressed in his Sunday-go-to-meeting blue suit, ready, it appeared, to conduct funerals over in Squirrel Flats for the victims of the ammunition factory explosion. "Never made it to the guestroom, I see."

"Sally treated me to Mozart on the piano," I explained. "Guess I fell asleep."

"I'm sure that pleased her," he returned gruffly. "I just had another long talk with her. She thinks you're crazy. Thinks I'm crazy too for letting you go to that damn place. And do you know something? I can't blame her. So is there any chance you've returned to reality? Changed your mind?

I shook my head. "I gotta go, Pastor. Sorry."

"You'll be sorry, alright," he grumbled sourly, and then flicked his hand in the general direction of the road. "I want you to stay off Route 9. You can cut across my property to Knight's farm. He hasn't worked his land in years so it's all scrub grass now. You can go across his field to the river and then follow the river to the trail. It'll take you a little longer but it'll be safer."

"Safer from what?"

"Think about it. Sheriff Nibbs knows you're staying with me. So you can be assured that most of the community knows by now too. If people see you out walking up the road toting a shotgun and wearing a knapsack, they're going to wonder why a boy who had just lost his mother is going hunting."

I had to admit it—he was thinking. "Okay, but what about Knight? If he sees me on his land he might call Nibbs or someone else and, well, word will get out."

He shook his head. "The old coot can't see more than two feet in front of his nose. Besides, even if he does spot you, his phone is on the same line as mine phone."

When the storm took the lines down last week and I couldn't call Sally, Nurse Bilodeau had said that things happen for a reason. I humored her outta respect, cuz for the life of me, I couldn't see a positive coming outta a broken phone line. It looked now like I was wrong.

"As you requested, I had Ester pack a knapsack of provisions for you. You've got a canteen, bedroll, matches, a hunting knife, a bottle of catnip oil for the insects"—he shrugged—"It'll help a bit. And I also had her pack about three or four days worth of food. It's all the knapsack will hold. So use the food sparingly. If you run out, live off the land. You'll have Sally's shotgun, and I know you know how to shoot, so don't be afraid to shoot a rabbit or possum if you need to eat."

I nodded a 'thank you'.

"Remember, it's going to be hot, so drink plenty of water. I haven't been up the trail in years, but I remember there were spots along the way to top up the canteen."

"There's a good drinking pond near the campsite," I told him. "It's about half way between here and where I'm going. If I can make it before nightfall, I'll spend the first night there."

He nodded. "Okay, good. Now where's the crucifix I gave you?"

I pulled it outta my pocket by the chain and held it up so he could see it.

"Keep it on you at all times. Don't put it in the knapsack. Because you can get separated from that, and though you might disagree, that crucifix is your best line of defense."

I figured the shotgun was my best line of defense, but what did I know? So I put the crucifix over my head, adjusted it so it sat properly around my neck, and then tucked it inside my shirt.

"Alright," he went on. "I'm letting Sally tag along with you to the river. She's no good around here today anyway, and if she keeps pestering you, maybe you'll change your mind about going."

That was unlikely. It was also unlikely he was allowing her to tag along for that sole purpose. No doubt Sally had requested to go and no doubt the Pastor, wanting to keep me happy cuz I knew his Possum Hollow secret, agreed. Not that I cared about his reasoning. I was just happy to have company for part of the trip.

"Once you get to the trail, she can cut through the field to Route 9. I should be coming back from Squirrel Flats around noon, and can pick her up along the way. Oh, and remember to keep your wits about you—especially when you're with my granddaughter. Because you're not out on a picnic."

Actually, with Sally tagging along, we were kind of out on a picnic. Course, I didn't say that to him.

"Oh, I almost forgot, Sheriff Nibbs mentioned last night that he found an abandoned banged-up Chrysler Airflow with Louisiana plates just past the town border on the way to Jackson. There might not be anything sinister about it because Conklin and his merry band of thieves were last seen driving a Packard with Illinois plates. Still, don't let your guard down."

"I won't."

"Okay, now we have to figure out what we're going to do about your mother."

"What do you mean?"

His brow knitted together with annoyance. "What do you want done with your mother's remains while you go off hiking?"

"Ma told me she had made all the arrangements."

"I know. Sheriff Nibbs told me last night. Still, they need a signature of next of kin to transport the body from the hospital to the funeral home. And the funeral home needs information as well. Like when do you want visitation? And when do you want the funeral service? Also, do you have a dress picked out for her to be buried in?"

It suddenly came clear that I couldn't leave. Not then anyway. The paperwork for the dead superseded my trip to Limbo, and as I went to say just that, the Pastor cut in, unknowingly saving the day.

"I'll tell Nibbs you're ill." He turned out his lips in mild disgust. "It's a sin to lie, but how much of a lie is it really? Anyone going up to Limbo to look for the ghost of their dead father has got to be sick in the head. So if you want, I'll sign the papers for you. I'm her pastor, yours too, so if you give me permission, I'll sign the necessary papers. And if it's okay with you, I'll have Ester go into your house and pick out a dress for your mother. I'm sure she'll make a better choice than you would anyway."

He was right about that. What did I know about picking out dresses?

"Okay, whatever you decide is fine with me."

He nodded and jerked his thumb over his shoulder in the direction of the kitchen. "Ester has made breakfast. So go eat and get moving. You've got a long walk ahead of you." As I stepped around him, he gently grabbed my arm at the bicep and pulled me in close to him. I smelt strong tobacco on his breath. "Word of advice, McGrath—there is no shame in running."

"I'll remember that."

He maintained his grip on my arm and added, "You asked me a question last night I forgot to answer."

"I did?"

"Clark Gable," he said. "For some reason, my son's mother admires him." He shrugged. "Clark is as good a name as any, I suppose. And though I care little for Gable as an actor, I do like reading Superman."

(2)

Breakfast consisted of hot baked rolls, fried eggs and bacon. It smelled great. It tasted great, too. The only problem was Sally. She sat beside me at the table and continued to harass me about how crazy I was to go hiking up to this mystical land of Limbo to look for my dead father.

I took it all in stride, not saying too much, concentrating instead on chewing. Before long, thankfully, the Pastor joined us at the kitchen table and Sally concentrated her efforts on him. She didn't get far, though. No one ever did with the Pastor.

"I don't have time to listen to this now," he told her bluntly. "I've got four funerals to conduct and I'm not sure what I'm going to say."

"But Pastor..."

"Don't 'but' me. If you've got something to say to your boyfriend, then say it. I got my own problems."

"But Pastor...I—"

A heavy knock on the kitchen door made her pause.

Ester, drying her hands on a kitchen towel, opened the door, and in walked the thin, grizzled-looking Mexican who had stood guard on the porch last night. His face was strained, his dark eyes were wide with excitement and his lips were puckered sourly as though he'd been sucking on lemons. Who knows? Maybe he had.

"What's the problem, Miguel?" the Pastor asked at once, rising to his feet.

Miguel walked up to the kitchen table and, in lighting fast Spanish helped along with wild hand gestures, addressed the Pastor. Spanish is a beautiful language, but I only know a couple of words and just about everything the Mexican said went right over my head. I did, however, hear through the mish-mash of sounds the words, "Knight" and "Conklin" so at least I knew what he was talking about.

The Mexican babbled on for another thirty seconds, and than ran outta words, letting his hands drop to his side. The Pastor turned to me and translated the exchange. "Miguel says the G-Men are at Knight's house."

Well ain't that great, I thought, and assumed they had captured both Conklin and his buddy. Hopefully there would be a speedy trail, followed by a speedy execution.

"Miguel says Conklin and his men broke in and murdered Knight."

Every thought in my head came to a dead stop and a sick, punch-in-the-gut feeling made me woozy. Was I responsible, at least partly, for Knight's death? After all, I had known where the killers were going, but had failed to inform anyone.

"Have they captured Conklin?" Sally spoke up.

The Mexican shook his head, and in perfect American, said, "Mr. Knight's car is gone. Sheriff Nibbs says the G-men think the murderers have fled in it."

"Makes sense," the Pastor muttered, nodding as though he was an authority on such matters. "No doubt they are on their way west, or south to Mexico." He cleared his throat and added, "The law will get them for sure now."

I had my doubts, but said nothing.

Chewing on his pipe stem, the Pastor instructed Miguel to get everyone back to work. "But keep the rifles handy," he finished up. "Just in case."

Miguel regarded the Pastor's callousness with a raised brow, but said nothing. He obviously had worked here long enough to know who he was dealing with. He nodded and left the kitchen, tipping his straw hat at Ester as he left.

As soon as the door closed behind him, the Pastor turned to me. "Okay, change of plan. Avoid Knight's property altogether, unless you want to chat with the FBI. You can get to Breckinridge's trail by going through the cemetery."

Ester, quiet until now, came over to the table and rested her hand on Sally's shoulder. "Since you're all a going to the cemetery, why don't you bring some cut flowers for your Ma and Pa and baby sister?"

Sally brightened to the idea, and followed Ester out the kitchen door and into the garden. With them gone, the Pastor gave me final words of advice.

"Remember, when you get to Limbo—if you get there—no further than the graveyard. Understand? Because if you go further you'll get trapped just like Breckinridge and his men did. And for the sake of my granddaughter, I don't want that to happen. For some reason, she loves you."

"I love her too."

He ignored my statement and, with all the exuberance and warmth, of a dead fish, muttered, "Good luck…because you're going to need it."

(3)

Within ten minutes, we were ready to go.

And so, with my baseball cap snuggly on my head, I slung the green canvas knapsack on my back, picked up the shotgun and, with Sally at my side, set out across the Pastor's land for Limbo.

The sun had only been up for an hour and already it was a scorcher of a day. The temperature was in the low nineties, and the humidity was thick enough to cut. It was only gonna get worse, and I feared by noon I'd be walking in triple-digit-heat. By then, with luck, I'd be in the woods and under a canopy of green. For now, however, we were out in the open, crossing an increasingly hot cookie-sheet of earth.

We walked in silence between rows of short, soy-bean stalks. It was odd for us not to talk. Well, it was odd for Sally not to talk cuz she could talk the ears off a mule without breaking a sweat. Today, however, she was quiet, and I figured her quiet somberness was cuz we were gonna visit the graves of her Ma, Pa and sister.

I remembered the day they died as if it was yesterday. It was a day much like this one, hot and muggy. Late June. I had stood on the driveway with Sally that morning as her parents and sister, Becky, climbed into the car for the drive to the hospital in Jackson so Becky could undergo treatment for the polio. Sally was suppose to have gone with them but, at my urging, had decided to stay home at the last minute and spend the day with me. A short time later, a truck lost control and flattened their car like a pancake. I understand, the police had to use shovels to pick up their remains. It was a closed-casket funeral, of course.

A twist of fate had spared Sally's life, and to this day, I still wonder 'what if?' What if I hadn't been so persistent to have her stay home with me? What if I had been doing something else that day? Of course, for that matter, you could ask, 'what if they had left five minutes sooner? Or five minutes later? Or if they had gone the next day? These were questions akin to asking how many angels can dance on the head of a pin. I suppose it would all depend on what sorta dance they were doing.

What happened happened. It was that simple. Sally wasn't meant to die that day and her family was and this made me think of Sam Knight. What if I had alerted Sheriff Nibbs to where Conklin and Snake were headed? Would Sam Knight still be alive?

"Are you okay?" Sally asked suddenly. "You haven't muttered a word and you look like you're not so sure about things. Do you want to head back? No shame in changing your mind, you know."

"I was just thinking about Sam Knight."

Sally took a deep breath. "I know. I can't believe what those savages did to him."

"What do you mean?"

"My Spanish is pretty good, remember. And Miguel said Knight's head was cut clean off and stuck atop a fencepost in the front yard for all to see. Sheriff Nibbs almost drove off the road when he spotted it."

The gory detail left me stunned. It also raised the question: why had they displayed their work for all to see? Were they just showing off their work like a proud kindergarten kid showing off a finger painting?

I didn't think so.

Conklin was a smart guy, remember; no genius, sure, but unlike Sam Knight, Conklin had a head on his shoulders. He would know the first person to drive by Knight's farm would see the head and alert the Feds. They would come a running and be all over Knight's farm like fleas on a dog's back. They would discover Knight's car was missing and automatically assume the killers drove off in it. But what if the stolen car was a red herring? Something to throw the G-men off their trail? Maybe they weren't on their way to Mexico or out west. Maybe they were closer. Maybe they were headed to Limbo. Why else would Conklin have asked about it?

"Johnny, you look terrified. Are you okay? Why don't we turn around?"

"I'm okay," I assured her. "But I have something to tell you. I bumped into Conklin yesterday."

"What?" she gasped.

"It was near dusk. I had just passed our boulder. You know, where I painted the Valentine's Day message for you. I was walking up the path for home and bumped into Conklin and his partner, a guy named Snake."

"I can't believe this. Why didn't you tell me?"

I shrugged.

"A better question might be: why didn't they kill you?"

"Snake wanted to, but I gave him a good punching, and for some reason Conklin stopped him from going further." I shrugged. "He liked Ma a lot, so I guess that's why he spared my life."

"You are so lucky."

"Tell me about it," I reflected. "But I've got a guilty conscious now. See, I knew they were out there, and I knew they were headed to Knight's house and I never said a thing to anyone about it. Maybe if Nibbs had known, Knight would still be alive today."

She paused, thinking about it, and then asked, "Did they say they were going to murder Knight?"

"Well, no. Of course not. Actually, I'm kinda surprised they did kill him. Knight was Conklin's stepdad, and from all indications, Conklin liked him."

"Exactly. So how can you blame yourself? You can't predict the future. You didn't know what Conklin had up his sleeve."

"Yeah, I know. But I still feel guilty."

"You said you ran into them around dusk? Out by our boulder?"

I nodded.

"It must have taken you a good half hour to get home?"

"Less time, probably. I ran mighty fast after Conklin let me go."

"Still, it took a while. And even if you had come directly to our house and told the Pastor, we have no working phone. So how were we suppose to alert Sherriff Nibbs? Smoke signals?"

I grinned. "I guess the Pastor would have sent one of his farmhands."

"Which would have taken time. And we all know Nibbs. He is not exactly a go-getter. Knowing him, and knowing it was after dark, he most likely would have sat on the info till morning. And even if he did alert the G-men at once, how long would they have taken to get into position?" She shook her head. "My guess is, regardless of what you had done, Knight would have ended up with his head on a pole. So you have nothing to feel guilty about."

I sure liked her way of thinking. No wonder I love her.

(4)

Sally and I knew a lot about the cemetery cuz once a year, as celebration of All-Hallows-Eve, Ma would spend part of an afternoon discussing its rich history.

The cemetery had been around as long as the 'Gulch' and the first settlers led by Harry Goonberry moved into the area around 1750. So when Sally and I walked up to the cemetery's stone fence that morning, the boneyard had been around for close to two hundred years.

In that time, a large assortment of characters had been buried within. Among the notable internees were witches, warlocks, pirates, politicians, British and French soldiers and, of course, Confederate dead. No Yankees, though. They weren't permitted.

The place had also been home to some rather nefarious acts that included, among other things, pagan rituals, animal sacrifices, vandalized tombstones, and yes, grave robbing—the latest incident occurring just last summer thanks to town hero Betty Zuckerman. The former Olympic gold medal swimmer and renowned painter had dug up her husband and disappeared with him.

For her sake, I hope she reburied him elsewhere. Cuz if not, she better be wearing a clothes pin on her nose, cuz—whoa Nelly—he must be smelling awful gamey by now.

"Batty Betty," Sally suddenly spoke up. "Remember her?"

I cast a sideways glance at her and grinned. "I was just thinking about her."

"It's hard to believe someone you know well is accused of not only grave robbing, but of murder."

I didn't know Betty as well as Sally cuz Sally played the organ for the church choir, and like Ma, Betty had sung in the choir.

"Last month when our phone was working, I overheard the Pastor talking about her. I don't know who he was speaking to, but he sure made it clear that he thought she was innocent and that the Mayor might be responsible for her husband's death."

"What do you think?"

"I know both of them quite well," she replied. "Betty is a wonderful, sweet person and the Mayor is a two-faced, back-stabbing liar." She raised a brow at me. "So who would you believe?"

I smiled.

"Oh, speaking of Mayor Valentine," she went on. "Keep an eye out for his two yellow-bellied kids. They could be up in those woods, you know."

She was right. The Valentine boy's were hunters and experienced woodsmen, and if you wanted to stay hidden from the M. P's you'd surely go someplace familiar but remote—and you couldn't get any more remote than the Goonberry Gulch Woods.

As Sally harped on about the cowardly Clem and Clancy Valentine, proposing just punishments for their crimes, we arrived at the spot on the wall where everyone climbs up. I handed her the shotgun, and then picked my way up across the uneven stones to the top. Sally then handed up the shotgun, and climbed up beside me. I gave her the shotgun to hold again, and then climbed down, dropping the last few feet. I missed the landing, though, cuz my feet got tangled in the long grass and fell backwards, the weight of the knapsack dragging me down. I landed on my side with a loud thud beside a large, white granite tombstone.

Sally laughed, "You okay?"

Physically I was fine, but what I eyeballed two feet away left me breathless. For the epitaph on the white granite tombstone read:

I CAME. I SAW. I DRANK SOME SHINE.
AND ALL IN ALL, LIFE WAS FINE.
NOW IT'S OVER.
NOW IT'S GONE.
I WALK TOWARD THE SHINING DAWN

"Shining dawn," I breathed as a cold chill crept up my back.

Seeing I was lost in my own world, Sally ignored proper gun-toting rules, and jumped down from the fence with the shotgun in her hands. She came up behind me. "What's the problem? You okay?"

"I don't know," I said, and pulled aside a mess of weeds covering the rest of the tombstone. I gasped at what I saw.

"Charles Haddes," Sally read. "That name sounds familiar. I think the Pastor knew him."

"So do I," I said, standing. "I met him yesterday."

"You couldn't have. According to the inscription he passedon March 14th, 1941. He's been dead for over three years. You must have met someone else."

I knew that wasn't the case but said nothing cuz…well, I knew she would never believe me.

Who would?

(5)

The Pastor had deep pockets so when it came to buying a tombstone for his daughter, son-in-law and granddaughter, price was no object. Only the best would do, and he bought a behemoth granite monument a shade smaller than our tool shed at home. It was built in layers like a wedding cake, each smooth white granite slab slightly smaller than the one beneath it. A cross, thick as a two by four, stretched dizzyingly high toward the blue sky from the top slab.

It was quite something to behold, and as I beheld it now, I didn't know quite what to say cuz the monument (heck, the graveyard as well) was wrought with jaw-dropping neglect.

Crows had, and were, using the cross as a perch and, sad to say, a bathroom as well. Long streams of creamy pearl-white excrement ran in rivers along the cross and pooled in gooey droplets on the base slabs. Molted feathers stuck to the excrement. Weeds sprouted up from between the slabs. Knee-high grass littered with dried leaves surrounded the structure. It was enough to make Sally cry.

"I can't believe this," she gasped, the flesh beneath her eyes quivering as tears spilled out and rolled down her cheeks. "This is disgusting." She sniffled back her tears and began stomping on the knee-high weed infested grass that swallowed up the monument's lower tier, hiding her family's names and epitaphs.

"Don't fret, Sally. The Pastor told me he was gonna have some of his farmhands clean the place up."

She scoffed. "Once his farmhands see this, they'll run back to Tijuana, screaming."

I tried not to laugh, but dammit, it was funny, and a smirk creased my cheeks. I turned slightly so she couldn't see my growing smile. Not that it mattered. She was too busy stomping flat the knee-high grass that surrounded her family's monument to see my expression.

A few seconds later, she knelt on the crushed grass and, with an index finger, traced over her Ma's name which, like her Pa and sister's name, was engraved in the granite in two inch fancy French script.

"Flowers, please," she said suddenly, holding out her hand.

I had forgotten she and Ester had cut flowers for the occasion. I slung the knapsack off my back, fished out the paper bag holding the flowers, and handed it to her.

With tears streaming down her face, she took the flowers from the bag, divided them into three piles and placed a pile by each name. With that done, she crossed herself and recited a prayer. I quickly took off my ball cap for the occasion.

The prayer ended with an 'Amen' and she stood, wiping away her tears. "Coming here makes me so damn sad," she admitted, and looked me in the eyes. "You know I don't believe a word you or the Pastor told me. You know I think you're both crazy. But..." she paused, sniffled back tears and added, "If it is true, if at the end of that trail you get to the place where the dead go, I want you to do me a favor."

"Uhhhh, okay. If I can."

"If you see my parents or sister, will you tell them that I love them and miss them?"

"Yeah, sure. Consider it done."

(6)

A long time ago, some smart guy on the city council saw fit to place a wooden park bench outside the cemetery. Why anyone would wanna sit outside the cemetery beside Route 9 directly across the street from the city dump was a question beyond my comprehension, but since the bench was there, Sally and I sat on the creaky, weather-beaten planks and ate home baked bread and strawberry jam. We both liked the moist bread and sweet jam, but neither of us was all that hungry. Sally was in turmoil about the condition of her family's plot and I was anxious to get going up the trail. The crows from the city dump, however, seemed to have nothing on their minds but food. For about a half dozen of them hung out by the road's center white line, squawking for a handout.

While the crows squawked, Sally and I ate and made small talk. But our hearts weren't in it and our minds were elsewhere, and before long, we chucked the lasts of our sandwiches to the crows, got to our feet and said our goodbyes. We hugged and kissed, and Sally got weepy and made me promise not to get hurt. It was an easy promise to make cuz I truly believed I wouldn't get hurt. I might get killed or trapped on the otherside like Breckinridge had, but hurt? Naw. That was the least of my worries.

With our goodbyes said, I shouldered the knapsack, picked up the shotgun, gave her another quick smooch, and crossed the road. Once there, I turned back and waved. She waved, closed the cemetery's black, wrought iron gate and, without looking back, walked toward her family's plot, determined to rip out every weed on and around the monument.

I was on my own now, and I walked overtop the weed-thickened, knee-high grass beside the dump and soon hooked up with the dirt path that snaked across the field to the river over the horizon. Sam

Knight owned the field, and at one time (when he still had his head on his shoulders), he must have considered working it cuz all the trees had been cut down. It was a rolling minefield of rotting stumps poking up outta the tall, washed-out, dandelion infested grass. I couldn't imagine how much work it would take to get the field in proper 'crop' shape. No wonder Knight had abandoned the field to nature.

There wasn't, however, anything natural about what I saw a minute later.

A set of fresh tire tracks had shredded the grass to a moist goulash of green. The freshly made tracks, car width wide, had come from behind the dump, fishtailing wildly across the open terrain before hooking up with the path. The path was too narrow for a car, so one set of wheels ran down the center of the flattened dirt while the other set of wheels tore a strip through the grass. Both the path and tracks disappeared over an incline about fifty yards away.

I knew from traveling this route with Pa that the river was a scant few yards over that incline. If the car had kept going—and from all indications it looked like it had—then I sure the heck hope the occupants were wearing their swim trunks cuz—splish splash—they were going for a bath.

And just who the heck had been behind the wheel? It was impossible to say then, of course. It could have been anyone from a lost salesman to a drunken rube out joyriding? But I didn't think so. If I had to guess, I'd guess the driver knew exactly where he was going cuz he didn't hang the car up on a rotting stump.

I reached the incline a minute later and, sure enough, as expected, the tire tracks ended at the river's edge. I followed them until my toes touched the water and surveyed the still, blue water ahead for any signs of a vehicle. The bottom dropped off quick here, and I saw river grass, toady-frogs, and small shadows that were probably fish. As for a vehicle? There was no sign of anything resembling that, and since I wasn't in the mood for a swim, I would remain in the dark as to whose vehicle was at the bottom. But I suspected it was either the Valentine boy's truck or Sam Knight's car.

Only time would tell.

(7)

About a half mile north from where the tire tracks went into the water, the river narrowed to a four foot span and rose to an ankle-high depth. Every critter in the forest crossed here, and I easily skipped across the short, shallow expanse and started up the steep slope of Breckinridge's trail.

A minute later, my cafes screaming from the steep climb, I reached the summit. Before going on, I sat and leaned against a pine tree to catch my breath. The trail looked pretty much like I remembered it, which only proved, if nothing else, my memory was still working.

The trail was wide enough for two men to walk along side by side, and froth with pitfalls: half-buried rocks, tree roots, holes, dips and low hanging branches that could take out an eye. Cuz of the heavy humidity, the thick, green vegetation wilted over the path and dripped with so much moisture I could see water vapors shimmering in the sunlight. For the most part, here, under the canopy, I was protected from the sun, but not the humidity and it promised to be a rather steamy afternoon.

I straightened up, hitched the knapsack further up on my back and started off down the path at a good clip, hoping to make up some valuable time.

As I walked, my mind drifted like an abandon boat on the ocean. I thought about a whole lotta things, mostly trivial stuff, as abstract as a Jackson Pollock painting. I can't say if it was healthy thinking, but it did pass the time, and the path in front of me was soon behind me.

Before I realized how far I'd walked, I rounded a bend in the path and spotted far off in the distance, Lou Purdy's old cabin.

It was set off in the bush about fifty yards and looked—at least from the path—like it always looked—scary and abandoned. It was built in the 1890's, and though I don't know what it looked like back then, it reminded me of a wooden skull with a caved in cranium. The roof was a splintered mess and the white shingles had turned yellow with age and looked like polished bone. The two windows, void of glass, looked like vacant black eyes, and the doorway, minus a door, looked like a blackened, toothless scowling mouth. Even in the daylight it looked scary, and I got a shiver up my back imagining how scary it would be at night.

Since I didn't have the hankering nor time to explore the cabin, I kept on walking and soon spotted something ahead twinkling in the sunlight. It was most likely a bottle cap or tin can or shell casing. Lots of people hunt up here, after all, and at certain spots, the path can be littered with shell casings. So it was no big deal, and I didn't give it more than a passing glance as I walked by. But the glance I did give it made me stop.

The shiny thing was a necklace, and I plucked it up by its thin silver chain. Lo and behold, it was a set of dog tags, and I blew the dirt off them, laid them in my palm and read what was encrypted on the silver tabs.

Valentine, Clem. 17794305, O positive, Protestant

Well, I'll be damned. Sally was right. The Valentine boys—well, at least Clem—had taken to the woods, and I wondered if the tire tracks belonged to their truck? It was difficult to say, but the evidence was certainly leaning in that direction, and my train of thought skipped ahead and I wondered if I had to worry about them.

Again, it was difficult to say, but I knew the Valentine boys weren't killers. They were crazy, hillbilly southerners, with half a brain between them in their toothless heads, but not killers, and I suspected that if they did see me, they'd give me a nodding 'hey' and keep on going.

Right or wrong, the thought was comforting and stilled the fear crawling through the pit of my belly.

I pocketed the dog tags, aiming to give them to the Pastor if I was lucky enough to make it back. He could pass the tags onto Nibbs or the Army or hang them off the rearview mirror of his car for all I cared.

I started off along the path again, keeping an eye on the ground in case Clancy Valentine had discarded his dog tags as well—might as well bring both sets home, right? And sure enough, after going only a couple of feet, I spotted something of interest, and this something stirred up a bubbling, witches' brew of fear in my gut.

The cigarette butt was embedded in the dirt, and I nudged it up with the toe of my shoe and bent over to examine it closer. The butt looked new, but what did I know? Maybe it had been out here for weeks. The Valentine boys, I knew, were tobacco chewers. But did they smoke now, too? I couldn't recall a time when I saw a cigarette dangling outta their faces, but maybe my memory was off. For that matter, it could be a new habit. Something they picked up in the army. Or, maybe, the butt had been discarded by a hunter. Lots of people hunt up here and lots of people smoke, so maybe.

…or maybe not.

I was thinking the smoke belonged to someone else and that someone else was Cole Conklin, and boy I sure hated the thought, but hey, there's no denying the fact that Conklin smoked and here was what looked like a fresh smoke.

Then outta nowhere, way off in the bush, a bird squawked loudly and I jumped and nearly messed my pants. I heaved a sigh, angry at myself of overreacting, hitched the knapsack up on back and started off along the trail.

Who cares about a cigarette butt, right? Let's just get further up the trail.

The path elbowed sharply then and snaked to within twenty yards of the cabin. It was then that I heard a loud buzzing coming from the wooden ruins.

Lots of things buzz out here, but what I saw made me utter a long, dark "Uh-oh."

A black cloud of swirling flies swarmed angrily at the door to the cabin. Most likely the flies had gathered cuz of a dead animal. A polecat or possum or maybe even something a little bigger. It was no big deal, right?

Yet, a tiny voice in my head urged me to take a peek—just to make sure. After all, I had Clem Valentine's dog tags in my pocket and near where I found them I had found a cigarette butt, and Cole Conklin smoked and, well, need I go on?

I slipped off the knapsack so it wouldn't get caught up in the bushes and laid it on the trail. Then, using the shotgun barrel, I pushed aside some shrubs and stepped forward, crushing the vegetation underfoot. I kept an ear open for any 'hissing' cuz this was cottonmouth country. A snake bite now and I might end up in Limbo without even having to walk there.

Before long, I broke free of the vegetation and stumbled out onto the dirt expanse in front of the cabin. It was then that I noticed there were actually two clouds of flies—one directly in front of the doorway which I had spotted back on the path; the other to the left of the cabin.

Two dead animals?

Alarm bells went off in my head. And that tiny inner voice that had urged me to take a look was no longer urging me. The voice was now telling me that maybe I should turn around and forget the whole thing. Why did I need to see a dead animal anyway?

But for some reason I couldn't turn back. It was like I was in a trance and, without realizing it, I found myself standing directly in front of the swirling cloud of flies at the doorway, staring ahead.

The buzzing was as loud as a truck's engine, constant, full, and swelling. And now the flies were on me too, not many, but a few, and I felt their tiny feet crawl over my soft cheeks and along my bare arms. Their touch was repulsive, sick and horrifying.

I ignored the feeling best I could and crept forward, coming to within five feet of the swirling cloud. And it was then that I realized I was staring at the body of a man.

The body, sitting upright like an Indian about to smoke a peace pipe, was heavyset, thick through the shoulder and belly. Clem Valentine, I knew, was heavyset. I also knew Clem Valentine had thick, muscular arms heavily decorated with tattoos. Even with the thousands of flies swirling about, I could easily see that the body's arms, laying limply in the body's lap like soggy noodles, were muscular and decorated with so many tattoos you'd think the carny was in town. Also too, the body was dressed in olive green army pants and wearing army boots.

Well, I was no Dick Tracy, but if it looked like a duck and swam like a duck and quaked like a duck—it was a duck. So it had to be Clem, right? It just had to be.

But I couldn't be completely sure cuz the body had no head. All that was left was a jagged hole at the top of the neck that the flies were using as a swimming pool. Thick gobs of blood had cascaded up through the neck and had spilled over the torso, turning the shirt a crimson wet. And maybe my eyes were playing tricks on me or maybe it was cuz of the flies crawling every which way, but it looked like the man's Adam's apple was moving up and down as though the headless body was swallowing. Was that possible? Was there still a trace of life left in this headless corpse?

It was an odd question to focus on. It was even odder that I was standing still as I thought about it. I should have been running. I should have been running and screaming. But no, it was as though I was rooted to the ground, and as my brain filled with more irrelevant questions, I heard a voice cry out, "Help me..."

A hand of cold dread seized my heart and, slowly, I turned in the direction of the voice, in the direction of that other cloud of flies. What I saw made my knees weak. I gasped and tried to suck in air, but for some reason no air would come.

"Help..." the voice cried again.

I was seeing things. I was hearing things, too. Cuz severed heads can't talk. So it all had to be in my imagination, right? It was the only explanation I could think of. None of this was real. It couldn't be. It couldn't be real cuz it went against nature. It went against science. It went against what I'd been taught. It was wrong. It was as wrong as wrong gets.

I teetered on the brink of madness then, my thoughts popping, my brain short-circuiting, unable to comprehend what I was seeing.

"Please help..."

I blinked and said, "You're not real. You can't be." Then I giggled. I giggled like a mad scientist on the verge of a great discovery. "Naw...I'm seeing things."

"McGrath???? Is that yuh?"

"Uh..."

"McGrath...help me."

The fact that the head knew my name made it real. It couldn't be real, of course, but hey, it knew my name. The damn severed head immersed in a cloud of flies and sitting upright on a chopping block in a wide pool of blood, knew my name.

"McGrath...it's me...Clem Valentine."

Now there was something I couldn't argue with. I knew Clem Valentine and that was certainly his severed head. Those were his fat cheeks dotted in blood. And those were his brown eyes still filled with life.

A thick stream of blood ran over his lips and down his chin, and he croaked, "McGrath…get the flies off me. I can't stand it."

I wanted to run but I couldn't move.

"Put my head back on my body, McGrath—please."

Over trembling lips, I wheezed, "I don't think I can…"

"They've got my brother," he said. "They're makin' him take them to Limbo."

Somehow I managed to ask, "Who?"

"Conklin…Cole Conklin."

Suddenly my paralysis broke, and I ran.

And I ran…and ran…and ran.

(8)

I ran until I could run no more, stopped by a scorching stitch that blistered my side like a blowtorch. I looked back along the empty path, half-expecting to see the severed head rolling after me. The notion was absurd, I knew; then again, so was the notion of a severed head talking.

Or was it?

I remembered reading a story about a man from France guillotined for his crimes whose severed head had sworn at his executioners. The story quoted a doctor as saying that as long as there was blood in the head, the brain would remain alive, and thus, be able to function as it always had.

Perhaps the explanation was as simple as that. Perhaps Clem Valentine's brain was still working cuz it still had a supply of blood. A macabre sight, yeah. And sure, it was downright terrifying to witnesses. But, like a lotta mysteries, explainable.

Knowing this didn't make me feel any better, but at least there was a possible explanation for what had happened, something I could hang my hat on.

In my mad dash from the cabin I'd had the presence of mind to snatch up the knapsack as I crashed back onto the trail, hooking it over one shoulder as I ran. Now that I was walking, I took the time to hook it over the other shoulder as well and adjust it so it sat properly on my back.

With that done, everything was now back to normal. It was as though I hadn't even ventured off to the cabin. Well, I did have the memory of a talking, severed head to haunt me for the rest of my days, but at least I was back on course.

It came without surprise, of course, that Clem's decapitation was no accident. And so, like I feared, Cole Conklin and Snake were in the woods and headed to Limbo. Pardon me why I pat myself on the back for coming to this conclusion earlier.

The question now taking center stage was why would these two killers go to Limbo? Did Limbo have a bank begging to be robbed? Or were they looking for the ultimate hiding place? A place where they could relax and not worry about running into the law. Or perhaps, like me, they were going to Limbo to check on a loved one. It seemed a bit out of character for these psycho killers to care about anyone other than themselves, but hey, I suppose it was possible.

And it did make perfect sense with what they had done with the Valentine boys. Cole, after all, was no outdoorsmen cuz he never went in the woods on account his Pa took off on him at a young age and his stepdad, Sam Knight, for the most part anyway, was a boozer, who, instead of taking Cole hunting, sat around drinking and telling stories. As for Cole's partner? Well, I read Snake was a city slicker from Brooklyn and no Yankee city slicker from Brooklyn would fair well out here in the Mississippi woods. Cole would certainly realize that and would want a guide. Maybe that was the real reason he had wanted me to join his gang. Since I was unavailable to lead them through the woods, he looked elsewhere, maybe to Sam Knight. I hadn't seen Knight in months, maybe a year, but knew he was damn old and way too fragile to hike through the woods. That wouldn't matter to Conklin and Snake. If Knight was breathing and could walk—like it or not—he was gonna lead them. Reading between the lines though, I speculated that Knight had either refused to go or had been unable to due to his health. So they had killed him and went looking for another guide. And you couldn't get a better guide for these woods than Clem or Clancy Valentine. Since the killers didn't need both of them, they killed one. I guess Clem drew the short straw.

So I felt I had most of it figured out, and what I didn't know, really didn't matter. All that mattered was that I had two psycho killers in front of me. This made me think of what the Pastor had said, "There's no shame in running."

Truer words have never been spoken.

Turning around was not only the smart thing to do, it was really the only thing to do. Sure, I wanted to go to Limbo, but if I wanted to go swimming instead and there were sharks in the water, I wouldn't go in cuz going in was downright stupid. And since I wasn't on a death wish, going further was stupid.

Just then, with that thought playing in my head, I rounded a bend in the path, and before me, twenty yards ahead was a three-way-fork in the trail. The main trail continued north with tributaries running east and west.

At one time or another, Pa and I had taken the east and west routes so I was familiar with them and knew that they eventually joined back up with the main trail. The route that ran west, I remembered, was as bumpy as an armadillo's back; the route that ran east twisted back and forth like an angry snake, and ran, at times, up and down like a rollercoaster. Also, for a good mile, this eastern trail emerged from the bush and ran outside the tree line. At this point, if you looked east across the swampy bogs and scrub grass fields, you could see, way off in the distance, the road that ran to Jackson.

Which way would Clancy lead the killers?

Going straight was the easiest route. It was the way I wanted to go, and so, I figured Clancy would lead them straight. Why make things harder on yourself, right?

I looked over my shoulder at the way I had come. Turning around would get me home the fastest so it was the smartest way to go. But if I turned around and followed the same path home it would lead me by the cabin, and I didn't relish that idea in the least cuz I knew if I heard Clem Valentine's voice on the wind I would go completely mad.

So I hitched the knapsack further up on my back and took the path to the east, planning to hike to the road once the path emerged for the bush.

What the heck? I would thumb home. We could bury Ma on Friday like the Pastor wanted, and the next day, before Nibbs could take me to the orphanage, I would make another attempt to reach Limbo. It was not exactly what I wanted to do, but hey, did I have a choice?

(9)

The day wore on and the sun shone and crept across the blue sky above me.

I walked and thought, and as I've said before, sometimes too much thinking is bad, and looking back on it now, I think this was one of those times cuz I made decisions I probably wouldn't have made if I hadn't over thought things.

See, I knew the killers were ahead of me and I knew they were heading to the same place I was heading to and I knew that if they saw me they'd try to kill me, and still, instead of accepting that and running from the woods like anyone with half a brain would do, I tried to think around the problem. How could I still go to Limbo, achieve my goal of looking for Pa, without getting killed in the process?

If there's a will, there's a way, and sure enough, my brain flicked on the switch that ran my ego, and though Pa always told me to leave my ego at home, it reared its ugly head and made me realize I had an advantage over the killers. I knew they were on the trail headed to Limbo but they didn't know I was behind them. In other words, I was invisible to them, and as long as I stayed invisible—which I thought I could do—I was safe. They were the underdogs in this match, not me.

Still, part of me (the sane part) wanted to bailout, and before long, my chance to do so arrived.

I emerged outta the forest and was now on a section of the eastern trail that ran outside the tree line. On my left was the forest; on my right, down a gradual slope of dirt and rocks and roots, was a semi-dry swampy bog that led to a knee-high grass field that led, far off in the distance, to a paved highway. The two-lane blacktop ran north to Jackson or south to the Gulch. The road was empty now, but surely a vehicle would happen by eventually.

Pa and I had hiked this way once before when an unexpected storm blew up from the south. With the sky as black as the Devil's heart and the rain falling so hard we could barely see ten feet in front of us, it took us about fifteen minutes to reach the highway and another fifteen minutes for some charitable soul to drive by and pick us up. Pa claimed we were lucky to get a lift so fast, what with the war only a few months old and gas all ready in short supply.

So if I took the easy way out and hiked to the highway, I knew getting a lift was not a sure thing. It might take a while. Gas was rationed, so joyriding was a luxury few could afford. Sides, cuz of the war, there just weren't that many people around these days to joyride. I might stand on the shoulder for a good long time before a car happened by. And who was to say the driver would stop. Remember, the weather was fine so driving by a hitchhiker wouldn't conflict with a driver's moral conscious. Plus, and perhaps most importantly, I was toting a shotgun and shotguns tend to make folks nervous.

Still, here was my out, and a smart man would have taken it. Unfortunately, my ego was running the show between my ears and I kept walking along the path as if it was the yellow brick road and I was Dorothy on the way to OZ.

I kept thinking: *Why bailout when I'm in control?*

Sides, I had cooked up a scheme (an ingenious scheme I thought) and felt, with a little luck, I might be able to pull it off and not only save a life but do me some good in the process. See, if I could rescue Clancy Valentine from the clutches of those killers, maybe Mayor Valentine would scratch my back. I didn't need a paved driveway like he'd given the Pastor for services rendered, but maybe the Mayor could save me from the Vicksburg Orphanage and our farm from the auction block. It was a long shot, sure, but sometimes long shots payout and, you have to remember, fifteen-year-olds don't think like adults.

I was, however, mature enough to know that thinking about saving Clancy was a heckuva lot easier than actually doing it. I imagined a scenario where I could sneak up through the bush to where they were camped for the night and cut Clancy's bonds (if, in fact, he was tied up) while the killers slept. We could then creep away and be long gone before the killers realized their tour guide was gone.

On the surface, it seemed like a great plan, something you'd see in the movies. But I wasn't Tyrone Power and this wasn't the movies. The bad guys shot real bullets and if you got shot you stayed shot.

Job number one, of course, was to locate them, which might be damn hard to do cuz the forest, after all, was a mighty big place. I knew they were ahead of me, though, and after weighing the possibilities, I figured Clancy would lead them to the campsite where I had planned to spend the night. If he had, then this might just work as planned cuz I knew the area well.

If they weren't there, well then, they could be anywhere from here to Timbuktu. As I ran different scenarios over in my head on how I might free Clancy, the path before me snaked to the left and I reentered the woods and kept on going, knowing that if things turned 'bad', I could easily run back this way. Just knowing that soothed my worries (a bit anyway).

With my thoughts occupied, time seemed to bolt ahead. Before I realized it, the sky in the east had turned a purple-blue and, cuz the canopy was thick, deep pockets of shadows thickened and spread out over the forest like a slate-gray cloud, casting a pall of somber eeriness over the area. Here, on the cusp of darkness, every faint rustle or creak or twig-snap stroked my fear and had me spinning about and pointing the shotgun in the direction of the sound.

Nothing was ever there, though. Nothing I could see, anyway.

Along with the growing darkness came the mosquitoes. At first, it was just one or two. And yeah, they were annoying, but I was able to easily squash them into paste before they could bite. But the whining in my ears and bobbing black dots in front of my eyes intensified and soon I was smacking them with my free hand like some bongo drummer gone mad.

Finally, unable to take it any longer, I stopped, fished the bottle of catnip oil outta the knapsack, and lathered the oil over my body. The funky stench kicked my nose like two mule hoofs, and for the first time on this trip, I was relieved to be alone so no one could smell me. I was also happy there were no cats around.

The skitters cared little for the odor as well and, except for a few brave ones that I easily mashed, kept their distance. So, for the time being, I wouldn't be tortured by them. But when the oil ran out, that would all change.

I didn't wanna think about it and, luckily, a couple minutes later, I found something else to occupy my thoughts. And that something else was a cloud of smoke.

At first I thought I was imagining the odor. But it got stronger with each step I took, and I soon stopped and sniffed the air like a hound dog. Yeah, it was wood smoke alright. No doubt about it.

Wood smoke, of course, meant that someone had built a fire, and that fire—if my nose knew anything—was coming from the direction of the campsite. It also meant that, like I had theorized, Clancy must have led the killers there. If so, it appeared I might be able to put my crazy Tyrone Power rescue plan into operation. The thought made my heart beat a tad faster. What happened next made it boom like a bass drum.

Suddenly, the undergrowth beside me began to rustle. Fear spiked through my belly, and I aimed the shotgun at the shaking bushes, my finger pressing slightly on the trigger. I took deep breaths to calm my growing fear. If I fired, I did not wanna miss.

Then two things suddenly dawned on me: if I fired, the shot was gonna make one helluva noise—so say goodbye to rescuing Clancy; and two, whatever was shaking the bushes had to be small, and if it was small, then it couldn't be Cole or Snake, and thus, I had nothing to worry about. Most likely it was a possum or polecat, and I backed up cuz I smelt bad enough already without being sprayed with polecat juice.

A few seconds later the bushes parted and a small child no older than seven crawled out. The child had a thick mop of long black hair, and cuz this was the forties and males kept their hair short, I immediately assumed it was a girl, a girl from a poor family cuz the child's shirt and pants were frayed and threadbare and so old looking I wouldn't have used them to polish my boots. The child reminded me of a downtrodden Oliver Twist type character with one major exception: this kid wore sandals.

Why a child would wear sandals in the forest was certainly a head scratcher, and as I puzzled over it, the child, completely unaware I was standing a mere ten yards away, stood and turned in profile to me.

Now it was dusk remember, and the woods were awash in dark shadows, but my eyesight was excellent and I realized that no, it wasn't a girl after all, but a boy, a boy with a dark complexion. Not dark like Ester, but darker than me, and I quickly concluded that the boy must be sunburned. I also noticed that the child held in his hand a New York Yankee baseball cap.

Well, it all made sense now. Only a Yankee would wear sandals in the forest, and though I cared little for the boy's choice of teams, he was obviously a baseball fan so he couldn't be all that bad, right?

"Hey kid, what are you doing out here?"

The child never responded. Never even flinched. He continued to eat wild raspberries outta his white cotton, dog-eared baseball cap as though he hadn't heard me, which couldn't be cuz I had spoken in a loud, clear voice from no more than ten yards away.

"Hey kid?" I yelled out.

Again, there was no reaction.

The kid continued to munch berries from his hat so nosily I could hear him sucking the juice over his tongue. He then casually turned his back to me.

I approached him slowly, meaning to tap him on the shoulder, when my nose was suddenly assaulted with a strong whiff of pepper. The smell was coming off him like stink off a garbage dump. It was as though he had just crawled outta a pepper shaker. I noticed then that he wasn't being bothered in the least by mosquitoes, and connecting the dots, figured that whatever was making that smell was driving away the bugs. Though I hated to admit it, it appeared that Yankee ingenuity was alive and well and being clearly demonstrated out here in the Goonberry Gulch Woods.

"Hey you."

Again, no reaction, and I thought, *The kid must be deaf.*

As I reached out to tap his shoulder, he turned and faced me. For half a second he just stared into my face. Then his eyes exploded wide with shock and his mouth dropped open as though a weight hung from his chin. He stumbled backwards like a drunk comedian, and lost the grip on his baseball cap. It landed on the path between us and a mess of berries rolled out in different directions.

I scooped up his cap and held it out to him. "Sorry for putting a fright in you," I said, and as I went to add more, I caught a real good look at him and realized something that scared me so much it damn near ripped the words outta my head.

"A Jap…" I whispered.

The boy screamed. But cuz he couldn't hear his scream, it sounded thin and crackly and far off. Then he turned and took off running as though I was the Devil.

Pearl Harbor was as fresh as a daisy in my mind, and my true patriotic spirit shone through like the noontime sun. I didn't care how old this Jap was or whether he was deaf or not. If he thought for one minute he could come in here and take over the Goonberry Gulch Woods, then he had another thought coming.

"Stop," I screamed, angry as a hornet and wanting blood.

He didn't stop. In fact, I think he ran faster.

For some reason I held onto his baseball cap. It was a good thing for him that I did, cuz with the cap in my free hand, I couldn't aim the shotgun properly, and thus, decided to run him down instead of shooting the warring Jap in the back like he deserved.

He beat me to the main trail, staying a few steps ahead, and turned right, headed to the campsite. Then, as I reached out to grab him, a man appeared on the path up ahead. He too was a Jap, and dammit, they were multiplying like hobgoblins. It looked like I had just uncovered a major invasion, and maybe I didn't need Mayor Valentine to scratch my back after all. Maybe someone a little higher up the food chain would scratch my back. Maybe good old Franklin Delano Roosevelt would save me from the Vicksburg Orphanage and our farm from the auction block. It's the least he could do for me after I saved the country from this Japanese scourge.

The boy jumped into the man's arms, grasping his neck. I tried to stop, but the dirt beneath my feet was loose and I slid as though I was trying to steal home and collided with them. The collision sent all three of us to the ground in a tangled heap.

And that's how I met Mr. Yume.

(10)

I scrambled to my feet with fire-alarm urgency and snatched up the shotgun. My sweaty palms slid across the cool steel as I took aim. My breath was ragged with panic.

"Don't move," I ordered in a choking, constricted voice.

The man, still hugging the crying child, sat up, blinking at me in terror. He was a thin man, a hundred pounds soaking wet, and though he was seated, I knew I was much taller than he was—perhaps as much as six inches. His hair was thick and black like the hair on a polecat, and he had two or three day's worth of spotty beard growth. His light brown suit jacket and matching pants were so dirty they were probably beyond cleaning.

His left hand was bandaged from the tip of his fingers to his wrist, and he raised it in a-please-don't-hurt-me gesture. "Please, I have no weapon," he croaked weakly, his bloodshot eyes filling with tears. "Please do not kill us. Please do not kill my son."

Your son, I thought. And yeah, come to think of it, there were similarities between the two. Since Pearl Harbor, however, I had heard often enough that Japs were crafty devils so for all I knew the kid was really a midget.

"What are you Japs doing out here?" I barked. "You out here spying?"

Hearing those words aloud made me realize how absurd a question that was. What the heck could they be spying on out here? Bears? The trees? It didn't make sense.

"Not Japanese," he replied. "Korean."

"You look mighty Jap to me."

He shook his head. "Japan is close to Korea. But like you, the Japanese is our enemy. They invade Korea before I was born. That's why we come to America. We are Americans."

"Americans, huh?" I returned, not believing a word outta this guy's pie-hole. "Okay, then, where are you two Americans living? Out here?"

He shook his head. "We come from New Orleans."

"You're a heck of a long way from New Orleans."

"Car broke down." He motioned with his head in the general direction of the eastern path. "Hit rock in the road and the axle broke."

The Pastor had told me a car with Louisiana plates had been found abandoned on the road. So it looked like this guy was telling the truth.... maybe.

"I try to get lift to town, but no one pick up," he went on, his speech so stilted every word seemed like its own sentence. Obviously, American was not his first language. "They think I am Japanese. Then these two men come by. They dress in army clothes—lots of tattoos."

"Tattoos?" I muttered, and immediately thought of the Valentine boys. They were so covered with tattoos it was hard to determine what was clothes and what was ink. Too bad I hadn't brought along Clem Valentine's head. I could have pulled it from the knapsack now and asked it to confirm the man's story.

"They shoot at us." The scared man continued. "They chase us into the woods. Threaten to kill us." He shivered slightly at the thought.

I was starting to believe him...kinda. "What were these guys driving? What kind a car?"

"A truck. A black pick-up truck—all dented."

"Huh-huh," I said, nodding. And yeah, maybe this guy was telling the truth—well, at least the part about the Valentine boys. It would be just like them to pick on an innocent family. And my train of thought leaped ahead and I imagined a scenario where they thought that capturing what they assumed were Japanese spies would make the army forget all about this AWOL business. "If it's who I think it was, you don't have to worry about them anymore."

"You know these men?" he gasped.

"I think so. But again, you don't have to worry about them." I suddenly realized I was still pointing the shotgun at them. I didn't completely believe the man's story, but I was starting to. Sides, he didn't look like he was armed. I lowered the shotgun. "I'm Johnny McGrath."

He set the boy down beside him and climbed to his feet. "I am Dae Yume." He held out his hand and we shook. His grip was firm and his skin was callused from physical work. He put his arm around the boy and gestured at him. "This is my son Pack."

"Yeah, I met him. Tried to talk to him but he didn't hear me. Is he deaf?"

Mr. Yume nodded. "Since birth." He shrugged. "I told him to stay close. But he is hungry and went off looking for berries."

"You hungry?"

"Yes, we have eaten nothing but berries in the last two days."

"Well, this is your lucky day. Cuz I got food for you."

The man nearly wept with relief. "You can spare food?"

"I got more than enough. And if I run out, I'll hunt what I need." I glanced down then and noticed the boy's Yankee cap in the dirt by my feet. I bent over, scooped it up and held it out to him. The boy snatched it outta my hand at once, and put it on, his face brightening. "I see your son likes baseball."

"He loves baseball." Mr. Yume answered. "He wanted to play with the other kids, but he can not hear, can not communicate, so the young boy's league in our area refused to let him play. He cried for weeks. My brother-in-law, the one we are going to stay with in New York City sent him the Yankee's cap to cheer him up. He loves it. I hope that one day I'll be able to take him to a game."

"I'm sure he'll love that."

The boy tugged on Mr. Yume's sleeve, and once he had his father's attention, flashed him a series of hand signals. I had never seen sign language before, but figured this was what I was looking at.

Mr. Yume signed something back and turned to me. "Pack thanks you for returning his cap and wishes to know about your cap. He does not know that team."

I took off my cap and looked at the large G above the bill. "This here cap is a Goonberry Gophers cap. It's a church league team. I used to pitch for them. Then the war came along."

He sighed. "Yes, the war. I understand."

Just then I heard rustling up the trail and my heart leapt into my throat cuz I thought it might be Cole or Snake. I stepped aside and leveled the shotgun in the direction of the approaching noise, squinting ahead in the semi-darkness.

"Don't shoot," Mr. Yume said with alarm. "It is my wife."

"Your wife? How many are you?"

"Three." He flashed a grin. "But soon there will be four."

Sure enough, it was Mr. Yume's wife, and sure enough, Mr. Yume was right—soon there would be four of them—for she was pregnant, about as pregnant as you could get without giving birth.

She was nearly as wide as she was tall, with long black hair that was littered with bits of twigs and leaves and flowed like a cape as she ran. She came to a stop between her husband and son, and though it was near dark, I could see that both her eyes were rimmed black and bloodshot. Her cheeks were scraped too, and puffy. A cut stretched across her forehead from temple to temple. It looked nasty, and I thought it should have been stitched.

"Johnny, this is my wife, Sue-Lyn," Mr. Yume introduced. "She speaks no English."

She bowed and smiled and I shook her hand, which was as dainty as bone China. How could anyone hit a woman? And I turned to Mr. Yume and asked, "Did the men that chased you into the woods hit your wife?"

He shook his head. "They shoot above our heads and chased us. We were too fast for them, and I think they are lazy. They did not follow for long."

"I see," I muttered, and was now wondering how Mr. Yume hurt his hand. Was he smacking the Mrs. around? He looked gentle enough, afraid of his own shadow, but looks could be deceiving.

I was familiar with domestic abuse, for a kid about my age named Doris Peters who used to sit behind me in school would show up damn near everyday all black and blue from her old man's fists. Doris's Ma didn't fair any better, for I'd seen her eyes black a time or two also, sitting in the back pew of the church wearing sunglasses, trying to fool the congregation into believing her eyes were sensitive to the light. The surprising thing about it was no one ever said a thing. It was one of those 'it's-none-of-our-business' type things. Thankfully, however, Mike Peters, the abusive husband and father, died suddenly from food poisoning. Couldn't have happened to a nicer guy, right? The odd thing about it was, though his wife and daughter had eaten the same meal at the same time, they never came down with it. Thankfully, Sheriff Nibbs decided that Mike Peters' accidental death fell into the 'it's-none-of-our-business' type category.

"There is a campsite along this path," Mr. Yume said. "My wife made fire hoping her men can bring home food. Will you join us?"

I nodded, and motioned for him to lead the way, happy I had company now that it was dark.

But what kind of company? Japanese spies pretending to be Korean? Or a Korean family with an abusive father and husband?

Only time would tell.

(11)

The campsite was an open spot of dirt, an oasis really, surrounded by a mass of green vegetation that, in the light summer breeze, swayed and rocked like the arms of a monster. In the center of this oasis was a fire pit surrounded by several sitting logs of various sizes and lengths. A burned-black metal grill shaped like an overturned box sat atop the pit.

Luckily for the Yumes, Mr. Yume smoked and luckily he had a working lighter so Mrs. Yume had no trouble making a fire. It cracked merrily away like popping corn and shot high between the grill. It threw a soft, moving, eerie light that distorted our shadows into the blackness behind us. I was happy to have company cuz if I'd been by myself I would have been bug-eyed paranoid.

We sat on logs: Mr. Yume and I on one log; his wife and son, directly across the fire from us, on another. I took off the knapsack, placed it in front of me, and dug through it, pulling out the food Ester had packed for me. We ate sandwiches, beef jerky, and molasses cookies. The Yumes ate it up as though they hadn't eaten in weeks. My appetite had waxed and waned all day, and though I didn't feel hungry, I forced myself to eat half a sandwich.

As we ate, Mr. Yume and I made small talk, talking about stuff so trivial I forgot about it half a second later. Yet, once again, I noticed that the Yumes seemed immune to mosquitoes. It was as if they had an invisible barrier around them and I asked why.

Mr. Yume nodded proudly. "Old Korean remedy," he said, and pulled a rolled up green and white oval leaf from his pocket. "Pepper weed. It is all over the place—if you look hard enough." He handed it to me. "Mash it with your fingers to release the juice and then rub it on your skin and clothes. You will not have to worry about the bugs."

I did as he said and crushed the leaf in my palm. The smell hit my nose with the force of a punch. My eyes watered and my nose ran. I then rubbed the leaf over my skin and clothes. Before long I couldn't smell it anymore. The mosquitoes could, however, and kept their distance, which, after all, was the end game.

"So Johnny," Mr. Yume began, and fished from his coat pocket a crumpled deck of cigarettes. "What are you doing out here? Hunting?"

"Uh, actually, no," I retuned, and shook my head at his offer of a cigarette.

He looked relieved I wouldn't be smoking off his deck and, before lighting up, pursued the matter further. "Hiking?"

I was still undecided on how much of myself and story I wanted to reveal to this man cuz frankly, I wasn't convinced he was telling me the whole truth. "Yeah, you might say I'm out hiking."

He nodded amicably. "Awful thick woods to be hiking in."

He was fishing for more of an explanation—well, fish away, cuz for now anyway, that was my story and I was sticking to it.

Still, upon reflection and regardless if he was a Jap or wife beater or both, he did have a right to know about Cole Conklin and Snake Richards.

"Uh, Mr. Yume, have you seen anyone else out here in the woods?"

His eyes narrowed suspiciously. "No. Only you. Why?"

"There are other men out here," I told him, and though I didn't have to worry about scaring his wife and child cuz one couldn't understand American and the other was deaf, I still lowered my voice when I added, "Dangerous men. Killers."

His eyes grew wide with fright. "Killers?"

"Have you heard of the Conklin gang?"

He swallowed hard. "I have heard of them. I hear about them on the radio. They are the men that use straight razors to kill with. Yes?"

"Yeah, that's them all right."

"They are in these woods?"

I nodded.

He gulped loudly. "Are we in danger?"

"To be honest, when I smelt the smoke from your fire, I thought the killers were at the campsite."

"So we are in danger?"

"Maybe not. They may be further up the trail. North of here." I shrugged. "I really don't know."

"But they could be south of here, heading north?"

"It's possible."

"What should we do?"

"For now—nothing. It's dark so they're most likely bedded down for the night."

"And if they are not?"

"Don't worry." I gestured at the shotgun leaning against the log. "If they come around, I'll convince them to leave."

He grinned wearily. "I hope you are a good shot." Before I could respond, he quickly rushed on and added, "I do not understand. Why would they come out here? Are they hiding from the law?"

I decided then to tell him the truth. What the heck? We had nothing else to talk about. Besides, it had occurred to me over the last few minutes that revealing my mission to Limbo, even to a Japanese spy, would not hinder the war effort.

"I'll be honest with you Mr. Yume, these men are out here for the same reason I'm out here," I said, and explained in length about Limbo and my life of late. As I spoke, I kept waiting for him to call me a lair or at least scoff. But amazingly enough, he didn't scoff once. He smoked and listened patiently, taking it all in, seemingly believing every word I said. Who knows? Maybe in Korea this sort a thing goes on all the time.

"So let me get this straight—you are going up to this 'Limbo' to look for your father's spirit?"

"Yeah, that's right."

"And these men are going to Limbo, too?"

I nodded.

"Why? Are they searching for a lost relative, too?"

I shrugged. "I'm not sure."

He was silent for a moment, thinking it through. Then he asked, "Are you sure you want to do this?"

I nodded. "I have to find out if I'm an orphan."

"Old Korean proverb says some questions are best left unanswered."

"I'm sure there is an old American proverb that says something similar. Still…"

He sighed heavily. "The dead should not be disturbed."

"I don't plan on disturbing anyone. I just plan on looking."

"It sounds like an unholy place, Johnny."

"You're not the first person to tell me that," I admitted, and shrugged. "But I have to do this. A man has to do what a man has to do. I feel it's my destiny."

"I don't believe in destiny. Or fate. I believe we decide what happens in our lives by our own choices. Our own decisions."

"Do you believe in God, Mr. Yume?"

"Yes," he said at once. "I prayed for help, food for my family, and before long you came."

I smiled. "Glad I could help."

"Maybe you came for us, and maybe we are here for you. Maybe I can convince you not to go further."

"Others have already tired to do that."

"Yes, but perhaps after you hear our story you will change your mind."

"Oh?"

"You said that you feel in your heart that it's the right thing to do. Believe me, Johnny, it is not wise to listen to your heart. Commonsense and logic is what you should trust. Commonsense told me to leave New Orleans a long time ago because it was not safe for me or my family. But my heart told me to stay. So we stayed." He held up his injured hand and then gestured at his wife. "If we had left earlier, gone to New York to live with my wife's brother, none of this would have happened and we would be there now, safe and sound."

"What happened in New Orleans?"

"After the attack on Pearl Harbor we became targets. It did not matter that we were Korean. We look Japanese so people would yell and throw things at us. We had a small dog. Pack loved that dog. Someone cut the dog's throat and used the blood to write bad messages on the sidewalk in front of our flat."

I cringed at their misfortune.

"Sometimes I was happy that Pack was deaf and could not hear the bad words. I am sure he knew they were making fun of us. Anger gives off a feeling not lost on the deaf."

"Did you go to the police?"

He nodded. "They told us to leave."

"That's mighty neighborly of them," I muttered, and wondered what Sheriff Nibbs would do in a similar situation. Probably the same thing.

"We went on with life the best we could. Then three days ago, I took Pack to the doctor for a checkup. When we were gone, they broke in and attacked my wife. They punched and kicked her and dragged her into the street. Then they set fire to our flat. I came home and saw my wife being beat up. I tried to stop it, but they grabbed me and closed my hand in a car door. I passed out from the pain. When I awoke, the police were there. They told us again to leave." He shrugged. "What other choice did we have? Our home was burned, and with it, all our possessions. All we have left are the clothes we are wearing and the car. And now we do not even have the car."

It seemed I wasn't the only one having a crappy summer. In fact, I felt better off. I only had myself to worry about; he had a growing family to take care of.

"It was a poor decision that led us to where we sit now," he went on. "Not destiny. So please Johnny, think about not going on. Do not listen to your heart. Listen to commonsense because you do not want to end up like us, in a trouble that you can not get out of."

He threw the last of his cigarette into the fire and sniffled back tears.

"If only we had left earlier. We would not have been attacked. And that rock would not have been in the road. And we would likely have made it to New York with no trouble. Instead, my wife and I have been injured and we are here in the middle of nowhere with no car and little money—a thousand miles from our destination." He looked me in the eye. "And what happens when my wife goes into labor? I do not know how to deliver a child."

And to think—I thought I had problems.

"Okay, I think I know someone who can help you."

"Really? Who?"

"The pastor at my church."

"Is he a good man?"

I thought about it. "Yeah, he's a good man. He doesn't care all that much for me, but that's another story. He has a good heart. And that's what counts. He'll help you get to New York. Now all we have to do is get you to him."

(12)

So I told him about the Pastor and about how to proceed through the woods and about how to cross the Goonberry Gulch River and about how to find Route 9 across the open field beside the city dump and about how to find the Pastor's mansion.

"Once you get there, you tell him everything that has happened to you and about meeting me. Okay?"

He nodded and thanked me, and was about to say something else when Pack stepped up to him and signed a message. I didn't understand the finger waving but cuz he kept looking at me as he signed, I assumed I was the topic of conversation.

Sure enough, I was. "Pack would like to know about your baseball days and about the team you played for."

I wasn't really in the mood to discuss my past, but since we had finished discussing the serious business of survival and had nothing else to talk about but the weather, I agreed, talking slowly so Mr. Yume could sign my words to his son.

"I played in a church league. We played other churches from all over the state. I started playing second base, but cuz I could throw, a lefty ta boot, the coach soon made me a pitcher."

I told them about throwing my no-hitter, trying not to sound like I was bragging (which was damn difficult to do), and when I finished, Pack signed a message to his Pa.

"Pack wants to be a pitcher so will you show him some of your pitches?"

What the heck—I had nothing else to do. So Pack and I collected some baseball size rocks, and I set up a rusty tin can on a tree branch about four feet off the ground. We stepped off about twenty-five or so feet—approximately half the regulation distance from the pitching rubber to home plate—and for the next ten minutes I showed him how to position his fingers so he could throw a curve, a sinker and a split-finger fastball. Then I showed him my wind up, leg kick and delivery, holding up from throwing the rock cuz we didn't have many to spare.

Pack soon mastered how to position his fingers for each type of pitch, but cuz he was as coordinated as a drunken arthritic man on stilts all his pitches missed the target by a country mile. Who knows? Maybe his hearing problem had something to do with it. He didn't give up though, and kept at it until we ran outta rocks.

When I returned from the bushes, retrieving seven of the rocks he had thrown, I found him curled up asleep next to his Ma, who was also asleep. Mr. Yume had gone to the pond for water, and so, finding myself alone, I decided to pitch the rocks away myself, curious to see if I still had some magic.

My first pitch sailed about five feet wide and two feet high of the target, and my next six pitches didn't come much closer. Right then, I didn't think I could have hit a barn door with a beach ball. So much for my magic, huh?

Pitching so wildly was disconcerting, but hey, what could I really expect after such a long lay off? Besides, I was pitching lopsided rocks after walking all day. This was hardly a fair test, hardly something to worry about or dwell upon for more than a few scant seconds. Still, I did dwell on it. And it bothered me. It bothered me a whole lot.

(13)

I awoke with a start and sat up, my back creaking from sleeping on the cold ground. An instant later, the reality of my situation flooded my thoughts and I looked around.

All that remained of the fire was white ash and listless threads of smoke that slowly curled upwards. Overhead, the sky was black and filled with stars. To the east, the sky was more blue than black and rimmed with a light glow. If I had to guess, I'd guess the time to be somewhere around five a.m.. For a farm boy like myself it was time to get up, and by the looks of things, Mr. Yume must of had a bit of 'farm boy' in him too, cuz he was no where insight. His family, however, was. Pack and his Ma hadn't were still sleeping soundly.

I climbed to my feet and stretched, and as I was stretching I caught a whiff of cigarette smoke. I thought of Cole at once, but after a couple of sniffs, I determined the smoke was blowing in from the pond. Mr. Yume, it seemed, had gone down to the pond to enjoy a smoke. Still, in case my nose wasn't working as well as I thought it was, I slung the shotgun over my shoulder before hurrying along the path to the waterhole.

Thirty seconds later I emerged in an open area about the same size as the campsite. The pond was roughly the size of a backyard swimming pool and inlayed with bulrushes and Lilly pads. Thankfully, as expected, I found Mr. Yume seated on a boulder, smoking a cigarette.

He greeted me with a smile and motioned me over. I sat beside him on the boulder and, noticing the tired black bags under his eyes, said, "You look a might tired."

"I can not remember a time when I have been more tired."

"You'll sleep better tonight," I assured him.

"If we make it," he muttered around his cigarette. "I have been thinking a lot about those killers, Johnny. If we run into them, I do not know what I will do."

"Do you want me to walk you outta the woods?"

He looked away. "You have done so much for us already. I can not ask you to put your plans aside for us. But I will not lie to you. I would feel better if you came with us. And not only for our sakes—but for your safety as well."

"I'll be fine."

He raised a brow at me. "You are not going to a country club."

I smiled at his humor.

"The only people who should go to the land of the dead—are the dead."

Not wanting to discuss the matter further with him, I changed the subject. "Have you ever fired a shotgun before?"

His eyes widened slightly. "No."

"I'll show you. It's easy."

"You are going to give me your shotgun?"

"I'll loan it to you."

"What about you? You will need a weapon, no?"

"I don't think buckshot will work on a ghost," I returned, smiling. "Sides, I still have the knife."

He shook his head. "No. You have given us too much already."

"I've only got myself to protect, Mr. Yume. You've got a family. So take the shotgun and don't be afraid to use it. Cuz Cole Conklin and Snake are dangerous men. They have no morals or values. If you cross paths with them, they will kill you and your family and not think twice about it."

He sighed heavily. "I wish you would come with us."

"I can't. I must see this to the end."

He nodded glumly.

I laid the shotgun in his lap. "When you get to the Pastor's house tonight, give the shotgun to his granddaughter, Sally. It's her shotgun. She's my girlfriend."

"Oh, you have a girlfriend?"

"Yeah. She's about the only friend I do have, so if you don't mind, could you pass on a message to her for me?"

"Okay, sure."

"Tell her I love her."

He grinned and nodded.

(14)

For the next twenty minutes as the sky brightened above us, I showed Mr. Yume how to hold the shotgun and how to aim the shotgun and how to load the shotgun. As for firing the shotgun?

"You better not," I cautioned when he asked for a test fire. "Sounds carry a long way out here. Cole and Snake could be in earshot."

"Okay," he grumbled. "I wish I knew what shooting it was like because I feel I will need it today."

I didn't argue with him or try to put his mind at ease, cuz frankly, I thought he was probably right.

"Now remember, it'll kick like a mule when you fire it. So hold it tight. As hard as you can. And don't jerk on the trigger. Squeeze it. Squeeze it smoothly."

"It seems simple enough."

"It is. But the most important thing to remember is to remain calm. Don't panic. Cuz if you panic, you'll miss, and believe me, you don't wanna miss. Not against these guys."

He asked a couple more questions, trivial stuff really, and once I answered his questions, he returned to the campsite to wake his family. With him gone, I knelt by the pond and drank up as much water as I could. Then I topped up the canteen and returned to the campsite to find the Yumes ready to start the walk south.

Pack was all smiles as he practiced gripping a rock, and I motioned him over with a wave and put the knapsack on his back.

"No, no, no," Mr. Yume said at once. "We will not take your food. Thank you. But no."

"You'll need it more than me," I told him. "Besides, there's plenty of wild fruit out here." That much was true. Finding something to eat would not be a problem.

I then slipped the canteen off my belt and tucked it in the knapsack.

Mr. Yume was aghast. "No. We will not take your water."

"Take it," I said. "There's plenty of water out here." That was boarding on a lie. Finding water could be a problem. But again, I only had myself to worry about and he had a young child and a pregnant wife to care for. So what the heck? They needed the canteen more than me. Sides, I figured if anything happened to me it wouldn't be from lack of water.

And so, with that done, and with everyone ready to go, I led the way along the narrow path to Breckinridge's trail. Once on the trail, we stood in a loose semi-circle, looking at each other.

I pointed south. "Follow this trail all the way to the end."

Mr. Yume nodded.

"Any questions?"

"No. You have explained things well." He stepped up to me and we shook hands like old buddies. "You have saved our lives."

"I'm glad I could help."

Mrs. Yume said something in Korean, and Mr. Yume nodded at once and said, "If the baby is a boy, Sue-Lyn wants to name him Johnny."

I blushed and told her to have a happy, healthy baby; Mr. Yume translated for me.

Pack caught his father's attention and signed a message. Again, Mr. Yume translated for me. "Pack thanks you for teaching him to pitch. He wants you to come and visit us in New York. We will go to see the Yankees together."

"I'd like that," I said, and took off my Goonberry Gulch cap, holding it out to the boy. "Here Pack, something to remember me by."

His face lit up like a sunrise, and he took the cap outta my hand, took the Yankee cap off his head and replaced it with the Goonberry Gulch cap. He then held the Yankee cap out to me.

I shook my head. "Give it to your Pa. He'll need a hat in the sun."

"Please Johnny," Mr. Yume said strongly, almost begging. "Please take the cap."

It occurred to me that for the sake of this man's dignity I needed to take something from him. But of all things, why a Yankee cap?

The damn thing actually fit, and so, unable to think of an excuse for not taking it, I resigned myself to wear it and thanked them for it. I then wished them luck, waved goodbye and walked off toward Limbo, saying a prayer, asking God to bless them and me. If I ever saw them again, I wanted it to be under better circumstances. Most importantly, I didn't want to see them walking the streets of Limbo, and that was what I feared most of all.

(15)

Minutes ticked on into hours and the path stretched on before me and I trudged on toward Limbo. I thought about a lotta stuff: the Yumes, Sally, the Pastor, Cole and Snake, and yeah, I thought about baseball. For some puzzling reason, last night's throwing display bothered me like a bad rash. I suppose I was troubled cuz somewhere deep inside me I still dreamed it was possible to make it to the majors. But I knew now the magic was gone. Sure I was throwing rocks and not baseballs and sure I hadn't practiced in a long time and sure I was dead-tired from the long walk and sure I was emotionally drained cuz of Ma's passing and Pa's disappearance and so it was surely not a fair test of my talent. Still, I felt in my heart the magic was gone and that disturbed and saddened me.

Eventually though, I soon had something else to think about and that something else was even more disturbing than a bad pitching performance.

See, without even realizing it, outta know where came a low-grade anger that seethed through me like the sickness from eating semi-turned meat. Where it had come from I couldn't say, but as time wore on it steadily grew stronger. Before long I was steaming mad and hating the Yumes with a passion. It was as though they were the cause of not only my troubles but the world's troubles as well.

I hated them for taking my possessions. Why the heck were they so puppy-dog-lost pitiful? And what really irked me, what nearly drove me to curse aloud, was this stupid baseball cap. I hated it, hated it with a passion and considered throwing it into the bushes. I didn't, though. I didn't cuz I wanted to stay angry at it and keeping it on my head was the best way of doing that.

So I trudged on with the cap on my head, storming up the path, hating myself for not driving the Yumes off with the shotgun the second I came upon that stupid deaf kid and his old man.

The thoughts were so vile it scared me and I actually stopped walking, wondering where the heck these thoughts were coming from. This was not like me. I was a Christian, a good Christian, and sure, I strayed off course from time to time like anyone cuz hey, I wasn't perfect, but dammit, I wasn't like this. I didn't hate people, especially innocent, nice people like the Yumes, who obviously had done me no harm. I wasn't selfish or greedy either but I was sure thinking that way, and now I started to think about Ma and Pa, and dammit, I got angry all over again.

Why the hell did Ma die? Why the hell did Pa leave? They shucked their responsibilities. Sure it wasn't like a drunk abandoning a child on the side of the road, but dammit, the end result was the same. What sort of parents would do that to their child?

Then I realized something that sent a shiver of fear through my belly. I must be thinking these evil thoughts cuz I was getting close to Limbo. It was the only thing that made sense. The Pastor warned me I would think like this, and dammit, he was right.

Forewarned is forearmed as the saying goes, and I found some comfort in the fact that I knew why I was thinking such vile thoughts. It didn't stop them from coming though, and with all this mental turmoil going on between my ears, time passed and I covered a lot of ground without realizing it.

The next thing I knew I rounded a bend in the path and came to the spot on the trail that I had always considered to be the end of Breckinridge's trail. This was as far as Pa and I had ever gone cuz the trail narrowed here to what could only be described as an indentation in the bushes. On the rare times that we had even ventured this far, we had always either turned back or had taken the trail that ran downhill and southwest.

Ahead was virgin territory, and without a second thought, I continued forward, pushing and pulling aside branches and crushing vegetation with vengeful force. It helped work out a little of the evil swirling in my head, though at times, I wished a cottonmouth or rattler would happen by so I could stomp it to death.

That didn't happen, though. Maybe all the forest critters knew to stay outta this area.

Within minutes, the path, thankfully, widened, and kept widening. I soon found myself walking in an open, treeless area. The ground beneath my feet was relatively flat and covered with moss and in spots, large flat rocks. It was easy walking, as easy as any place I'd been on this trip, and the evil swirling in my head backed off a bit. I relaxed some, feeling good about my whereabouts.

I felt the wind more out here, of course. It gusted and swayed the undergrowth, which made an almost constant swishy, crinkly sound. It was all I could hear, and that put me on edge a tad cuz I relied a lot on my hearing to warn me of danger. Since it was harder to hear, I kept turning my head from side to side and looking behind me. As I was doing that, I spotted something which made me stop.

A thick section of bushes about thirty yards away on my left was shaking fiercely, a lot more fiercely than what the wind was blowing. Something was in those bushes and the last time I saw bushes move like that a child had popped out. It was most likely a four-legged critter this time. It's rare to see a polecat or possum moving about during the shank of the afternoon, but what else could it be?

A second later I got my answer. And no, it wasn't a polecat or possum.

The undergrowth shuttered violently and out popped a cinnamon-brown bear the size of a small car. It stood erect on its back legs and raised its snout, sniffing the air. Half a second later, it caught my scent, and roared savagely as though a pipe wrench was clamped on its privates.

My bowels groaned.

The bear dropped to all fours and charged me like Teddy Roosevelt heading up San Juan Hill. The only weapon I had was a knife, and it didn't take a genius to figure out that in this situation a knife would do me little good. Heck, for that matter, I didn't think the shotgun would have done me much good either. Cuz shooting at the damn thing would probably just make it madder.

So I did what comes naturally: I took off running, head down, legs chugging like the pistons on a race car.

It's funny what you think about in times of danger. This time I thought about the National Geographic Magazine. It's a fine read—always has been—and lucky for me, the Pastor was a subscriber. Whenever I had to wait for Sally to get dressed or do a chore, I'd sit in the parlor and flip through the latest issue. In one of those issues I had read up on bears, and a good deal of the information had stuck with me.

I knew my best chance to survive was to run, and a bear, I knew, could run up to 30 miles per hour. I was a fast runner, and thought I could go faster than that. The question was: for how long? Eventually I would tire and my legs would weaken and I'd slow down, and when I did, if the bear was still chasing me, it would overtake me like a tidal wave. I had to hope it would tire before I did. If it didn't, if it kept chasing and over took me, I had to use survival tip number two—again from that National Geographic article. That tip was to simply play 'dead' like a possum. All I had to do was drop to the ground and curl up in a ball. It sure seemed easy enough. Crazy, yeah, but nonetheless, easy. I had a sneaky suspicion, though, that the fella who wrote the article suggesting to do such a foolhardy thing had only seen bears—well fed bears at that—in the zoo. Cuz playing 'dead' for this moving muscular mass of fur, teeth and claws chasing me would only get me dead. And a painful death it would be.

So I kept running, praying I wouldn't trip; and the bear kept running too, closing the gap between us. I could hear the thunderous boom of its paws slapping the ground and its ragged, grunting breath, growing louder behind me.

My only chance now was to get outta this flat, open area and into the thick foliage. If I could get there, I felt I could dodge and weave around the trees better than the bear. I wouldn't be able to lose it, though—not with its keen sense of smell—but maybe I could find a good climbing tree. Bears could climb too, of course, but having the high ground gave me the advantage, and maybe my knife would come in handy then. I figured catching that thing in the face or paw with six inches of serrated steel might persuade it to climb down and find another meal.

It might not have been a great plan, but nonetheless, it was a plan, and as I was thinking it over, I suddenly tripped over some uneven rocks and sprawled belly first in the dirt. I shot up into a kneeling position, and as I did, the shadow of the beast fell over me. Escape was impossible, I realized, and drew the knife from the sheath. Such a weapon, I knew, would do little good against this thing, but still, it was better than fighting it with foul language.

It stood up on its hind legs. It looked as tall as a Douglas Fur tree and as angry as a bull with a sore hemorrhoid. It roared so loud the sound hurt my ears. And it was then that I spotted its injury—a wide gash of dripping blood ran across its shoulder blade and up into its neck.

Now there are plenty of dangers out here in the forest, so any number of things could have happened to it, but if I had to guess, I'd guess it was a gunshot wound.

Even back in 44 it was illegal to hunt bears. That didn't mean it didn't go on. It just meant it was illegal. So maybe a hunter had taken a potshot at it. I hadn't seen or heard any hunters out here, but hey, the woods are a big place, so it was possible.

And do you know what else was possible?

It was possible that Cole and Snake had shot at the animal.

In fact, as I waited for it to attack and kill me, I became convinced Cole or Snake had shot it.

The damn cowards.

(16)

Snarling fiercely, the bear stepped forward and coiled its arm back to strike me. Its paw was the size of a frying pan; its claws, black as night and eight inches long, curled out like fishhooks. I knew one swat from its mighty paw would tear me to shreds and rip out my guts. I cringed, waiting for the end, knowing that nothing could save me now but a miracle.

And then, suddenly, that miracle happened. From outta nowhere, a gunshot blast thundered overhead. The bear held up, whipping its head about from side to side in distress. Another gunshot blast rolled across the open expanse.

This time the bear got the message. It shook its head, growling angrily, and hightailed away in the direction it had come from.

I was safe—at least from the bear.

I scrambled to my feet and looked around, expecting to see Cole or Snake. Instead I saw a woman fighting her way outta the underbrush.

"Well, I'll be damned," I whispered, thinking *I can't believe it*

"Heidi-do," she yelled out, and waved. "Yuh okay?"

"Yes," I returned as she approached me.

She had a few inches on me, thin but muscular, with broad shoulders. Her white t-shirt was cut off below her ribcage and I could see her stomach muscles. It was rare to see stomach muscles on a woman, but she had them, defined like the muscles on a Greek statue.

Her blond hair, shoulder length and choppy, looked like it had been hacked by a blind hairdresser. I figured she had cut it herself, maybe with a dull pair of scissors.

She needed a bath, for a thin dusting of dirt covered her face and forehead. But her beauty still shone through. Her cheekbones and chin were tight as stone and her eyes were robin egg blue, piercing, hypnotizing.

She flashed me a smile. Her teeth were yellow, but for the most part, straight.

"Thank you for saving me."

"Yer a welcome," she said, her eyes narrowed with suspicion. "I know yuh, don't I? Yer Katie's boy, right? Yer Johnny McGrath? Southpaw Johnny?"

I nodded.

"Well, I'll be dipped in dawg's do-do," she said so cheerily it sounded much like a bird's chirp. "I sang in the choir with yer Ma."

"Yes, I remember."

She held out her hand to me. "I'm Betty Zuckerman. Though I understand the kids are callin' me Batty Betty cuz I stole my husband's dead body from the boneyard."

Well, if nothing else, at least she was open about it.

"Yeah, I heard," I said, and shook her callused hand with the tattooed Olympic rings below her knuckles. Her grip was as firm as a man's grip. But there was more to that handshake than a firm grip. Her hand was as cold and as clammy as a dead fish and alarm bells went off in my head cuz now all I could think about was Charles Haddes. Shaking hands with him felt mighty similar to shaking hands with her.

The wind picked up then and I caught a whiff of her, and now those alarm bells were ringing even louder. She smelled. Not of B.O. or of dirt, but of rot. She smelled like a dead animal.

She had no flies orbiting her head, though, and cuz of this, I couldn't positively say if she was a ghost or not. Not that it mattered, I suppose. She could have been a leprechaun for all I cared. She had rescued me from the bear and that was all that mattered. And now, after a friendly— and hopefully short conversation—I could be on my way.

"Yuh shoot that bar?"

I missed what she said cuz her Mississippi accent was as thick as Ester's biscuit batter. You could take the girl outta Mississippi (and oh boy, she had traveled plenty when she swam for America) but I guess you couldn't take the Mississippi outta the girl. I ask her to repeat what she said. She did, talking a might slower this time.

"No," I replied. "I don't have a rifle."

"Well, someone sure shoot that bar."

"Maybe a hunter."

"Yeah, maybe."

Since we were on the subject of hunters, I fished around to see if she'd seen Cole and Snake. "Have you seen anyone around here? Two men that look outta place?"

"Naw." She muttered, looking me in the eye. "Speaking of lookin' outta place, what are yuh doin' up here? Yuh lost?"

"Uh...no."

"This ain't no place to be walkin'," she went on. "This ain't friendly territory, yuh know?"

"Thanks for saying."

"Does yer Ma know where yer at?"

"No." And without even having a valid reason for passing along the information, I said, "Ma passed a couple days ago."

The words she was about to deliver died in her throat, and she stood before me, her mouth agape, her eyes blinking. "Huh..."

"She died of the cancer."

"I heard she'd been feeling poorly," she said, and shook her head slowly. "But to pass." Tears bubbled up and ran down her cheeks. "I can't believe it."

I know how you feel, I thought.

"She was a wonderful woman," she said, her voice thick with grief. "Beautiful singin' voice."

"Thank you for saying."

She wiped the tears from her cheeks with the back of her hand, and in those few seconds, the grief ran outta her face and her eyes narrowed. She now looked as serious as a judge about to hand down a long sentence. "Are yuh a fixing to go to that evil place? Is that why yer up here?"

"What evil place?"

"Don't yuh be pretendin' to old Betty. I know what's goin' on. I know why yer so far from home."

"It's not what you think."

"Oh no? Then what is it?"

"I'm looking for my Pa."

She raised a brow, urging me to explain. So I explained. I told her that Pa was missing in the country where she won her gold medal, and that

Sheriff Nibbs wanted to put me in an orphanage cuz I didn't have any kin, and that the Pastor wouldn't take me in cuz I was a southpaw and, in his opinion, not good enough for his granddaughter, and that the bank was gonna take back our family farm at the end of the month unlessing I could pay the mortgage, which I couldn't do unless she actually was a leprechaun and was willing to give me her pot of gold.

"So as you can see I'm in a bit of a spot. So I'm going up there to see if I can find him. If I see him then I know he's dead and I can plan accordingly."

"Plan accordingly? What does that mean?"

I shrugged. "I don't know. I love Sally Dickerson a whole lot but I don't wanna spend the next three years in an orphanage. So maybe I'll just take off. Go out west. I really ain't sure."

"Okay. What if yuh don't see him?"

I shrugged. "My hope stays alive."

"Hope's a wonderful thang," she said, nodding. "And yeah Southpaw, I don't much blame yuh for wantin' to take a gander at those evil streets. But yer a walkin' into a mess of trouble. Are yuh shore yuh know what yer doin'?"

"I feel I have to do this."

"Well then, I'm please to say, yer purt near the land of the dead." She pointed north. "Limbo is over yonder about a two hour walk from here."

"Only two hours, huh?"

"Are yuh all in a rush?"

"Uhhh…sort   of,   I   guess."

"Since I can see yuh ain't got no provisions, why don't yuh come back to my campsite. Take some food. Take some water. I could sure use the company."

"Maybe I better get a move on. Thanks anyway."

"My campsite is just a hoot 'na holler from here. Maybe a ten minute walk. And I've got a story about Limbo yuh might wanna hear."

"Huh? Really?"

"Yeah, it just came to me now," she said, "But knowin' it could come in handy."

"I just plan to look. I ain't gonna go any further than the graveyard."

"I ain't no carny medium, Southpaw, so I ain't gonna argue with yuh, but I suspect yer gonna need to hear what I hafta say. So how about it? Wanna spend a half hour talking to a crazy old coot?"

Not really, I thought. But unable to come up with a real good excuse not to, I surrendered with a nod.

(17)

Betty led me into the undergrowth, instructing me to "Step careful like", explaining that, "Yuh never know when something might happen by and take a bite outta ya."

It was good solid advice, and I did 'step careful like' and stuck close to her despite the rotten odor wafting from her. I kept telling myself the smell was explainable. Like maybe she had been handling dead animals. It didn't make a whole lotta sense, I suppose, but hey, it was all I could think of at the time.

We soon hooked up with a path that snaked away through the undergrowth and disappeared over a dip. Again, she instructed me to "Step careful like."

As I was doing that, following close behind her, she glanced over her shoulder at me. "So? Yuh gonna tell me who shot that bar?"

"What makes you think I would know?"

"Ya'll asked about two fellas that looked outta place. Who are they?"

"Have you heard of the Conklin Gang?"

"Those pecker woods are up here?"

"I think so. Two of them anyway. Cole Conklin and a man named Snake."

"Conklin, huh?" she muttered with distaste. "I've seen him a time or two 'round town. He looked harmless enough. I guess hangin' out in New York turned him evil."

"I don't know if New York had anything to do with it. Maybe."

"That's a dangerous bunch, Southpaw," she went on. "Are they headed to the same place yuh are?"

"I think so."

"Any idea why?"

"No."

"Ain't yuh afraid of runnin' into them?"

"Not really. Cuz I know they're out here, but they don't know I'm out here."

"I see," she said, making it sound like she thought I was making a mighty big mistake. "Might be harder to stay hidden then ya'll think."

"They're both city slickers."

She chuckled and fell silent, which was good cuz I didn't feel like talking all that much right then anyways cuz now I wanted to think about what she had just said. I had gone along assuming I could easily avoid them, but now, thanks to her, I was having doubts—doubts that ebbed and flowed until we reached the entrance to her cave.

"Now that yuh know the secret entrance to my campsite I guess I'm gonna have to kill yuh." She glanced back and laughed.

I grinned nervously and wished I was back on the trail—alone with my thoughts.

"Home sweet home," she said, and pointed out the thorn bushes ringing the cave's entrance. "Duck yer noggin comin' in, Southpaw."

"You want these thorns up here?" I asked. "I could easily—"

"Don't touch them. Those thorns are to snag bad spirits."

"Oh yeah? Does it work?" I asked, ducking my head as I followed her inside.

"It failed terribly a couple days ago," she said with a hint of annoyance, making it clear she didn't wanna talk about it, which was fine with me, cuz to be honest, I didn't wanna hear about her crazy superstitions anyway.

I soon discovered the cave was really a tunnel. A wide swatch of light slanted in from the far end, taking a bit of the gloom outta the place and providing enough light to see. The dirt walls were as bumpy as a half eaten cob of corn and crisscrossed with roots. An army cot sat against one wall. Beside the cot was a cardboard box turned upside down which she was using as a nightstand. A gas lantern sat atop the box. A dozen or so other cardboard boxes of various sizes were neatly piled near the cot. Beside the boxes were four wooden crates with 'CANNED GOODS' stenciled in black on the side.

"It's a might cold and damp in the winter," she commented, leaning her shotgun against the wall. "But I think I'll be a movin' on before the cold weather hits. Actually, to be honest, I think I'll be a movin' on pretty soon."

"Might be a good idea," I said, and spied something hanging from the corner of the cot that blotted out all other thoughts. "Is that your medal?"

She picked it up by its blue ribbon and handed it to me. It was heavier than I expected, and I ran my fingers across the raised lettering in apt wonder. The inscription read: Paris, France, 1924. 200 backstroke.

"I'll let yuh in on a secret, Southpaw, I always hated swimmin' the backstroke. But for some damn reason I was good at it."

"I'll say."

I had only been a twinkle in my Pa's eye when she won her medal, but I'd seen the black and white newsreel footage at the Bijou Movie Theater of her gold medal swim and the parade down main street on her return to the Gulch. She was a beast in the pool, a shark with limbs, and I felt proud that I lived in the same town as such a talented athlete.

"Backstroke is like kissin' your sister. It ain't fun to do and it ain't fun to watch, but dammit, it was the only stroke I qualified for."

"I'll have to take your word for it cuz I don't have a sister and I only swim doggie style."

She laughed and motioned me ahead, and we exited the back end of the tunnel, emerging onto a wide dirt expanse of land surrounded by bushes.

"My husband, John and I found this place a long time ago. We were out huntin' and chased some game through here. We loved the place so much we used to camp here all the time."

"Uh, about your husband…"

"Yuh wanna know why I dug him up and where he is now?"

"Well, only if you wanna tell."

"I'll tell yuh—in good time."

She pointed ahead at the smoldering campfire. Above the fire, suspended on black metal posts was a large pot with a lid. Surrounding the fire was an old wooden log, and she gestured for me to sit on it. I did as she asked, and watched as she lifted the pot's lid. It should have been scolding hot, and I suppose it was. For some reason she seemed impervious to the heat and I wondered, *Do ghosts feel heat?*

"We'll eat first. Then I'll tell yuh what yuh need to know."

I had no idea what she was talking about. How did she know she had to tell me anything? It didn't make sense.

"Is this about Limbo?"

She nodded. "I don't know how I know this but I know I gotta tell yuh about my relative. About Lou Purdy."

"You're related to Lou Purdy, the murderer?"

"He's my Ma's oldest brother. My uncle. And he's in Limbo. And yuh have to know about him."

(18)

We ate the stew from ceramic bowls she had in one of those boxes in her cave. The meat was chewy and foreign tasting, though eatable and filling. I didn't wanna know what the surprise meat was, but the conversation sort of died out for a time, and I guess to help get it started again, she let me in on the recipe. "Few people like squirrel and polecat. But I think it's as good as chicken or beef. Would yuh like more?"

My stomach groaned, and I politely shook my head. "I think I've eaten enough."

She didn't try to force anymore on me, and with the bowls and spoons piled up on the ground beside the log, she began her story, the story she was convinced I needed to know.

"I was only five when it all happened, but I remember Lou quite well. He was a big burly fella, kind of like Sheriff Nibbs, but with muscles. And he was as bald as a cucumber, and had a scruffy beard. Though every so often he'd surprise everyone and come into town with it shaved off. He also had a big, hearty laugh."

"Yeah, I heard about the laugh."

"I guess you'd think of him as a hayseed," she went on, not missing a beat. "Heck, people think I'm a hayseed. Anyway, he lived in that cabin along Breckinridge's trail. I gather yuh've seen it."

"Oh yeah," I put in, and thought, *I've also seen a talking severed head there too.*

"It started with animals," she went on. "Cats. Dogs. Possums. Polecats. Yuh name it. Lou would trap them, torture them, and then skin them alive." She shook her head. "It's a sick mind that does that to an animal. And the sickness worsens. One day yer killin' animals, the next day yer doin' it to kids."

I felt a sick swirl in the pit of my belly, and once again, I wished I was on the trail —alone. At least I wouldn't have to endure this macabre story.

"Then kids started goin' missin'," she continued. "The whole town was soon in an uproar. I remember Ma not lettin' me outside to play. She would walk around the house totin' a pistol in case the kid monster showed up. Little did she know it was her own brother." She sighed and added, "The day we learned the truth he had come over to the house for coffee and had bounced me on his knee for a spell. I still get the willies thinkin' about it."

"Looks can be deceiving," I offered with a shrug.

"Yer right about that, Southpaw," she returned. "Luckily, later that day before he could strike again, a hunter happened by Lou's cabin wanting to borrow some traps. Lou weren't home, but the man found all the bodies stored in the cabin. Skinned and gutted. Of course, the town formed a posse to find Lou. A lynch mob really. If they had gotten a hold of him they would have strung him up sure. That's how things were done back then."

As far as I knew, things were still being done like that, especially if the accused was anything other than white.

"But ole Lou was a sly one," she continued. "He caught wind that the posse was a comin' and hightailed it deep into the woods. Someone spotted him and the mob gave chase. Chased him all the way to Limbo."

"I heard he crossed over."

"He found sanctuary. No one, of course, was too eager to crossover and try and haul him out. They had other worries. See, the evil was so strong near the gates of Limbo, the men started attackin' each other. A lot of people got hurt from what I hear."

"Someone I know says that cuz of Limbo, Goonberry Gulch is the center of all weirdness. That's why we have so many crazy people."

"Like me."

"Uh...I didn't mean..."

"It's okay Southpaw. If I were in yer shoes I'd probably think the same way. But believe me, I ain't crazy." She shrugged. "Maybe Limbo caused Lou to be the way he was. I don't know. Whatever is waftin' off that place does affect the mind. So maybe it is botherin' folks in the Gulch. But it's worse the closer you get. So be mindful of that evil. And be mindful of Lou."

"I don't think I have to worry about Lou. I'm not planning on going into Limbo, I'm just gonna sneak into the graveyard and look in. That's all. In and out. Besides, wouldn't Lou be mighty old by now?"

"In this world he would, but we're talkin' about Limbo. And in Limbo, I suspect, things are a might different."

"Well, in any case, I don't have to worry. Cuz I ain't gonna crossover. So I ain't gonna see him."

"Southpaw," she began hesitantly. "I don't know how I know, but I know yer gonna have to be careful of Lou. And yuh also need to know that Lou likes baseball. He was a big baseball fan. So use that to yore advantage."

Thinking she was crazy, but being too polite to say it, I merely shrugged. "Okay. Whatever you say."

(19)

With her story told and her warning given, she led me away from the fire in the opposite direction of the tunnel. I saw no path ahead, only thick green foliage, moist with humidity, and wondered where we were gonna go—surely we weren't gonna crash through the underbrush like a scared animal.

"Right here at this rock," she said, pointing. "This is where the path is." And sure enough, she leaned over, and with a sweep of her arm, pushed aside a thick bush. Ahead, as promised, was a level dirt strip that ran off into the undergrowth. "Will yuh remember where this path is at?"

"Sure, I guess," I said, punctuating the sentence with a shrug.

"It's important. Cuz all goin' well I'd like yuh to bring the Pastor up here."

"Why?"

"Yuh'll see."

She started along the path. I followed, keeping a couple yards between us cuz of the rotten stench rolling from her. A few minutes later we arrived at an open dirt area about the size of a large room. In the center of the area was a dirt mound.

"John is buried here," she said sadly. "I haven't had time to chisel him a proper burial stone. And I know there won't be time now. So could yuh ask the Pastor to handle it? He can get the money from sellin' off my gold medal."

"Uh—are you sure you wanna do that?"

"Please Southpaw, just listen. Ask the Pastor to do this for me. I trust his taste. Somethin' simple like John's marker back at the cemetery."

"Why don't you just use that one? This way you can keep your gold medal."

"I did somethin' else with that," she said, but failed to explain what. "So just tell the Pastor. Okay, Southpaw?"

"Okay. I promise to tell him."

"And I'd like him to conduct a small service—somethin' simple will do."

"Okay," I said, thinking, *He'll sure be in practice from all the funerals he's been conducting lately.*

"And I want yuh to tell him my story as well. Okay? Cuz I don't want people thinkin' I'm crazy or a murderer. I know it probably don't matter much in the grand scheme of things but it matters to me."

"Are you sure you want me doing this? Why don't you tell your own story? If you've done nothing wrong, you have nothing to fear."

"Trust me on this, Southpaw—I can't do it."

A brief moment of silence ensued, and sometimes I can't keep my mouth shut and this was one of those times. "Uh, Betty…are you… dead? Are you a ghost?"

Her eyes widened slightly with surprise but she didn't recoil in staunch denial. "What makes yuh think that?"

"I met a ghost the other day and, well, you're kind of giving off the same feeling. He was covered in flies and you're not." I shrugged. "Still…"

"I suppose it would explain things," she said. "I'm missin' time."

"Missing time? I don't understand."

"There's gaps in my memory. I know what I did a couple days ago, but not today. The only memory I have is savin' yuh from that bar. I kind a came awake and found myself walkin' through the undergrowth to where the bar had yuh. How I got there I can't say."

A nervous shiver went up my back.

"But let's not worry about that. I wanna tell yuh somethin.'" She paused for dramatic effect and said, "When I returned from Paris with my gold medal I met John, an educated man who, frankly put, was a might outside my social class." She shrugged her brows. "I suppose the gold medal helped me git my foot in the door with him. But John was one of a kind who loved me for who I was—not for what I'd done. So we got engaged and planned to settle down in the Gulch and raise youngins. But almost from the start things went wrong. I couldn't have children. With John workin' long hours for the Mayor, I grew listless, bored. That's why I took up the brush. My granddaddy painted so I guess I got his talent."

"The Pastor has one of your paintings hanging in his office," I said. "I really like it."

Her face brightened. "That's good to hear," she said. "Do yuh know that work of his church is the last one I did?" She grinned. "I suppose if I am a ghost, it's my last paintin' ever."

"That's too bad," I said. "I wish you had done a painting of the school. With Ma gone, I think that before long they'll tear down the school and build something new and I'll only have the memory of the place to hang on to."

"I wish I had painted that for yuh. But I guess those days are over, Southpaw. Blame the Mayor."

"Mayor Valentine?"

She nodded abruptly. "Yuh think that peckerwood Conklin is dangerous. The Mayor is worse."

She was obviously no fan of politicians. Who could blame her?

"He paid Mountain Man Cameron Mitty to kill John."

"Oh?"

There were two stories circulating about John Zuckerman's death. The original version had him dying of a heart attack at the Goonberry Gulch Diner. Version two had him being poisoned by Betty. How Cameron Mitty played into this remained to be seen.

"I know Mitty did it cuz he told me." She pointed up the path that ran north. "When yuh leave here yuh'll run into him. He's lying off the path. Spoilin' in the sun."

"How do you—"

"Cuz I killed him. Killed him as dead as dawg's dirt."

I didn't think being as dead as dog's dirt was any worse than being plain old dead but who was I to argue with a ghost.

"The Mayor sent Mitty up to get me. He knows these woods like the back of his hand and was able to track me to my campsite. He's the bad spirit that my thorns didn't snag. Except it was me that was faster on the trigger."

Again, who was I to argue with a ghost? But it stood to reason that if she was a ghost, she had to have died, and if she was dead, then maybe Mitty was faster on the trigger than she thought.

"Should of seen the look on his ugly mug when I plugged him. I betcha he was wishin' he had killed me like he killed John—with the cyanide."

"Cyanide killed your husband?"

"As Mitty lay dying, he confessed," she said. "The Mayor was behind John's murder. See, my John saw a lot when he worked in Valentine's administration. He saw the corruption up close. Bribery, kickbacks, payoffs, you name it, it went on. Valentine is as crooked as a dawg's hind leg. And that's why John wanted to run for Mayor. Cuz he wanted to clean up the Gulch. Valentine knew John could have sent him to jail, so he paid Mitty to slip cyanide into John's coffee at the diner. The cyanide made it look like he had a heart attack, but I knew different, and started makin' noise. Next thing I know, Sheriff Nibbs is at my door lookin' hound dog sheepish and carryin' a search warrant. He told me he was under orders from the Mayor to carry out the search."

"That's a recurring theme with him," I commented. "He also blamed the Mayor for wanting to throw me in an orphanage."

"I know yuh and Nibbs are feudin' on account of him wantin' to bring yuh to the orphanage, but he's a smart, honest man, Southpaw. I don't blame him for any of this. He knew somethin' was up, even before findin' the cyanide tablets under my bed."

"The Mayor planted the poison?"

"Mitty confessed to it," she returned. "And once the tablets were in the house, the Mayor made Nibbs carry out the search. Nibbs knew he would find them so he gave me a head start. Told me to take off for Mexico or Canada. Since I like good old Mississippi so much, I decided to stay."

"I understand," I returned. "But why did you bring your husband up here?"

"John loved the woods, loved this campsite. So I decided he should spend eternity someplace he liked. So that's why I did it. I dug up his tombstone first and took a sledgehammer to it. Then I threw the crushed stones in front of the Mayor's mansion. Awful lotta bad luck is associated with throwin' crushed tombstone in front of a fella's house. So yuh watch. The Mayor is gonna befall to a whole lotta bad luck."

Though I kept quiet, I realized there might be something behind the crushed tombstone superstition. For as of now, the Mayor had lost at least one son. And if what Clem had told me was true, then Clancy was as good as dead too.

"So if yuh would, Southpaw, please tell the Pastor my story."

"Okay."

"If yuh bump into John in Limbo, would yuh tell him 'hey' from me? And tell him I love him?"

"Eh, okay. Sure, I guess. If I see him."

"Thank yuh, Southpaw. I owe yuh big time." She then pointed north. "Yuh better get a goin'. If yuh follow the path it'll lead yuh right to Limbo. Shouldn't' take yuh more than a couple hours."

I thanked her again for saving me from the bear and for having me to lunch. I didn't practically want to shake her hand, but forced myself to cuz proper etiquette dictated I do so.

With that outta the way, I said "Bye" and hurried along the path.

(20)

The smell of death was in the air.

It was hard to say where the smell was coming from cuz the wind was gusting from all over, but if I had to guess, I'd guess the smell was coming straight down the path toward me. This made sense, of course, cuz Betty had said I'd find Cameron Mitty just off the path, gunshot dead and spoiling in the sun, and by the stench of death clinging to the air like an outhouse-reek it looked like she was telling the truth.

The bushes were thick here and the trees behind them were pines and evergreens and cottonwoods, so tall they blocked out a good portion of the light, casting the area in shadows and smothering me with a closed-in, buried feeling that increased as the stench of death grew thicker. I wished I had the shotgun to hold for comfort. Heck, for that matter, I wished I had two shotguns and a couple of grenades to hold. Instead all I had was the crucifix, and I remembered what the Pastor had said: "… *it's your best line of defense.*" Boy, I sure hoped he was right.

Seeing a dead body didn't bother me much; especially since I'd been warned in advance that I'd be seeing one. So I was prepared. Well, as prepared as anyone could get who was about to glimpse the grisly remains of a human. What bothered me, though—and oh boy it was sure playing on my mind—was what if the ghost of Cameron Mitty was still hanging around? After all, if the ghost of Betty Zuckerman was still hanging around, why not the ghost of Cameron Mitty?

So far all the ghosts I'd encountered had been friendly, or at least non-threatening, but maybe the ghost of Cameron Mitty would be different. I knew he had been a mean-spirited-son-of-a-gun in his earthly-body so it stood to reason his ghostly form would be the same. Another thing to consider was just how well was he taking this 'being dead' thing. Maybe he was as mad as hell cuz of it and was wanting to bring a few of us living souls along for the ride. More the merrier, right? And if the ghost of Betty Zuckerman was toting a shotgun, maybe the ghost of Cameron Mitty was toting one too. Heck, he might be toting his entire arsenal: guns, knifes, crossbow, etc.

Course, maybe I was just being paranoid. Seeing ghostly apparitions had a way of doing that to me. So maybe it was all in my head. Maybe the ghost of Cameron Mitty had moved on to another plain of existence. One could only hope, right?

Thing was, my intuition kept telling me I was heading toward trouble, toward danger. Course, my intuition had been wrong before and I sure hoped this would be one of those times.

The path bent sharply to the left then and as I got to that bent elbow I heard the sound of flies. The carcass was close, and my heart started to pound harder. Then I heard something else—a sound I couldn't recognize at first. But I did know one thing: the sound was not being made by flies.

I paused and listened closely. It was a guttural sound mixed in with the sound of...*chewing?*

I had done my share of chewing to know what chewing sounds like and this was definitely chewing. Obviously some meat-eating varmint was chowing down on Cameron Mitty. Hardly a big surprise when you think of it. Cameron Mitty, after all, was a big, beefy fella, and any meat-eating varmint in the woods would consider his carcass as good eats.

If Mitty's carcass was being eaten—at least in my mind anyway—it meant that his ghost had moved on cuz I strongly doubted a son-of-a-gun like Cameron Mitty would allow an animal to eat his remains while he stood nearby watching. Most likely his ghost was up in Limbo or down in Hell. In any event, I didn't have to worry about it.

I might, however, have to worry about who was chowing down on his body. Cuz if I had to guess, I'd guess it was a bear or mountain lion. Not wanting to be next on the menu, I considered turning around. It would be the smart thing to do.

Well, smart or not, I decided a 'look-see' wouldn't hurt. So I crept forward, walking as quiet as a mouse but ready to run.

My heart pounded and I was so nervous I was having trouble breathing. I wanted to 'chicken out' and run, but a curious fascination tugged me forward. I needed to see what was doing the eating. Once I saw, I could run.

I rounded the bend, sticking close to the bushes and saw a cloud of buzzing flies. The fly cloud was about ten yards away and within the cloud was a pair of boots sticking up outta the bushes and there were legs clad in buckskin sticking outta the boots. The legs disappeared down behind thick green foliage and though I wasn't Dick Tracy, I was willing to bet the legs belonged to Cameron Mitty. As to what was standing on his chest eating him? Well, I wasn't so sure what that was.

There were so many flies it was hard to see, but whatever it was, it had feathers—a glossy black plumage smeared with blood. Feathers meant it was a bird, a buzzard of some kind, and for a few seconds anyway, I felt a sense of relief cuz a buzzard couldn't hurt me.

The feeling was short lived, mind you. Cuz I soon realized that this was not your run-of-the-mill buzzard. Sure, things grow big here in Mississippi, but not that big. This thing was huge. Close to my height; its body thick and meaty. It was like something outta a horror movie, except this was no man dressed up in a costume. This thing was real—and it looked awful mean and dangerous.

So where had such a large creature come from? Africa? South America?

Though I had no way of knowing, no proof anyway, my gut said it had come from Limbo. And if I was right, what else would I encounter there? A squirrel the size of a pig? An ant the size of a dog?

As all this went through my head, the buzzard unexpectedly batted its wings, clearing flies, and I got a good look at it. If I live to a hundred, it's a sight I'll never forget.

Its neck was long and featherless and crisscrossed with tiny blue veins. Its round head was bumpy, veined as its neck and covered with whiffs of sparse white hair that swayed in the breeze. Its hooked beak, toe-nail yellow and lined with tiny cracks, held a glistening wet, pink section of Cameron Mitty's intestine. I couldn't say if it was the large or small intestine, but the buzzard sure seemed to be enjoying it.

It made gurgling, wet, sucking sounds and its gizzard twitched as it swallowed inch after inch of the flattened pink tube. I'd seen children eat spaghetti like that. This, however, was a hundred times more revolting.

Since it was looking down at its meal, oblivious to my presence, I decided to risk going forward. Sure, it was a scary varmint, something you wouldn't wanna meet in a dark alley, but still, it was just a bird and if it did see me, I didn't think it would attack, And if it did challenge me, I could run into the thick brush where it couldn't fly. It could follow me on foot, I suppose, but it didn't look so quick. It was built for the open sky, after all, not walking on land.

I wanted to run of course—anything to get by this creature quickly— but running makes more noise than creeping, so I fought the urge to run and crept instead, walking backwards so I could keep an eye on it. And that turned out to be a big mistake.

I don't have eyes in the back of my head and...*Crack.* I stepped on a branch so brittle I bet the crack was heard in Tennessee. It was certainly heard where Cameron Mitty's remains were being munched on, and the buzzard suddenly looked in my direction, its evil black eyes riveted on me. My stomach bottomed out as though I'd just swallowed a bucket of rocks.

For a few seconds it didn't move, and a false sense of relief swept through me. Maybe it would go back to eating and pretend I wasn't there. Then again...my luck wasn't that good.

The creature snapped off Mitty's intestine, extended its wings, leapt outta the fly cloud and landed on the path no more than five yards from me. I gulped in terror and stepped backwards, hoping it would back down the further I got away from its meal.

Again, my luck wasn't that good.

As I walked backward, it walked forward. Its talons and lower legs glistened with Mitty's blood, and flies clung to the red gore, drinking hungrily. It was enough to make one scream, and I suppose if I'd been able to collect enough air in my lungs, I might have done just that.

The creature suddenly squawked loudly and the sound sliced through my paper-thin courage like a straight razor through hot butter. If only I had the shotgun, and I reached down with a trembling hand and drew the knife from the leather sheath. It gave me no comfort whatsoever. Certain tools are for certain jobs, after all, and this job required a shotgun, or maybe a bazooka, not a six inch knife.

I stepped back again and again. And now I had opened a wider gap between the creature and myself, and *Should I make a run for it?*

It had the wing span of a small plane, and I knew it could take me down in less time than it would take a hawk to take down a three-legged toad. So I needed to open up a slightly wider gap and find a good place in the undergrowth to run to before I made my move.

I crept backwards another two steps. It held its ground, and *Phew…* maybe it was gonna leave me alone. Maybe all it was doing was protecting its meal—which was fine with me. Bon appétit, Mr. Buzzard, the meal is all yours. I'm not fond of intestine anyway.

I took another step back. Again, it held its ground, and now I was really feeling relieved. *I think I'm gonna get outta this in one piece.*

And that's when a creepy, 'something-is-behind-me' feeling came over me. Couldn't be, right? I wanted to believe it was only a feeling, nothing more. Still, I slowly turned my head—just in case—and spotted something black out the corner of my eye. My heart burned with a lit match of fear and I whipped my head about and…"Oh my God…"

This buzzard was approximately the same height and size as the first one. It stood no more than ten yards away, blocking my path. It too had been eating, for it held in its blood-coated beck a forearm and hand. On that limp appendage was a tattoo of Olympic rings. I had found Betty Zuckerman…well, at least her hand.

My fear suddenly crested and, oddly enough, in mere seconds, a calmness washed over me. Seeing no possible way to escape, I resigned myself to the inevitable. I was gonna die. I was gonna meet my Maker in a matter of minutes. Right here and now on this path. Well, so be it.

And to think, I thought if I died on this trip I'd be killed by either Cole or Snake. Never would I have dreamed that two horror-movie-size buzzards would take me down. You just never know, huh?

Still, if I was gonna die, I decided to go out fighting. I would have no respect for myself if I didn't at least make it hard on them. If they attacked at the same time—and I figured they would—I planned to stab at one using the knife while I kicked at the other with my foot. Who knows? Maybe these things were all squawk and no fight, and would fly off if I did that. In any event, if they did take me down, they were gonna know they were in a fight.

As they approached, moving slowly, savoring every moment, the bushes directly in front of me began to shake, drawing not only my attention but their attention as well.

A few seconds of apt curiosity ensued. The bushes shook some more.

What the heck is causing that?

I held my breath in anticipation.

Then the bushes exploded as though someone had thrown in a grenade. Branches and leaves filled the air like confetti, and bounding through it all was the injured bear that had chased me earlier. It went by me as though I was invisible and leapt at the buzzard eating Betty Zuckerman's hand. The bird dropped the hand, squawking wildly, and tried to raise its talons in defense. The bear was too fast, and in one felled swoop of its paw, ripped the buzzard's head clean off. The head tumbled end over end into the bushes like some weird ball thrown by a child. A jettison of reddish-black blood shot out the top of the severed twisting neck. It reminded me of an unmanned fire hose turned on full blast.

The bear, oblivious to the shower of blood engulfing it, savagely sunk its teeth into the buzzard's underbelly. The buzzard, amazingly enough, still fought despite having no head. It beat its wings crazily and clawed at the bear with its bloody talons. Then the bear dropped its weight on the bird and the sickening sound of hollow bones crunching filled my ears.

The other buzzard had seen enough of the carnage and took to the air with a screaming squawk, disappearing over the trees like a black rain cloud.

I had seen enough too, and skirted by the bear and its meal, running up the path as fast as my legs could carry me.

I ran until my wind was used up. Panting like a plow mule at the end of a long, hot day, I dropped to my knees and looked back at the empty path, praying the bear was still at the killing sight enjoying its fowl dinner.

Then I noticed an intermittent reddish light on the bushes. I turned, looked up, and saw, far off through the foliage, a flashing red light.

I had reached Limbo.

(21)

Without taking my eyes off the light, I climbed to my feet.

All of a sudden the bear, the buzzards, Cameron Mitty and Betty Zuckerman seemed a million miles away; for that matter, so did Goonberry Gulch and my mountain of problems. All that mattered was what was flashing on and off in the forest. Nothing like reaching your goal to eliminate all the bad memories of getting there.

I glanced skyward then and was a bit shocked to see that the sky was darkening. If I had to guess, I'd guess it was between seven-thirty and eight p.m.. Somehow time had jumped ahead on me. I remembered Betty Zuckerman saying she was missing time. Now I knew what she felt like.

I continued along the path, and before long, the incline became as steep as a ski hill. Soon my leg muscles screamed with hot pain, my breath became labored, and sweat built up on my face. As I grabbed hold of branches and bushes to help pull myself along, the evil waves wafting off Limbo returned, pounding me hard. Suddenly I hated pretty much anyone I'd ever met. And unlike before, I didn't try to stop the thoughts. Maybe I was too tired. Or maybe I just didn't give a damn at this point. I let the thoughts come and enjoyed each one.

I was puzzled though on why the evil was just returning now, and concluded that maybe the lay of the land had something to do with it. Since Betty took me to her campsite, I'd been in a shallow valley, and maybe the evil wafting off Limbo was going over my head.

Well, not any more.

The steep incline, thankfully, soon became a gentle rolling hill that even a youngin could climb. Within a few minutes the trail leveled out flat and I came to a T-junction and stood directly in the center of the T.

The top of the T was, of course, Breckinridge's trail. To my left was south and home; to my right was north and Limbo. I turned right and walked forward.

A whispery hush stretched out in every direction. Where were the sounds of the forest? The tittering or chattering of four-legged varmints? For that matter, where was the buzz and whine of skitters?

I knew I should turn and run. If the varmints kept their distance from this place, there had to be a reason, right? If they had no business being here, I had no business being here either. Heck, no one alive had any business being here. Still, I pushed on, and before long, my evil thoughts fell away, and a sick nervousness wormed like a slimy snake through the pit of my stomach. I preferred the evil. But you get what you get, right?

I soon came out into an open area that ended abruptly at a rocky outcropping. The foliage was sparse here and I could see Limbo clearly.

The land of the dead, oddly enough, looked pretty much like any nineteenth century town except for the flashing red light and the weak glow of the wood buildings. What was making the wood structures glow like a dim light bulb was a puzzling question. So too was the question of the flashing red light. What was powering that?

From where I stood, it looked to be about a hundred yards away at the end of a long dirt street with wooden buildings on either side. It was suspended by four metal wires over what looked like a grassy knoll. The grass—at least from here—looked as pristine as a golf green. Obviously Limbo's groundskeeper was not off fighting Japanese in the Pacific.

As for ghosts? Well, I saw none. The place looked abandoned, as abandoned as—well, for lack of a better term—a ghost town.

I stepped up to the edge of the outcropping and looked down. The hill below was thick with weeds and stunted bushes. I saw no path leading to the graveyard. The stone fence surrounding the graveyard was waist-high, so if I wanted—if, now—I could easily hop over it.

The thing was, I had a decent vantage point from here. Going forward, fighting my way through the weeds and bushes to the graveyard, seemed like too much trouble. Maybe if the place was teeming with ghosts a closer look would have been warranted, but as it stood, the place was as abandoned as main street on Christmas morning. So why go to all the trouble of fighting through the foliage?

The graveyard, however, did itch my curiosity some. I could see six tombstones—two rows of three—and I wondered who the heck buried their dead way out here? Talk about having an excuse for not dropping by with flowers.

Also—and though I couldn't be completely sure from where I stood cuz of the shadows—it looked like one of the graves was open. Why? It was tough to say. Either there was gonna be an upcoming burial or, perhaps—thinking about what the Pastor said about hearing noises coming from beneath the ground—someone had dug their way out.

The need to know—however compelling—was not compelling enough to entice me to go down for a closer look. I'd seen enough horror movies to know that going into a dark room—or in this case, a graveyard—was not always a wise decision.

Call me chicken if you want, but I think I'll sit this one out, thank you very much.

I was quite comfortable where I was and decided to stay put. The evil thoughts had slowed to a trickle for some reason (maybe I was just getting use to them) and, for now anyway, there was no sign of ghosts. It seemed like the perfect spot to spend the night cuz there were no skitters or four-legged critters to worry about. Now if I only had some firewood, matches and a bag of marshmallows, I'd be happy as a pig in slop.

But I forgot about something. I forgot about the two-legged critters.

(22)

"Well, looky here."

I spun about so fast I nearly gave myself whiplash.

Snake stood by himself at the mouth of the open, dirt area and pointed his pistol at my head. "So you followed us to Limbo."

It was easy to see that the last two days had not been kind to Snake. The bags under his eyes were deep and dark, and that 'shiner' I'd given him was purple and puffy. His long hair was tangled like clumped spaghetti and littered with bits of twigs and leaves. His face was covered with welts from mosquito bites. Obviously he had never heard of the old Korean remedy of pepper weed. Obviously he should have stayed in Brooklyn, where the only critters you have to worry about stand on two legs.

"You've come a long way to die," he hissed around his yellow teeth. "Why?"

A lie came to me at once. "I changed my mind, I wanna throw in with you."

He chuckled evilly. "Is that so?" He shoved the pistol in his jacket pocket, and for half a second I thought he believed me. Then he drew out his straight razor, flicking out the blade. "I'm gonna do to you what I should a done to you two days ago." He giggled. "Time for your first... and last shave."

As if by magic, the small amount of fear bubbling in my belly melted away and was replaced with a building anger. I guess the evil wafting from Limbo came in waves cuz now every fiber in my body was tuned to one thing and one thing only: smashing this guy's face into a bloody pulp.

He sure picked the wrong guy to mess with today, and as he pulled back his arm, preparing to slash me, I made fists, leapt forward and threw a haymaker at his head. He saw it coming, his eyes widening in fright, but was too slow to react and my fist connected squarely below his nose. It sounded like a heavy slap. His eyes squeezed together in bitter agony as the impact spread out across his ugly face. He grunted and stumbled backwards, but not far, and I screamed savagely and jumped at him. I socked him square in the face again and again, and then a third time. I had so much force behind that last punch that his two front teeth flew outta his mouth with a jettison of blood droplets. He cried out in pain like a baby and fell backwards, landing hard on his back with a loud thud. The straight razor flew from his hand, missed my ear by an inch and clanged on the rocks behind me.

I jumped on his chest like a crazed monkey and rained down blows into his face until my hands got sore. Then, I grabbed a fist-full of his long hair, raised his head up and bashed it down onto the hard dirt. I did it over and over, four or five times at least. His body became limp beneath me.

He couldn't defend himself anymore, and you know what? I didn't care. In fact, in some fiendish way, I was happy about it. Maybe now he'd know what his victims had gone through.

I made fists again and pummeled his face with every ounce of strength I could muster. Blood spurted up from his mouth and nose and his eyes rolled back white in their sockets. I kept punching, and I knew I couldn't stop.

I was gonna kill him—and that made me happy. The evil wafting off Limbo was gonna make me a murderer and there wasn't a blessed thing I could do to stop it.

Then, outta nowhere, something kicked me hard in the ribs and I rolled off Snake onto my side. I came up on my knees, my fist balled, still ready to fight and looked up into the barrel of a pistol.

Cole squinted down the barrel, and for half a second I thought he was gonna pull the trigger and end this once and for all.

Then he lowered the pistol and smiled. "You know something, McGrath? I betcha old Snakey sure wishes he never met you."

(23)

Cole looked as haggard as a man lost at sea. His eyes were rimmed red from lack of sleep and his face was dirty and mosquito bit. In all fairness, though, he did look better than Snake, who was lying comatose (or dead, I really didn't know) bleeding from his nose and mouth.

Cole didn't seem to care about his partner, who lay at his feet. He did care about my knife, however, and ordered me to remove it from its sheath and throw it into the bushes. I climbed to my feet and followed his orders, doing it real slow, not cuz I was afraid he'd misinterpret the move as hostile and shoot me but cuz my hands were throbbing from beating on Snake's hard head.

With the knife outta play, he looked relieved and relaxed some, actually grinning at the condition of his partner, who hadn't moved a muscle or groaned since Cole's arrival. Maybe I had killed him. Maybe it was the head banging. It had sure sounded awful nasty.

"Wow, you really beat up on old Snakey this time," he said with admiration. "I didn't think you had it in you, McGrath."

Frankly, neither did I.

He crouched beside Snake and patted him down like some junior G-man. He came across Snake's pistol almost at once and tucked it in the waist band of his pants. I thought it was odd that he would disarm his partner but said nothing. He then turned out the rest of Snake's pockets, muttering to himself.

"Where's his straight razor?" he asked bluntly, staring at me through narrow slits.

I jerked my thumb behind me. "He dropped it over there during the fight."

"Now ain't a good time to be lying, McGrath."

"I ain't lying."

He climbed to his feet. "You'll forgive me if I don't believe you. See you're a savage sonofabitch. Anyone who is savage enough to do this to someone can lie. Believe me, I know. And I think you're lying."

The evil waves wafting off Limbo was still working on me, and though a tiny voice in the back of my head cautioned me that saying too much could land me in hotter water than I was already in, I didn't listen. I didn't listen cuz I didn't care what happened to me. I was obviously gonna die so why hold back now, right? What difference would it make? I looked him square in the eyes. "You're a murderer. A low-down good for nothing killer. So who cares what you think?"

The grin ran off his face by the time my last word made it to his ears. His eyes narrowed; his face twisted into a knot. "You're gonna regret saying that," he muttered over bitter lips. He pulled Snake's pistol from his waist band and pointed it at my head. "Last chance to tell me where the straight razor is at."

That tiny voice in my head was back, this time screaming at me to cooperate, and above all, to be respectful. Maybe I could 'sweet talk' my way outta this. Then again...

"Clean the wax outta your ears, Cole. I told you the truth. Now either believe me or shoot me."

"Nice knowing you, McGrath," he said.

"I wish I could say the same."

He pulled the trigger. Before I could flinch or cry out, the pistol's hammer fell. A dull 'click' sounded and Cole chuckled and tossed the pistol into the bushes.

"Snakey emptied it shooting at a bear."

If this had been more of a social setting, I would have recanted the story of my bear encounter. Since this was the farthest thing from a social setting as one could get, I said nothing.

"You better be telling me the truth, McGrath," he went on. "Cuz if I find that straight razor on you, I'll cut off your privates and make you eat them."

"I'd like to see you try, you son-of-a-bitch."

He raised his arm to hit me, thought better of it, and then lowered his arm to his side. He heaved a sigh and said, "Okay, McGrath, first things first—what are you doing here?"

Since I had used the 'I-wanna-throw-in-with-you' lie on Snake, and since Snake was currently in no position to voice an opinion, I offered up the same lie to Cole. "You still need another partner?"

He smirked. "You know something, McGrath? You ain't that good a liar. Now I wanna know what you're doing here."

Okay, so the 'I-wanna-throw-in-with-you' lie had fallen on deaf ears. It happens. So, seeing no other way around it, I opted for the truth. "I came here looking for my Pa. Like I told you, he's missing in action. So I came up here to see if he's here. If he ain't, then maybe I ain't an orphan. And maybe we ain't gonna lose our farm."

Cole digested the explanation with all the emotion of a houseplant. "When I asked you about Limbo, you claimed never to have heard of the place."

Since the truth seemed to be working well, I stuck with it. "I lied."

He barked out a short laugh. "Okay McGrath, you wanna look for your old man. Fine. I'll make sure it happens. But for now—get over there next to Clancy. You remember Clancy, right?"

In all the confusion, I hadn't noticed Clancy, but there he was, lying on his side at the mouth of the path, shirtless and tied up with clothesline cord like a Christmas goose. His green army t-shirt was stuffed in his mouth. The mosquitoes had lunched on his walrus-like girth and I couldn't tell where his tattoos ended and his mosquito bites began. It was a safe bet that he wished he had never gone AWOL.

I stepped over to where he lay, still shaking the sting outta my hands. He looked up at me, his eyes pleading, whimpering around the shirt stuffed in his mouth. I shrugged, wondering what he wanted me to do. Save him? Ha. Right now I was more concerned about saving myself.

Cole stood before us, beaming like a politician after a landslide win. "Clancy, I got some good news for you. Your services are no longer required. I'm gonna go with my new partner, McGrath. So I'm giving you the night off." He laughed at his wit. "Also keeping with good news, I ain't gonna butcher you with my straight razor."

Clancy muttered something around the shirt in his mouth that sounded a bit like "You're letting me go?"

"What I'm gonna do is a lot quicker—and less painful." And as the last word fell from his mouth, he aimed his pistol at Clancy's head and pulled the trigger. The blast felt like ice picks in my ears, and I watched in stunned horror as Clancy's cubby face contorted in savage furor. A violent splatter of red, gray and black yuck exploded out the back of his head. He pitched forward like a sack of potatoes and landed with a deadened thud in the dirt. A pool of blood formed around his head.

I looked up to find a sick, satisfied smile plastered on Cole's weary face.

"You could have let him go," I said.

He snickered. "They'd drum me outta the killer's union if I had."

"You're quite a comedian, Cole. You should be in Vaudeville or on the radio. With the country at war, we need all the funny men we can get."

"You think I'm funny, huh? Let me tell you something McGrath, you're gonna look awful funny with a hole in your head." He snapped his fingers and pointed at Clancy. "Now untie him, quickly."

"What? Are you kidding? Untie him? Why? You wanna save on rope?"

"You wanna be my new partner, don'tcha? Then do as I say. Untie Clancy and tie up Snake."

"Really?"

"Yeah, I'm deciding to terminate my partnership with him. He was becoming too much of a liability."

Since I really didn't wanna untie a dead man, I raised the obvious point with him. "Why bother? If you like killing so much, then just kill your good-for-nothing partner and be done with it. Do us all a favor."

He shook his head. "Timing ain't right, McGrath. Cuz if I do kill old Snakey, his good-for-nothing spirit might end up hindering your mission."

"My mission?"

"Yep, your mission into Limbo."

(24)

Before the war when life was fun and, above all, normal, Pa had raised a small heard of milking cows, and during that time I learned to hogtie calves. It's a rather simple procedure: get the animal on its back and start wrapping and tying the four feet together much like you'd do with a Christmas turkey. Except, of course, a Christmas turkey ain't thrashing about and mooing. Thankfully, Snake was more like a Christmas turkey than a calf, and though he groaned in pain, he didn't thrash in the least as I rolled him over on his belly. Then, with about thirty feet of clothesline to play with, I tied his hands behind his back, pulled the cord tight, and then bent his legs at the knees, tightly tying the cord around his ankles. With that done, he looked ready for the dinner platter. All he needed was an apple in his mouth.

"You tie him tight?" Cole asked, perched now on a rock over looking the graveyard.

I nodded.

"You better have."

"What makes you think I wouldn't tie him tight? Do you really think I want him to get loose? Remember, I'm the reason he's lying there with less teeth."

Cole grinned. "Okay McGrath, I believe you. Now come sit over here in front of me. We gotta talk."

I did as he ordered, sitting Indian style in the dirt.

"I gotta question for you, McGrath. Do you trust me? And be honest now."

Since he was gonna kill me anyway, I decided to be brutally honest. "Trust you?" I fired back, finding it impossible to muzzle my growing smirk. "Oh come on, Cole. I don't believe a word that comes outta your mouth. I used to. I used to think you were a decent person. But not anymore. You're a thief and a killer. A good one—I'll give you that. Though I hardly think that's something to be proud of." I jerked my thumb over my shoulder in the direction of Snake. "You're not even trustworthy to your partner."

He was stoic for a moment, his mouth a straight gash, and I thought maybe I had gone too far, that maybe he was gonna kill me right here and now and be done with it. But the corners of his mouth soon curled up and he laughed quietly. "That's good, McGrath. Wonderful."

"You told me to be honest."

"That I did," he said. "And yeah, you're right not to trust me, but you ain't in a position where it matters. You're gonna have to trust me. And you better be damn respectful and do as I say cuz I'm feeling a might poorly on account that I ran outta cigarettes. My head is throbbing like a drum. So I'm warning you to behave. And if you do, when all this plays out, you're gonna be mighty surprised—and rich."

I raised a brow. "Rich?"

"That's right. You're my new partner, and once I get my hands on the money, I plan on giving you a cut."

Again, I found it impossible to muzzle my growing smirk. "Oh please. You're gonna give me money? C'mon. Don't waste your breath."

"Think what you want, McGrath. But I'm telling you the truth. See, through out my life there has only been two people that ever believed in me. Your Ma and my Ma."

Boy, were they both way off base, I thought.

"Since your Ma is dead, I'm gonna honor her memory by not killing you."

"You're gonna let me go?" I asked. "Oh, please."

"I could have killed you two days ago, but I didn't. And I don't plan on killing you now. In fact, I'm gonna help you save your farm. You said you owe the bank money? Well, I got seven hundred thousand dollars and no one to split it with. And since I ain't greedy, once I get my hands on the money, I'll give you enough to save your family's spread. It's the least I could do for your Ma."

"Your hands on the money?" I questioned. "Where's the money now?"

"Well, that's the problem, McGrath. I ain't sure." He pulled out a crinkled sheet of paper from his pocket and handed it to me. "Here. Take this. You'll need it."

I plucked the paper from his hand and unfolded it. It was a wanted poster, the kind you see at the post office, and the face staring up at me from the poster was somewhat familiar. I had seen this ugly mug before in the newspaper.

"That there is Charlie 'Big Ears' Bernard."

"Yeah, I see his name here," I said, and wondered why his nickname was 'Big Ears' cuz to be honest—at least in the picture I was looking at—his ears looked no bigger than my ears.

He was a homely looking thing with a face like a rat: eyes too close together at the top of a long nose and no chin to speak of. It was a face only a mother could love. Or maybe a bounty hunter, for the price tag on 'Big Ears' was ten thousand dollars. Granted, it wasn't six figures like the price tag on Cole or Snake, but ten grand was—and I suppose still is—a handsome figure.

"He was one of the founding members of my gang. It was me, Doc, and 'Big Ears' that pulled off the first few bank jobs in New York. Snake and 'Tonsils' Peterson came later."

Snake started to moan louder. He was coming to, and at any moment, I expected him to start yapping about why he was tied up.

Cole, seemingly oblivious to his former partner's moans, continued to talk. "Tonsils Peterson went first." He shook his head in dismay, grimacing slightly. "It was a helluva thing what happened to Tonsils. He was running from the bank and got hit by the trolley. It cut his legs clean off. He was still moving about though, crawling along like a worm. And then—if you can believe it—some treasure hunter ran off with his legs." He shrugged mildly. "As far as I know, his legs still ain't been found."

"That's the trouble with legs, they're always running off on you," I put in dryly.

Cole grinned at my wit. "Anyways, a few months after that Doc bought the farm on the Chattanooga job, gunned down by G-men. Then, three days ago, 'Big Ears' got blasted outside Squirrel Flats." He pointed at the wanted poster in my hand. "That's who I want you to find."

"What makes you think 'Big Ears' is in Limbo?"

"I don't know where he is, McGrath. But for your sake he better be there."

"I take it he knows where your money is?"

"Our money."

I rolled my eyes. "Yeah, sure. Whatever you say."

"We split up after the Philly job," he explained. "It was safer that way. I knew I could trust 'Big Ears' but I wasn't so sure about Snake. My instinct was telling me to watch him. So I made sure 'Big Ears' had most of the money. I ordered him to bury it in the Squirrel Flats Cemetery. He was suppose to meet us outside the Gulch afterwards, but the G-Men gunned him down right by our rendezvous spot. Snake and I watched from a hilltop overlooking the road. Even before they bagged his body, they went through the car looking for the money. They found a shovel, but not the money sack, and believe me, it was big enough to see right off. So the loot—over seven hundred thousands clams—is buried in some grave in Squirrel Flats. So that's your job, McGrath. Go into Limbo, find 'Big Ears' and ask him what grave he buried the loot in."

"Cole, what you're asking me to do is insane."

"I want the money, McGrath—and I don't see another way to get it."

"Go to Squirrel Flats and dig up the fresh graves." I suggested at once. "It's bound to be in one."

"I thought of that. But there was an ammunition factory explosion near by."

"I heard."

"Hundreds are dead and a lot of them are being buried in the Squirrel Flats boneyard. So there could be hundreds of fresh graves."

I smiled. "It's a good thing you didn't kill Snake, huh? You can put him to work digging."

He shook his head. "We're gonna do it my way."

"Cole, I don't think you've got any other choice."

"It's you who ain't got the choice, McGrath. You're going into Limbo, even if I have to throw you in."

I shook my head. "Cole, I don't know what you know about Limbo, but let me fill you in on something real important. Once you go in, you can't get back. So how do you expect me to get out?

"Knight did it. And if he can do it, so can you."

"Knight is a liar...and a drunk."

"True, but I got proof." He fished from his shirt pocket a 4X8 black and white photo, creased and yellow with age. "Here, look at this."

I took the photo from him and studied it closely. It was taken at the bottom of a wide set of stairs leading up to a wooden structure with a double door opening. Through the opening, cast in a gloomy grainy haze, was a train platform and railcars leading off in a long line. The railcars looked giant size, though I suspected it was just the angle the picture was taken at.

"That was taken in Limbo." He pointed ahead. "See, it's that building way at the end of the street. Near the flashing red light. That's the train station."

I winced dubiously. "It looks a bit like that building, but..."

"That's the building."

"Cole, this picture could have been taken anywhere. At any railway station."

"It wasn't," he barked, and snatched the photo outta my hand. "I ain't lying."

"I didn't say you were. I think it's Knight that's doing the lying."

"Naw." He shook his head strongly. "See, before me and Ma moved in with Sam, he lived there with his Ma. She was ninety-nine when she passed. Sam couldn't find her bag of gold coins, and there was enough gold in it to buy the Pastor's mansion. So, he was in the same sort of predicament I'm in now."

"You're telling me he crossed over to ask his dead Ma where her gold was at?"

He nodded. "Knight claimed he was short of money and was gonna loose the farm. He knew the Pastor would buy it at auction. And since he hated him so much, he risked going into Limbo to find out where the gold was stashed."

"And he had no trouble getting back?"

"You have to come back at 'Dead Time'."

"And just when exactly is that?"

"I ain't sure. Sam said time runs different in Limbo. He said one of the clocks he saw ran backwards. So you're gonna have to work it out on your own. And wait until the train's conductor, Lou Purdy, yells 'Dead Time'. Have you heard of him?"

"Oh yeah," I said, thinking, *Recently too.*

"Sam knew Purdy well from the Gulch, and was even in the posse that chased him to Limbo. Sam said he nearly crapped his drawers when he saw Purdy. He hadn't aged a day since they chased him into Limbo and he was wearing a conductor uniform and acting like a boss. Sam stayed hidden, found his Ma and got the info he needed. Then when Purdy yelled 'Dead Time' and the train pulled out, he was able to come back over the graveyard fence." He shrugged. "I guess the train can't leave until the invisible barrier that surrounds the place is lowered."

I shook my head and smirked. "That's insane. Are you sure Sam Knight didn't get drunk and imagine the whole thing?"

"Sam hasn't worked his land in twenty years. What do ya think he's using for money?"

"I don't know, Cole. Sounds like he's pulling your leg."

"He ain't, McGrath," he snapped. "Remember, he still owns the farm. So that's proof enough. He found his Ma's gold coins. His story is true. It's gotta be."

I sighed doubtfully. "If you're so sure, why don't you go?"

"Cuz I got you."

"I won't be any good to you if I can't get back."

"If a drunk like Sam Knight can make it back, a smart kid like you shouldn't have a problem."

"I ain't that smart, Cole. Cuz if I was that smart, I wouldn't be sitting here."

"Smart or not, you are going in and you are gonna be motivated to succeed. See, cuz not only is your life on the line, so is your girlfriend's life."

"Leave her outta this."

"If I don't get my money, I'm gonna go to find her. And let me be blunt with you, McGrath, it ain't gonna be pretty when I do find her. I'll torture her for a month before I kill her. So you're not only doing this to save yourself and your farm, you're doing this to save your girlfriend. Do I make myself clear?"

I swallowed hard and tucked my hands under my armpits so he couldn't see them shaking. "Uh, listen Cole, suppose I go in and suppose I do find this 'Big Ears'—and believe me, it's a big 'suppose'—what makes you think he's gonna tell me where the money is buried? He doesn't know me from a hole in the ground."

"I'm way ahead of you on that, McGrath," he said proudly. "I'll write a message on the wanted poster. I ain't got a pen so I'll find a thin branch to use as a quill and there's enough blood bubbling outta the hole in Clancy's head to write a book."

"I don't know," I said skeptically. "This guy may still say no. It's not like you can do anything to him."

"That's where you're wrong. See, 'Big Ears' was a momma's boy. And I'm gonna make sure he knows that if he doesn't tell you where my loot is, I'm gonna make my way back to New York and slice his old lady to ribbons." He grinned wickedly. "Believe me, that'll do the trick."

"You got it all figured out, huh?"

"Almost," he returned. "The only thing I ain't figured out yet is where I'm gonna spend my retirement."

(25)

The scene was something outta a macabre nightmare. Before me, with the red light of Limbo casting an intermittent eerie red pallor over the area and turning the ankle-high ground mist into a tomato soup, Cole sat on Clancy's back as though he was riding him like a horse. Once in position, Cole plunged a skinny stick into Clancy's massive head wound and stirred it as though mixing up a can of paint. With that done, he began scribbling on the wanted poster. Occasionally, he would wave the paper back and forth to dry his bloody words. Occasionally, he would wipe the skinny stick on his pant leg to remove bits and pieces of Clancy's brain. All the while he whistled a happy tune. Whistle while you work, huh? It was enough to make me wanna scream.

"Okay, I'll read it to you," he said suddenly, tossing away the stick. "It says, 'Dear 'Big Ears' tell this kid where the money is buried or your Ma dies. And don't think I'm kidding, cuz I ain't.'" He stood, stretched and added, "I signed my name at the bottom. Okay?"

I shrugged. "I'll give him the paper—if I find him."

"You'll find him," he said in a threatening tone, and came over to where I sat.

He handed me the paper and I read it over. The script was slanted, the letters long, and the paper was littered with tiny dots of gray that looked like pepper. Of course it wasn't pepper. It was brain.

"Okay McGrath, time is a wasting. Move out."

I climbed to my feet and tucked the paper in my pant pocket. Before I could move a step, Snake came to. He spit blood outta his mouth and yelped, "Let me go, Cole. This ain't right."

"Shut your pie-hole, Snake. You knew it was gonna end like this. One of us was gonna turn on the other." He shrugged. "I beat you to it. So take it like a man."

He rolled over on his side so he could see us without straining his neck. "Let me go, Cole," he barked again. "We're partners."

Cole ignored him and pointed for me to head out.

"Don't do what he wants, kid. Cuz if you do, the second you get back, he'll cut your throat."

Cole's face creased with tobacco-starved anger, and he spun about, brought his foot back as though kicking a field goal, and booted Snake square in the face with brutal, eye-wincing force. The impact was blunt, and Snake's head whipped back as though invisible hands had tugged hard on his hair. His eyes rolled up white in their sockets like jiggling marbles. He groaned, expelling a sigh before falling silent.

"Did you kill him?"

"I hope not," Cole muttered. "I'd like to kill him but I can't take the chance. Cuz if he ends up in Limbo he'll try and stop you."

"Thanks for thinking of me."

"I ain't thinking of you. I'm thinking of my seven hundred thousand dollars." He pointed ahead. "Now move."

I stepped atop the rock outcropping, jumped down into the foliage below, my feet sliding in the slick dewy vegetation, and slowly walked toward the graveyard, surveying the area, looking for an escape route.

The hill was covered with knee-high grass and dotted with bushes. All the good- thick-hiding vegetation was a far distance away, making an escape attempt harder, if not impossible.

How good a shot was Cole?

He didn't look like much of a marksman, but looks could be deceiving. Besides, how accurate would you have to be anyway? If you shoot at something long enough, you're bound to hit it eventually. I preferred to go into Limbo alive rather than dead, for at least this way there was still a possibility I'd be able to get out. After all, if a drunk like Sam Knight could do it, then why not me?

Before I had gone ten feet, I heard a thump behind me and turned to see Cole.

I raised a brow at him. "You're coming along?"

"Just to the graveyard," he answered. "I wanna make sure you go in. Sides, Snake is starting to wake up and I ain't in the mood to listen to him jaw."

I nodded, turned and started toward the cemetery again. It was a walk I wished would never end. But it did end no more than a minute later.

I stopped at the cemetery's stone fence. It was waist-high, and if I wanted, I could have stepped over it without breaking stride. Instead, I crouched beside it as though someone from Limbo was watching.

Cole came up along side the fence but kept his distance from me.

"Okay McGrath," he began in a hush. "I'll be waiting right here for you."

"How brave of you," I mocked.

"Listen you sonofabitch—"

"No, you listen—coward."

He pointed the pistol at my face.

I laughed at him. "We both know you ain't gonna shoot."

"Don't bet on it, McGrath. Cuz if you don't get over that fence in the next five seconds, I'll blow a hole in your head, walk back to the Gulch and come back with your girlfriend. Do you want her to go into Limbo for me?"

His threat struck me in the heart, and I realized I had no other choice. So I reached up, touched the crucifix around my neck, said a silent prayer and slipped over the fence.

"Good decision, McGrath."

"Up yours."

He laughed at my reply.

The grass was ankle-high and choked with weeds. A ground mist rolled by me in thin layers like steam from a witches' brew. I ran in a crouch to the nearest tombstone. The inscription on the stone read: Joshua. There was no date of birth or death, not even a R.I.P.

I moved over to the next tombstone. Again, there was only one word engraved on the stone: Daniel. Again, the name was as Anglo-Saxon as names get and, to quote the Pastor, "Biblical".

I found another biblical name engraved on the next tombstone: John.

As I crouched there, trying to come up with some logical explanation for these bland inscribed tombstones, I heard banging beneath me and felt heavy thuds through the bottom of my feet. The occupants of these graves were banging to get out, and I froze, paralyzed with terror.

"Get going, McGrath," Cole yelled out.

"There's something alive buried beneath me."

Cole's eyes filled with alarm and he gulped. "Uhhhhh, it don't matter. Now get a going."

I suppose he was right. It didn't matter. Actually, come to think of it, did I really wanna be standing here if whatever was banging managed to dig its way out? I'd seen enough horror movies to know that anything that dug its way outta a grave was gonna be in a crappy mood and dangerous as a cornered snake. So perhaps it was best to move on while I still could.

With that in mind, I dashed to the next tombstone. The grave here was empty. It was just a well dug hole. Whoever was suppose to fill it was either still alive or laying out in some mortuary. His family was certainly on top of things, though, cuz the man's tombstone was already in position. Again, all that was inscribed on the granite stone was one name. And again, the name was a name right outta the Bible: Gabriel.

"C'mon McGrath," Cole barked from the far wall. "You ain't here to sightsee." And with that said, he pointed the pistol at me. I didn't think he'd shoot. Then again, who knows what a nut-job like Cole Conklin would do. Calling his bluff might just get me dead. So I ran over to the fence boarding Limbo. Ahead, I saw a dirt road that led off towards town. All the structures looked to be two or three stories high and made of wood. As for ghosts? I saw none.

I spotted a small rectangular wooden sign on a crooked pole near the first building. Written on the sign in jagged black paint was the following:

LIMBO
DEATH AWAITS THOSE WHO ENTER
SO STAY OUT
THAT MEANS YOU!

"You won't get many tourists that way," I whispered.

PART THREE—LIMBO

While there's life, there's hope—

Cicero

Never lose hope—

Source unknown

(1)

What was happening was surreal. Heck, it was beyond surreal, and I truly wanted to believe it was all a dream, a bad dream, a nightmare.

Pinch me please so I can wakeup.

If only.

What was happening was really happening and all the denial this side of the Mississippi wouldn't change it. I was in Limbo. The land of the dead.

But I wasn't dead.

Never say never, I guess, huh?

And to think: I'd been warned not to come here, warned not to go any further than the cemetery, warned many times, and still, here I was.

I huddled beside the stone fence and took deep breaths, trying to get my gut-wrenching fear under control. It helped a bit—a very small bit. I still felt like throwing up but the feeling was milder than when I first dropped into Limbo.

My thoughts came and went like flashes of lightning, and through it all, a small amount of hope surfaced. Where it had come from I couldn't say, but it was there—a small bit anyway.

Now hope is a wonderful thing and, cuz the barrier was invisible, and cuz I felt nothing crossing over, a smidgen of hope that maybe there was no barrier at all swirled through me like a stiff, cold January breeze. Maybe all this talk of an invisible barrier preventing folks from leaving was just that—talk. Something to keep the locals away. After all, you can't have folks coming up here whenever they pleased to say "Howdy" to dead relatives. Death didn't work like that. It was the final goodbye.

So with hope still dampening my rising panic, I extended my hand back over the stone fence, moving it slowly, praying with shear force that

I would hit nothing but air. Inch by inch, inch by suspenseful inch, I kept extending my arm back, twiddling my fingers, expecting the worse, but surprisingly finding the barrier not there. This was too good to be true, and my hope rose.

A second later my rising hopes died with the same finality as a gallows' hatch swinging open.

My fingers grazed something hard, something other than air. I hiccupped a gasp, and extended my fingers further. I touched something solid, though invisible. Panic tore through my insides with the force of a runaway train.

Nowadays, I suppose you'd call it a force field but back in '44 I thought of it as an invisible wall, and this invisible wall felt as solid as rock and as rough as sandpaper. I knew at once that no amount of force I could muster would break it. If I was ever gonna get outta here, I would have to do it when the barrier came down, which lead to the question, *When the heck does the next train leave?*

Relying on the word of a drunk was hard to swallow, and as I thought about it, Cole yelled out, "Go on McGrath. Go on—get! Go find 'Big Ears.'"

His voice sounded muffled and outta tune. Probably cuz of the barrier, though who knew for sure?

I could see him outside the graveyard, pointing his pistol at me. I didn't think he'd shoot—not now—but again, who could say what a nut-job like Cole Conklin would do. One thing for sure, mind you, if I could slip into Limbo, something traveling as fast as a bullet could cross the barrier as well. So I was still not safe from him.

And so, resigned to my fate, I turned and walked toward the town, heading to the closest building. I stopped a few feet before it and reached out, half expecting to put my hand right through the dull glowing wooden planks. But the planks were as solid as the wood planks back home. The building was real, and I thought *Why would the dead need a building?*

It was certainly a puzzler of a question. Well, I guess you gotta hang your hat somewhere, right? Everything has a home and I guess that goes for ghosts too.

Staying close to the building, I crept to the corner and peered around it. The street was empty and looked longer than it did from the perch overhanging the graveyard. In fact, the whole town looked bigger. Just how big it was I couldn't say, but I had a sneaky feeling the place was big, bigger than the Gulch, heck, maybe even bigger than Jackson.

From where I stood, I estimated the distance to the flashing red light to be about three or four hundred yards away, which was a heckuva lot further away than it looked from the outcropping over the graveyard. Either my eyes were playing tricks on me or the basic rules of measurement did not apply in the land of the dead. Cole had said time ran different here, so maybe distance was a bit askew as well.

I stepped out onto the street and looked at the building I'd been hiding behind. It was a two-story square wooden box with a sloped roof, one door and no windows. Where I come from folks call that a barn. What they called it here in Limbo was anyone's guess.

The building across the street did have windows though—one on either side of the door—and I hurried across the street to the closest window and looked in. What I saw both amazed and frightened me. It was total darkness. No floor. No walls. No nothing. Pure blackness. Yet, this blackness had a depth to it. It was a three-dimensional blackness that made me think of outer space, a starless spot in the night sky that gave off a sense of utter freedom.

So hypnotized by it, I continued to stare, unconcerned about anything else. Then a creepy I'm-being-watched feeling closed around me like a heavy blanket. Someone or something was around, and I turned away from the window and looked about.

At first I saw nothing outta the ordinary and heaved an annoying sigh at my paranoia. Then, as I turned to look back in the window, I felt a soft touch on my arm, a breath really, a ghost's breath, and if it had been possible, I would have jumped right outta my skin.

I stumbled back, looking all over, and zeroed in on what had touched my arm. What I saw made my train of thought stop dead as though it had hit a stone wall.

The last time I saw Becky Dickerson she was in her father's arms, being carried to the backseat of the car for the ride to the hospital in Jackson. She had the polio and needed treatment, but never got there cuz a truck literally ran over the car she was riding in, killing her, her Ma and Pa. It was a closed-coffin funeral, of course, and I never thought I'd lay eyes on her again.

Well, silly me. Cuz as the song goes, *There she was just a-walkin' down the street*. She wasn't singing "do wah diddy" though. In fact she wasn't making a sound. She stopped ten feet away and stared at me as though she couldn't believe what she was looking at. I suppose my expression looked similar.

Here in the afterlife, her ghostly spirit was, thankfully, in tact, and standing. If nothing else, death had glued her back together and cured her of the polio. How's that for small miracles. She was about the same height as when she died and shaped about the same too. She wore no clothes but didn't need any cuz she gave off a soft yellow glow like a light bulb. In other words, she was a glowing mannequin. And though she had no hair, her facial features were identical as they were on the day she died.

I wanted to say something but my mouth suddenly dried up like an Arizona desert. I managed a long "Ehhhhhhhhh," but nothing more. Thankfully, Becky didn't have the same problem.

"Leave," she said firmly. "Leave now."

Though I hadn't heard it in years, I knew that was her voice. Same pitch. Same timbre. Yup, it was Becky alright.

"Leave," she barked louder and flicked her hand in the general direction of the graveyard.

Well, how's that for a fine-how-do-you-do? We ain't seen each other in years and all ready she's telling me to leave. You'd think she'd at least wanna exchange 'how-do-you-dos' and get caught up with the latest gossip before sending me on my way.

"You must leave, Johnny. You're undead."

It was nice of her to notice, and I found my voice. "Yeah…I know."

"You are in danger. You must leave."

Now there was something she didn't have to tell me. "I don't know if I can leave," I explained. "There is a wall…a barrier."

"You must leave at 'Dead Time.'"

A wave of relief washed over me cuz she had confirmed the part in Sam Knight's story about 'Dead Time' being a time when the invisible wall was lowered. The old drunk was telling the truth. Well, at least about that.

"When is this 'Dead Time'?"

"When the train is full and the Crone's minions go for spirits."

"Huh? The Crone? Who the heck is that?"

She ignored the question. "You must hide," she warned. "If the living dead see you, they may squeal to stay off the train."

"The train? Why don't they wanna ride the train?"

"You don't want to go on the train. The train is bad. The train leads to a bad place."

"Worse than here?"

She nodded. "Much worse."

"What is this place, anyway?" I asked suddenly. "Isn't this the land of the dead? Don't souls stay here?"

"This is nothing more than a waiting room. The good souls stay longer because they are not as valued; the evil souls are treasured and ride the train first. But no one stays forever." She flicked her hand at me again. "Now go and hide and wait for the conductor to yell 'Dead Time'. When you hear that, run for the graveyard and don't stop until you're a long way from here."

It was good solid advice and as I went to ask where I should hide she drifted away, walking down the street as though a good strong wind was pushing her. "Becky, please don't go."

"I must."

I chased her down the street. "Becky…Becky…please stay. Please talk to me." Then I remembered something real important. It was the reason I had first ventured here in the first place. "Becky, have you seen my Pa?"

"No."

That was good news and I took out the wanted poster, holding it up for her to see. "Have you seen this man?"

"No."

"I need to find this man," I said, considering letting her know that my life and her sister's life hung in the balance.

"You need to hide from the Crone's soul catchers and their fire sticks."

I didn't like the sound of that. "Fire sticks?"

"The soul catchers may not be able to see your spirit because your body is protecting it. But we can see it."

"The living dead?"

She nodded. "Hide. Because someone will tell on you. And if the Crone or the conductor finds you, you'll ride the train. And that's a ride you don't want to take."

"Becky, where should I hide?"

But she was gone.

(2)

A minute ago I had been so alone I felt as if I'd been shipwrecked on a deserted island, but then Becky had happened by, and now, with her disappearance came a flood of other glowing spirits.

They were everywhere, walking slowly, virtually going at a snail's pace up the street like the mummy in the '32 movie classic starring Boris Karloff. The only difference between the two was that Boris moaned and groaned evilly as he walked. These spirits were silent.

They were all headed down the street toward the train station. If what Becky said was true about the train—and I assumed she was dead-bang-on correct—then I could understand why these spirits ambled along at such a slow pace. Cuz that was a train no one wanted to catch.

I backed up to the closest building and watched them walk by. They came in all shapes and sizes: Tall, short, fat, thin. I guess whatever body type you had in life you brought with you to the afterlife. If ever there was a reason to stay in shape I suppose this was it.

Before long, I heard a commotion to my left and whipped about in alarm. I saw a portly female ghost drop to her knees, screaming. She clasped her hands together as though saying a prayer and pleaded loudly to be spared. Cuz of the spirits filing past her I couldn't see who she was pleading with. But then the crowd parted and I saw—and what I saw made my legs go weak.

I had seen these things before at Ma's bedside, though at the time I believed I'd imaged them cuz of my Everest size mountain of worry. But there was no denying that the creature was there now, and I swooned with terror. If not for the building behind me I would have ended up on the ground.

197

This gray creature was tall—seven feet at least—thin as a beanpole with large pink eyes. In its oversized hands it carried a thin metallic tube that an electrician might use to run wire through. Except this was no metal tube. A thin curl of black smoke twirled out the end of the tube like smoke from a cigarette.

I had obviously found one of the Crone's soul catchers Becky had spoken of. It was also clear to me now what a 'fire stick' was.

"I don't wanna ride the train," the female ghost pleaded to the creature. "Please. I ain't bad. Really. I ain't. I'm just misguided sometimes."

The Crone's minion didn't seem to care in the least how good or bad she had been in her life. It uttered not a sound and pointed off down the street toward the train station.

"No," she cried weakly. "Pleeeeeeeeeasssssssseeeeeeee."

The creature aimed the metal tube at the pleading ghost, hesitated for a moment (perhaps giving her one last chance to reconsider), and then, as the ghost continued to beg for mercy, fired its weapon. A huge cloud of black smoke hiccupped from the bore of the tube and an instant later a tongue of brilliant orange flame lashed out. It engulfed the ghost in a firestorm of swirling flame, knocking her over in the dirt.

She screamed so loud it hurt my ears. If there had been a wine glass around I'm sure her scream would have shattered it. My heart burned with pity and most of all, fear. I teetered on the edge of madness as I watched her kick with her arms and legs like a child throwing a tantrum.

Burning ghost smells a lot like hot road tar and I gagged and cursed Cole Conklin for getting me into this. No human deserved to see such horror. No one.

Smoldering and whimpering, the ghost crawled away on her hands and knees. The Crone's minion hit her with another blast of flames. I couldn't stand it anymore. I had to do something. I had to intervene, stop this madness, and as I went to cry out, an entity rushed up, grabbed my arm and pulled me along the street at the same snail pace as all the other ghosts were walking.

"Boy, are you lucky I recognized you," the entity whispered. "C'mon Southpaw, this is no place for you to be standing."

The voice was familiar, but I couldn't put a name to it. I studied the lightly glowing face, thinking *Where do I know you from? Where?* Then it came to me. Hooked nose. Mole on the cheek. Weak chin. Genuine smile.

"Doc Rose? Is that you?"

"That's right, Johnny. Now keep walking."

A crazy thought floated across my mind and if we had been alone, just the two of us like I had been with Becky minutes ago, I probably would have asked him the pertinent question: *So Doc, what was it like to drown in a sea of cold waste?*

Now, however, walking up the street with a crowd of ghosts didn't seem like the appropriate time to ask such a thing. Maybe later, if time permitted.

"Are you gonna tell me what the heck you're doing here?"

"I'm trying to find someone."

"Who? Your Ma?"

"My Pa."

"Ain't seen him."

I held up the wanted poster. "What about this man?"

"That's a wanted poster," he shot back as though I might not have known. "Are you looking for a criminal?"

"A big time criminal," I answered. "Now have you seen him?"

He shook his head. "Maybe he's already ridden the train. The evil ones go first." Then, after a short pause, he asked, "Why do you want this fella anyway?"

"He's got information I need to stay alive in the real world."

"He could be inside the train station," he offered up with a shrug. "The train ain't left in a while, so maybe. But I wouldn't go in there. You might not ever come out."

"I don't intend to go in," I returned. And as the last word fell off my tongue, I spotted an entity that looked a lot like 'Big Ears.'

He was about twenty yards ahead, slowly mounting the train station stairs, looking all about as though searching for a loved one—or help. He turned too quickly for me to be certain but it sure looked like 'Big Ears.' I would need to get closer to be certain.

"Good luck, Doc," I said, and raced forward.

(3)

I bolted up the stairs, skirted by a throng of slow moving spirits and touched the arm of who I thought was 'Big Ears'. The ghost spun about as though I'd pinched him and we locked eyes. I studied his face in silence and quickly concluded that I had found—believe it or not—Cole Conklin's dead gang member.

Still, just to be sure, I asked, "Hey, are you 'Big Ears'? Charlie 'Big Ears' Bernard?"

His eyes were wide and disbelieving. "You're undead," he managed weakly.

"Yeah I know, and I wanna stay that way." I handed him the wanted poster. "Read what's on the back."

He ignored my request and stared at his picture. "Have you come to collect the reward?" he asked incredulously.

"No. Read the message on the back."

He chuckled. "Good luck collecting the money, kid."

Somehow my message wasn't getting through to him, and it donned on me that maybe everyone called him 'Big Ears' cuz he didn't listen.

"Look at the back," I snapped, and turned the wanted poster over in his hands. "Please read the back."

"Okay, kid," he muttered and looked at the message written in blood. "Cole?" he managed weakly a moment later, his face hardening with concern. "Is this from Cole? Cole Conklin? Did he send you here? Is he gonna hurt my Ma?"

"Not if you tell me where the money is buried."

"The bastard," he uttered weakly, his face clouding over with anger. "How dare he? How dare he do that?"

"What do you expect? He's a criminal and killer and a no good human being. Now please tell me where the money is buried so I can get outta here."

He shook his head curtly. "I don't think so, kid. Ma lives in New York and Cole would never go back there. Not in a million years. Every cop in the city is looking for him." He shook his head again. "That money can stay buried."

"Listen mister, if you don't tell me where it's buried, he's gonna kill me and my girlfriend."

He scoffed. "I'll let you in on a little secret kid—he's gonna kill you anyway. You'll be standing right here beside me—dead this time—two seconds after you tell him where the money is."

He was right, of course. Cole was planning to kill me, but I figured he'd do it once I dug up the money for him. After all, why would he get his hands dirty? Might as well keep me alive long enough to dig for him. Once he had the dough, mind you, he'd most likely shoot me and bury me in the grave I had just dug up.

At least that was the likely scenario. Another scenario—one twinkling in my mind's eye—had me bashing Cole in the head with the shovel he would give me to dig with. I clearly saw myself bashing him repeatedly with the shovel until his brains ran out his nostrils. Oddly enough, the images gave me a feeling of great satisfaction.

"Take my advice kid, run, and don't stop running."

"Ah c'mon," I pleaded, and was about to plead some more when a throng of spirits on the stairs below us parted and a soul catcher marched toward us as though we owed it money. According to Becky, the soul catcher couldn't see me cuz my body shielded my soul, but it could see 'Big Ears' and went right toward him.

'Big Ears', trying to act nonchalant about the whole thing, casually stepped back, looking away. The only thing he didn't do was whistle. Maybe he should have, for the soul catcher raised its fire stick and thrust it at the criminal's chest.

That got 'Big Ears' attention in a big way. "No," he cried. "Please no." He looked at me for support and I considered repeating the advice he had just given me. *Run 'Big Ears'. Run and don't stop running.* But this was no time for pettiness. I needed to know where the money was buried. Once I found that out, well...bon voyage Mr. 'Big Ears'.

"No, please," he begged desperately. "I don't wanna ride the train."

The soul catcher obviously didn't care and replied by jabbing the fire stick with brutal force into the spirit's chest. The blow sounded thick like a sack of oats falling off the back of a truck. It sent him reeling up the stairs toward the short landing before the open doorway. 'Big Ears' cursed a blue streak. I might have laughed if I'd been anywhere else but here.

I followed behind and to the right of the soul catcher, trying to catch 'Big Ears' attention, praying desperately that he'd see me and change his mind about revealing where the money was buried. After all, what did it matter to him? Sure, he didn't want Cole to have it but maybe I could convince him that Cole would never have it. That I had a plan all worked out for Cole—the shovel-in-the-head plan. Perform once, repeat, and keep repeating until Cole's head breaks or the shovel. Which ever comes first.

But 'Big Ears' refused to look in my direction. He screamed at the creature to spare him. The creature, in turn, struck him in the chest again with its metal pole, driving 'Big Ear's to the station's threshold. For 'Big Ears', his life and death, his very existence, was at a crossroads.

I ran up to the top stair, and though I didn't wanna call out to him, I was desperate. "Please," I hissed. "Please give me a name? Please."

His eyes zeroed in on me and he reached out and grabbed my sleeve.

"Let go," I snapped, shaking my arm rapidly. "Let go you bastard."

"Help me, kid."

I clawed at his fingers.

"Please kid," he went on with mounting dread.

"Let go."

The soul catcher struck him again in the chest with the fire stick and 'Big Ears' wobbled at the station's threshold. He looked like a man on a high wire caught in the wind, and he screamed a long "Noooooooooooo," as the creature delivered another blow to the chest with its weapon. That blow did the job, and 'Big Ears' tumbled into the station, dragging me along. I threw out my hands at the last instant, trying to latch on to the door jambs. But the door was too wide and all my hands hit was open air.

I tumbled inside, rolled overtop of 'Big Ears' and landed on my side, facing him. For one second we stared into each others eyes. I can't say what he was thinking, but in my head a voice screamed: *Do you know where you are????*

Oh yes I did.

When I stepped from the graveyard into Limbo ten short minutes ago I didn't think I could have been any more terrified. Well, stupid me. My heart was thumping so wildly I thought it might explode at any second and kill me, which, I realized at once, would not solve my problem. In fact, it might make things even worse. Sure I'd be dead, but I'd still be here, on the train platform and I heard Becky's voice in my head clearly say, *You don't wanna go on the train. The train is bad.*

'Big Ears' scrambled to his feet and ran to the entrance. He had a free path cuz the soul catcher had moved off. Ahead was freedom—well, as much freedom as any soul can expect to have in Limbo—and he muttered a desperate sigh, stepping toward the threshold with the urgency of someone fleeing a burning building. An instant later he crashed into the invisible wall and remained there pressed against the barrier, moaning softly. He then stepped back, grunted like a bull and ran at the opening, shoulder first as though he was playing halfback for the Packers. He hit the unseen barrier with a grunting 'Ugh', bounced off it, sunk to his knees and screamed to be let out.

I watched all this in a paralyzing-horrific haze, so terrified I had gone beyond feeling, beyond thinking. I was operating solely on instinct. I don't remember climbing to my feet. But one moment I was lying on the wooden platform watching 'Big Ears' scream and pound on the invisible barrier, the next moment I was standing next to a redbrick pillar that stretched up to the platform's roof. I turned then—why? I couldn't say. But I turned away from 'Big Ears' and looked at the train. It was pulled up along side the platform, steam from the locomotive casting the area in a thin white mist.

I had seen my share of locomotives but this locomotive was twice as high and twice as wide as the locomotives back home. Its wheels were a story high and the pistons driving them were the size of telephone poles. The cars it pulled were huge as well. They were rectangular boxes, half a city block long, completely solid and black as the inside of a cave. They stretched off to the horizon, car after car. Just how far I couldn't say. Infinity, maybe?

Then, out the corner of my eye, I saw movement and turned. I expected to see a soul catcher or a soul or, the way my luck had been going, Lou Purdy, Limbo's infamous train conductor. Instead, I saw a man in his late thirties, an undead man.

He was about my height, short black hair, thin face with a black eye patch over his right eye. He was clad completely in black leather: black leather shirt, pants and trench coat. The trench coat hung open, the two ends of the belt dangling down like black snakes. In his left hand, he held a wooden cane pointed at the floor. I got the impression by how he held the cane that it was more for show than necessity.

He shook his head in disbelief. "What are you doing here?" he asked bluntly, his voice as smooth as a radio announcer. Before I could reply, he added, "Are you crazy?"

I could have asked him that same question cuz I was damn sure his travel agent hadn't booked him through the Limbo train station.

"How do I get outta here?" I fired back, desperate.

Suddenly, I was being pulled away, and looked to see 'Big Ears' dragging me toward the entrance. He stared into my eyes. "Kid, you gotta help me. You gotta help me get outta here."

"I don't know if—"

"Please kid. Please. Look, I'll tell you. Okay. I'll tell you where I buried the money. It's in the Squirrel Flats Cemetery. It's buried about two feet down in a plot marked Kirby Fellows. Okay? So now you know. So help me get outta here. Okay? Which way do we go?"

"I don't know."

"What do you mean? You must know."

I shook his hand off me. "Wait here. I gotta talk to someone." I stepped back between the pillars and looked about. Patch was gone.

"Hey Mister? Where are you?"

I turned back to 'Big Ears'. He was looking up at someone approaching, and whoever that someone was, was tall. Real tall.

"No," 'Big Ears' whined. "No."

A hearty, booming laugh thundered along the platform and I hid behind the pillar, poking my head out just enough to see. What I saw made my stomach lurch with fear.

Lou Purdy, easily six-foot ten, was thick in the shoulders as a grizzly bear and plump in the belly. His massive girth was stuffed inside his navy blue conductor's uniform, held in place by gold buttons that were done up to his saggy double chins. His cheeks were thick as hanging slaughterhouse beef and his head was shaved smooth and shiny. Poised on his shoulder was a baseball bat. The bat was old school even for 1944. It was a Mohawk Indian Label with the mushroom knob, probably circa 1900 or earlier. The Pastor and Betty Zuckerman had said Lou liked baseball and it looked like he still did. So we had that in common. We had something else in common too. Lou Purdy was just like me—undead.

"Git on the train," he barked at 'Big Ears.' "Now!"

"No please. It wasn't me. It was Cole. It was Cole and Snake. They're the killers. Not me. I'm innocent."

"Innocent, huh?" He laughed loudly—a whooping horse laugh just like the Pastor had described to me. "No one here is innocent."

"I am," 'Big Ears' managed. "Honest."

"Stop yore whinin', melon head." He pushed the bat's end against 'Big Ears' chest. "Now git on the train."

"You like baseball, right?"

"So?"

"Please, if you let me go. I'll make you a deal."

Purdy's brows rose up. "Oh? Go on."

"How would you like a genuine Yankee's baseball cap?"

Uh-oh

"I hate the Yankees," he boomed, and then rushed on and asked, "Where are yuh gettin' this cap?"

"It's a secret, but if I tell you, will you let me go?"

"A secret huh? Okay, I like secrets. I'll let yuh go. The train is almost full anyways. So where are yuh gettin' this cap?"

"Behind the pillar is a kid—undead. And he's wearing a Yankee cap."

"What?" Lou Purdy roared. "Where?"

My heart leapt into my throat and I raced down the platform, weaving in and outta ghosts. I didn't know where I was running to. I was just running. Running away from this crazy, bald lunatic with the baseball bat.

"Stop!" Purdy yelled, his footfalls thundering behind me.

I kept going, too scared to look back, and then tripped over a spirit's foot. I went sprawling on my hands and knees. As I scrambled to my feet, Purdy was on me, knocking me down with the barrel end of the bat. I flopped on my rump and pulled my knees up to my chest, staring up at him. He looked as tall as a skyscraper.

"What are yuh doin' here?" he screamed.

Between Purdy's legs, I saw the guy with the eye patch move away down the platform. Obviously, he believed in the motto, 'every man for himself'. I could hardly blame him. He didn't know me from Adam. Sides, he was no match for this monster.

"Well?"

"I'm lost."

"Oh, yuh a-lost alrighty," he said smugly, and hauled me to my feet by the scruff of my collar. "Okay lost boy, time to meet the Crone."

(4)

Lou Purdy locked one of his large mitts around the back of my neck and dragged me along the platform as though I was a bad kid beginning brought home from the playground by his Pa.

"We're a-goin' to see the Crone," he thundered. "She ain't gonna believe it—someone undead."

Obviously finding someone undead was like finding a four leaf clover. It was rare, and needed to be brought to the attention of the person in charge. This, obviously, was the Crone.

'Big Ears' Bernard tagged along beside us like a second rate friend trying to join up with the group. "See. See. I told you he was undead."

Purdy said nothing.

"So I did good, right?"

Again, Purdy said nothing. He didn't even look at the ghost.

"I'd like my reward now."

"A reward, huh?" Purdy muttered, slowing his pace.

"That's right. I wanna be released. Not just from the station but from Limbo."

I knew 'Big Ears' was asking for trouble. If I had been him I would have wandered off with the hopes of being forgotten. But not him. Maybe his nick name should have been 'Big Mouth'.

"Yeah, you and the Crone owe me big time."

Purdy stopped abruptly and for half a second I thought 'Big Ears' was gonna feel the big man's bat upside his head. But we had stopped cuz we had arrived at our destination. Ahead was a closed wooden door with a frosted glass window. Stenciled in large black letters on the window were the words: CONDCUCTOR PURDY. If nothing else, Lou Purdy had his own office.

He leaned his bat against the wall and fished through his pockets for what I assumed was a key, allowing me time to take everything in. To the right of his office door was a window with no curtains. The window was armor thick and dirty from train soot. Still, I could see his office was nothing more than a high-ceiling closet with a desk, a chair and a small green sofa. Hanging on the white plaster wall above the desk was a clock in the shape of a large baseball. The clock's numbers were inside drawings of miniature baseballs and the arms were shaped like baseball bats. The second hand ran backwards. What else would you expect in this crazy place?

"Well, where's my reward?" 'Big Ears' wanted to know.

Without a peep or even a glance in 'Big Ears' direction, Lou pulled a ring of keys from his pocket, selected a large brass key that looked like it belonged to some 15th century dungeon master, and used it to open his office door.

"C'mon. C'mon. I want my reward."

Lou's cheeks began to redden and the loose skin under his eyes quivered slightly. You'd think 'Big Ears' would have taken notice of this and shut his pie-hole. But no. He kept on talking like he was untouchable.

"C'mon, it's time to pay up," 'Big Ears' went on smugly.

Purdy shoved me inside his office and slammed shut the door as though I was a vicious animal he'd just caged. I stumbled across the small room like a drunk on stilts and landed on the sofa. As I sat up, I turned to the window in time to see Purdy launch his attack. Like a woodsmen splitting lumber, he brought his bat down over the ghost's head. Though the door was closed the impact of the blow sounded thick and wet and reminded me of the times Ester would take the Pastor's carpets outside and beat the living daylights outta them. 'Big Ears' yelped and disappeared below the window ledge and kept yelping as Purdy savagely continued his attack. The big man kept taking wild hacks at the ghost, grunting heavily with each swing. Finally, mercifully, the screams of anguish and pain ceased and the attack ended.

Could you kill a ghost? It was hard to say, though Lou Purdy had sure given it the old college try.

Huffing from exertion, Lou bent over slightly and stared down at his victim, perhaps judging his handiwork. Had he inflicted enough damage? Apparently, he judged that he had, for he soon straightened up and entered his office.

"I hate tattlers," he grumbled and wiped sweat from his meaty red face with a hanky. "I hate them to death."

No kidding, I thought.

He leaned his bat in the corner behind his desk. The way he used it to pummel 'Big Ears', I was amazed he hadn't shattered it.

"So yuh like baseball, huh?"

I did, I thought, assured that if I survive this horror I'd never look at a bat the same way again. "Yeah," I returned, sitting up straight. "I used to play."

"It's a beautiful game," he declared. "A game where yuh can be twenty runs down in the last innin' and still come back to win." He grinned proudly. "There ain't no other game like it."

He was certainly right about that, and I agreed with a nod, expecting him to add more to the conversation. But he paused, silent now, heavy in thought. Then, without warning, he charged me and slapped the Yankee cap off my head before I could even cringe. It rolled off the sofa and landed upside down on the floor by my feet. I decided to leave it right where it lay.

"I hate the Yankees."

I considered letting him know I felt the same way, that the St. Louis Browns were my team, but thought better of it cuz for all I knew he hated the Browns even worse.

Brooding, and heavy in thought, he walked behind his desk, standing stoic. His desk was smaller than the Pastor's desk and made of what looked like cheap wood. The top was empty. Guess there wasn't all that much paper work to do in Limbo.

He opened a side drawer, pulled out a baseball, and tossed it to me. "Take a good gander at that. It's my most prized possession. A 1900 ball autographed by the Iron Man himself, Joe McGinnity."

I turned the ball around in my hand until I found the autograph. "Wow," I marveled. "It's quite a treasure."

"I'll say. I bet yuh it's worth a fortune."

Yeah, I thought. *It would fetch a handsome price. Not here, but somewhere.*

"28 wins that season," he boasted as though he had something to do with it. "Boy, I'd love to see him throw that tatter."

"I think he's dead."

"Huh? Really? Yuh sure? I ain't never saw him come through here."

I shrugged.

"That's the problem with livin' here," he muttered. "I've lost track of time. And I ain't heard any news. I'm so outta touch." He shook his head. "Who's president now?"

"Roosevelt."

"Theodore? He's still in office?"

I shook my head. "He's dead. It's another Roosevelt. A cousin of Theodore."

"Gal darn it. Things do change. Theodore was president last I heard."

"That was a long time ago—about ten presidents ago."

"I've missed a lot."

I'll say, I thought.

I handed the baseball to him and he put it back in the drawer, closing it.

"So tell me," he went on, straightening up. "Who's on top this season? Ya know, who's leading the majors?"

Before I could answer, his office door opened and a sickening smell of rot blew in. The smell hit my nostrils like a punch, causing my eyes to water. I gulped, blinking away the tears and focused on the figure standing in the doorway.

The Crone was short, slender, with a head too large for her body. It was misshapen like that of a pumpkin left unattended on its side while it grew. Her forehead was flat enough to rollout pastry and the left side of her head was as bumpy as a mountain range. Her eye sockets were as large as silver dollars. It made her look like a freakish skeleton with glowing red eyes. Maybe in Limbo she was considered a babe, but elsewhere? Uh-uh. She was a toad for sure.

She wore a long flowing black dress that hid her feet and the silver and gold bracelets on her wrists clanged as she walked toward me. The gold amulet around her neck attracted my attention. In the center of the amulet was a blue eye floating in liquid. The eye looked real. Maybe it was.

She looked me over, her eye lids narrowing slightly with suspicion. "Who do we have here, Lou?" she asked, her voice old and as crusty as a hundred year old smoker.

Lou hadn't gotten around to asking for my name so he simply shrugged and filled her in on what he did know. "He's undead."

"Yes, I can see that," she returned smartly. "And I can see that he's just a mere boy." She sighed heavily and turned to Lou. "Are they sending boys against us now?"

Lou shrugged.

She turned to me. "What's your name?"

"Johnny McGrath."

"McGrath, huh?" She glanced at Lou. "I've never heard of one of them with a name like that."

Lou shrugged again. "It'll fit easy on a tombstone."

"Yes it will." She turned to me. "You're giving off no regal qualities whatsoever. It's like you're simply a mortal."

At the time I had no idea what regal meant. For that matter I had no idea what mortal meant either. So, adhering to my motto of 'less said the better' I stayed silent. She could say anything she wanted to me; she could insult me till the cows came home and stamp her feet as she did as long as in the end she let me go.

She ran her bony fingers through her sparse, jet black hair and picked absently at a scaly red scab just above her ear. "How old are you?"

"Fifteen."

"It's a shame you won't make sixteen," she said, and paused, closely examining the scab she had just picked off her scalp. She played with it in her fingers for a few seconds, enjoying, I suppose, its rough, crusty texture. Then she popped it in her mouth as though it was a sweet bonbon and chewed it.

My stomach lurched with revulsion. Thankfully, it was pretty empty so nothing but spit came up in my mouth. I swallowed hard.

"Okay, who sent you?"

I thought about Cole, and yeah, I had no moral dilemma in ratting him out. In fact, it might be a good thing considering Cole meant to kill me once he had his money. Still, I couldn't bring myself to do it. "I came on my own." Which, in a way, was the truth.

"Is that so?" she muttered, making it sound like she thought I was lying. "Who are you here with?"

"No one."

She cocked an eyebrow at me. "Where did you come from?"

"Goonberry Gulch."

She looked at Lou for help. He said, "It's a small town just a hoot 'na holler from here."

"Please Lou, in English."

"Uh, the town is about a two day walk from here."

"I see."

"We should leave," he suggested strongly. "Too many mortals know we're here. We should leave and set up shop elsewhere."

"There's a lot of work in doing that," she said. "Besides, I don't feel like moving. I like this location. It's out of the way. We're isolated. And we've never had too much trouble from the surrounding inhabitants."

Lou motioned at me and spoke the obvious. "He's here."

"Yes, but I think his visit might be an isolated incident." She turned to me. "Why did you come here?"

I considered telling her about Pa, but decided it was none of her business. "I was hiking in the woods and stumbled upon this place by accident. Sorry to have bothered you. I meant no harm and I didn't mean to impose. If you'll be so kind as to release me, I promise never to return or tell anyone where I was." I shrugged. "Who would believe me anyway?"

She smiled around her crooked teeth. "When a mortal lies, it gives off an odd vibration. You're giving off that vibration right now."

"I ain't lying."

"You're telling half-truths at best."

She bent down close to me and I made the mistake of breathing through my nose. Her stench bore through me, strangling my airway. I gagged, gulped audibly and looked away, convinced now that she was not, nor ever had been, a human. She wasn't a ghost either, certainly not like those wandering around these streets. She was more than that. She surged with power, a force like none I'd ever encountered. She was evil, pure evil, a demon. It was all I could do to keep from wetting my pants.

"I want the truth," she went on evenly. "The whole truth. You came up here for a reason and I want to know what that reason is."

At this point, I decided telling the truth might be the wisest course of action. "I'm looking for my Pa."

"Did he die recently?"

"I don't know. That's the thing. He's in the war—missing. So—"

"So you came here looking for him?"

I nodded.

"Who told you about this place?"

"An old timer named Charles Haddes. Haddes' brother came up here during the Civil War with Major Breckinridge."

Her eyes lit up with recognition. "Ah yes, the Major." She looked at Lou. "You replaced the Major when he was lost during our last small problem."

Lou shrugged as though he could careless.

"I must say Johnny McGrath," the Crone went on, "you have lots of courage. No brains, but lots of courage. Most of your type would have turned back long before entering our town. Did the evil not bother you?"

"Well, yeah. Kinda."

"But still you came."

I shrugged. "I'm looking for my Pa."

"We should leave," Lou cut in. "I think we're in a heap of trouble."

"From him?" she said flippantly. "Oh please Lou. I think young Johnny McGrath is only a minor irritant—an isolated incident."

"I don't know," Lou said. "I get bad feelings sometimes. I got it that afternoon the posse came after me—that's how I managed to escape to here. I knew I was in trouble. And I'm a getting that same feelin' now."

"You're overreacting."

He shrugged and asked, "What about his Ma? Won't she come a-lookin' for him?" Or maybe the sheriff?"

She glared at me. "Does your mother know where you are?"

"I didn't tell her."

"Do you think she'll come looking for you?"

"Not up here. She doesn't' know this place exists."

"Mmmmmmmm, I see," she muttered wearily. "You're telling half-truths again. Not that it really matters. Your answers are irrelevant for the most part. I'll find out your whole story on my own."

"Can I have him?" Lou asked, suddenly giddy with joy. "It's been so long since I've enjoyed the company of a youngin."

She thought about it for a moment and then slowly shook her head. "Not yet. I can't say why, but I don't feel the time to kill him is right."

His cheeks soured. "Why not? Keepin' him alive is dangerous."

She turned abruptly to him, her eyes narrowing. "Are you questioning me?"

He cowered meekly under her gaze and bowed his head. "No. No. Course not. It's just that I need his company."

"When the time is right, you can have him. But for now, I want him locked up so I can check out his story. Let's see if his father is one of our guests. And I need to know about this Charles Haddes. Also, I'm not convinced he's alone. So release the wolves. If anyone is in the vicinity, they'll sniff them out."

I wondered if Cole had enough fire power to hold off the Crone's wolves. For that matter, what about the guy with the eye patch? Would the wolves sniff him out as well?

"Should I call 'Dead Time' to lower the barrier?" he asked.

She shook her head. "Release them through the emergency tunnel. I want our defenses in tact. So delay 'Dead Time.'"

"But our customers are a-waitin' for that train. It's already late."

"It won't take long. And before I lower our defenses, I want to make sure what we're dealing with." She stared at me. "If you're lucky, we can reunite you with your Pa, and the two of you can ride the train together. Of course, before that can happen you and Lou are going to become better acquainted." She paused then, her eyes suddenly focused on something below my chin. "I see you have a crucifix. Are you religious?"

I nodded. "I'm a Christian."

"That won't help you here."

I shrugged indifferently.

"Don't believe me?"

I don't know where I found the courage to talk back to her—but I did. "What I believe is none of your business."

Her eyes widened with surprise. I guess she didn't expect me to talk back to her. Her mouth opened slightly and a long pause ensued. Finally she said, "No, I suppose your beliefs are none of my business. I just don't want you to get your hopes up."

"Hope has nothing to do with it," I whipped back smartly. "And I suggest you follow your own advice—don't get your hopes up either."

Her look narrowed. "When I'm satisfied I don't need you breathing anymore, Lou gets your body. And when he's finished with it, I get your soul. And that Johnny McGrath is something you don't want to happen. You're going to need more than a crucifix when I'm finished with you. For I plan to tear your soul apart fiber by fiber like that flatten sorry sonofabitch outside Lou's office." She turned abruptly to Lou and snapped her boney fingers. "Lock him up."

(5)

At the bottom of a long staircase, at the end of a dimly-lit corridor, we stopped before a rusted metal door. Lou dugout his dungeon master ring of keys again, selected a long brass key and shoved it in the lock. The deadbolt clunked loudly open. He swung back the door, the hinges creaking with rusty protest. The dim light (the closest bulb was no stronger than forty watts) slanted into the room's blackness and I saw that the room was nothing more than a rectangular closet with a cement floor and brick walls.

"Hope you ain't scared of the dark," he joked, and shoved me hard inside.

The air inside the closet was hot and stuffy. I turned and stared at him.

He grinned back, his huge body silhouetted by the light behind him. "Remember, when this is over, yore mine…all mine." With that said, he slammed the door shut, throwing me into total blackness. I heard the 'clunk' of the deadbolt fall into place and the receding shuffle of his footfalls.

I hated the dark at the best of times and this, obviously, was not the best of times. I felt tears sting my eyes and panic seize my heart. I remembered the crucifix then, and touching it helped me maintain my composure and dampen my growing fear.

I sat then with my back against the wall, and allowed my thoughts to go where they wanted. I thought of open fields and bright sunshine and Sally and Ma and Pa. Then I thought of Patch. Who the heck was that guy?

Though I had no way of knowing, I strongly suspected this man, clad entirely in black, was a good guy in all this. So would this good guy attempt to save me?

I didn't think so. In this crazy place it seemed the motto 'every man for himself' ruled. Still, thinking that a rescue could be in the works kept an ember of hope lit and my panic at bay.

But the feeling didn't last long. As time wore on, my panic grew, and kept growing, and before long I was hyperventilating. I didn't know it was called that at the time. But whatever you wanted to call it, I was having trouble breathing and thought for sure I was gonna die right there in the darkness of that closed up room.

And then, when all seemed lost, when all hope was gone, I heard a noise outside the locked door. Then the deadbolt clunked open, and though I didn't think it was possible, my fear grew even worse.

It had to be Lou, right? He had come for me. He had come to do unspeakable acts to me and there wasn't a blessed thing I could do about it.

The door swung back and Becky stood on the threshold with a single key in her hand. How she got the key, I couldn't say but right then it was the least of my concerns.

She pointed down the hall. "Turn right at the end and keep going. It will take you to an exit. You will come out beside the town square where the light flashes."

"Thank you," I managed, still panting, trying to get my breathing under control.

She nodded and walked away.

"Becky, please stay with me."

She turned and faced me. "If the Crone finds out that I helped you, she will set my soul on fire and put me on the train like she did to my parents."

I sighed. "Okay, I understand."

"I miss you," she said.

"I miss you too." Tears welled up in my eyes. "Sally asked me to pass a message on to you if I saw you. She wants you to know that she loves and misses you a lot."

"I miss her too." She pointed down the hall. "Now go—quickly. You must return to her and tell her I love her."

"Becky, where is the tunnel where the wolves leave from?"

"I don't know."

I sighed with dejection. "Okay."

She started off along the hallway, only to stop a second later and turn. "Oh, Johnny, your Ma says for you to use your talent."

"My Ma?" I yelped. "Where—"

I never finished the question, for Becky was gone.

(6)

I followed Becky's instructions, and soon emerged from the station.

The town square with the flashing red light overhead was to my left; ahead, the street was empty. In fact, it was too empty, and I immediately got the feeling something or someone was watching the street. Going that way, I felt, was a mistake. Maybe it was my paranoia talking; then again...

In any event, to my right was an alley, and I followed it to another street. I knew Limbo was bigger than I imagined, but I got the feeling that the place was huge. New York City huge. Or bigger.

Again, my paranoia was running rampant, and feeling this street might be under watch as well, I stayed close to the buildings and moved at a swift pace, wanting to get to the graveyard. What I would do when I got there was a question I couldn't answer. But at least I had somewhere to go. It was familiar territory, and maybe if I got there, things would turn out okay. Like maybe Lou would bellow out 'Dead Time' and I could slip back over the fence. And maybe—maybe now—the Crone's wolves had killed Cole and Snake and I could merrily go on my way.

It was a nice thought, and as I thought about how fast I could make it back home, a spirit suddenly appeared ahead of me. My heart leapt into my throat and I stopped dead in my tracks. Then I realized it was just your average, every-day-run-of-the-mill spirit. I had seen plenty of them. It was no big deal, nothing to be scared of, and I moved to go around it.

"Excuse me, are you Southpaw Johnny McGrath?"

For half a second I considered denying it. After all, all I wanted to do was go home, not socialize with the dead, and admitting who I was would surely invite more conversation. Still, good manners prevented me from lying.

"Uh…Yeah."

"I can't believe it," the entity said in awe. "Finally someone I know. Maybe all isn't lost after all." He stuck out his hand to shake. "We have not been properly introduced. I'm John Zuckerman. We attend the same church. My wife sings in the choir with your Ma. Do you remember?"

"Yeah," I muttered in awe. "I remember."

He was a couple inches taller than me, glowing dimly like all the other spirits. If he hadn't of told me who he was I would never have recognized him. Now that I knew his name, though, I recognized his light southern drawl—smooth as silk voice with sociably correct diction—and his facial features—gentle eyes, eagle-hooked nose, thin mouth with a dimple on the chin. Yep, it was John Zuckerman alright. Well, at least his ghost.

"Could you help me find my way home?" he went on. "This sure isn't Goonberry Gulch."

"Uh, I don't think I can do that?"

"Oh." He looked sad. "You know, it's the strangest thing. I remember going into the Goonberry Gulch Diner, and then Cameron Mitty came in. He talked to me for a couple minutes, complaining about the price of a hunting license"—he chuckled lightly—"as if he'd pay for one. And then I found myself walking around here. It's weird. It's like I've been suffering from amnesia."

It donned on me that this guy had no idea he was dead. And though I hated be the barer of bad news, I felt obliged to break it to him. If I was in the dark over such a matter, I would want someone to tell me.

"Uh…it's worse than amnesia, Mr. Zuckerman. You're dead."

"What?"

"You died, sir. I'm sorry."

"How?"

"Cameron Mitty poisoned your coffee with cyanide."

He thought about it for a moment. "I suppose that makes sense." He looked at me sharply. "Are you dead, too?"

"No. I'm just some place I shouldn't be."

"Is this Limbo? Is this that evil place I've heard about that's up in the woods?"

"Yeah, that's right."

"Oh," he said sadly. "I see."

"Listen Mr. Zuckerman, I really have to get going if I'm gonna get outta here."

"Of course, Southpaw. I understand."

He looked so pitifully helpless and alone my heart nearly broke open. "Uh, listen, Mr. Zuckerman, I'm sorry I can't help you. Do you wanna walk with me?"

"No, it's okay," he said with a shrug. "I'm sure it's a mistake that I'm here. I have faith. Everything will be okay."

"I hope so, sir" I returned, and then added, "Whatever you do, stay away from the train. The train is bad. Okay?"

"Thank you for saying."

Though I wanted to leave, I felt he needed to hear the rest. "Uh, listen Mr. Zuckerman, I bumped into your wife on the trail. She brought me back to your favorite spot in the woods. Actually, that's where your body is resting."

"Really," he muttered reflectively. "She hauled me up there." He nodded happily. "Good for her." He laid his hand on my shoulder. "Do you think you can get back to her? Because she has to be warned about Mitty."

"Cameron Mitty is dead."

"He is? How?"

"Your wife shot him."

He stared at me in stunned silence.

"Mr. Zuckerman, I better get going."

"Is she okay?"

I considered lying for his own protection, then decided he deserved the truth no matter how terrible. "Uh, no. It looks like it was a Mexican stand-off. She shot him. He shot her."

He was silent for a moment. "Oh. Oh my."

"I'm sorry."

"Is she here?"

"I don't know. I spoke to her on the trail."

His eyebrows crinkled in dismay. "How could you have talked to her there if she was dead?"

"I don't know, Mr. Zuckerman. For some reason, I've been able to talk to ghosts of late." I sighed. "Believe me, I wish it wasn't happening to me."

"It must be happening for a reason."

"I guess." I stepped around him. "I really have to get going."

"Would you do me a favor, Southpaw?"

"Uh, sure, if I can."

"Tell Sheriff Nibbs that I have a safety deposit box at the Jackson City Bank on Fifth Avenue in Jackson. Tell him the number of the box is 1, 9, 6, 2. Think you can remember that?"

"I think so."

"Tell him that there is enough evidence in that box to put Mayor Valentine away in jail for fifty years. Okay?"

"If I survive, I'll tell him." Then I remembered something else that he needed to know. "Betty said that if I saw you, to let you know that she loves you."

"Thank you for saying, Johnny. That means a lot."

(7)

A few minutes later, as I hurried toward the graveyard, I spotted two red dots ahead in the darkness. At first I thought it was a reflection from the flashing red light behind me, and I moved out into the middle of the street, hoping that the change of location would confirm my theory. Then it occurred to me the dots weren't flashing. They were constant, and *Gee, this is plum weird.* Mind you, this was Limbo, and in Limbo weirdness was the norm.

Then two more red dots appeared beside the first red dots. A few seconds later two more red dots appeared, and then two more dots appeared after that. The damn things were multiplying like rabbits and now they were making a noise—a soft, low growl. It didn't take a genius to figure out the growling wasn't coming from a poodle.

My nerves lit up with terror and my bowels twisted and groaned. It was all I could do to keep from messing my pants. I came to an abrupt stop, swallowed hard, watching, wondering just what the heck I was up against.

A second later I got my answer.

They emerged outta the darkness, walking slowly. A spike of fear went through me, and if someone had been with me I wouldn't have been able to talk to them cuz I couldn't form words. I was just too numb with fear.

These wolves were much larger than your garden variety type of wolf. These things were the size of large grizzly bears. Their paws were the size of dinner plates. Their legs were as thick as fence posts. Their shoulders were large enough to ride. And worst of all, their snouts, thick as a tree branch, were lined with three inch long teeth that looked sharp enough to slice metal.

I took a step back and looked for a place to run to. The wooden buildings on either side of me were windowless. There were two doors close by—one on either side of the street. Were the doors locked? I had no way of knowing. And even if they were unlocked, where would they lead to? Hell? A parallel universe? Maybe entering one of those buildings would be worse than staying out here.

I hated the idea of retreating, of going deeper into Limbo, but what other choice did I have? I glanced over my shoulder, ready to run, and what I saw damn near short circuited my brain.

There were as many wolves behind me as in front of me. I was surrounded. And with no place to run to, I knew there was no way outta this. I was done for.

I reached up and touched the crucifix. A still calmness came over me and I sat down in the street, resigned to my fate, hoping my death would be quick. If nothing else, at least Lou Purdy wouldn't get his hands on me.

And who knew for sure? Maybe my soul would escape the bounds of this place and I'd be free of the Crone. It was stuff of dreams I suppose, but at times like this why dwell on things I couldn't change?

The wolves, savoring the moment, approached at a snail's pace.

I thought of Sally, and felt sad that I'd never see her again. Then, I heard the squeaky groan of hinges moving and turned in the direction of the sound. The man dressed in black and wearing the eye patch stood in the open doorway. "Hey kid, who's afraid of the big bad wolf?" He grinned. "How fast can you run?"

I climbed to my feet. "Fast."

"I suggest you prove it to me—now."

I took off running, hitting full speed after only two or three strides. The wolves took off after me. I could hear the thunder of their heavy paws striking the hard ground and their savage snorts.

"Hurry kid," Patch sang out with alarm. "Hurry! Hurry up!"

A solid, wet chomp by my ankle made me run just that much faster. In my peripheral vision I could see the blur of a huge brown head. The lead animal was almost on me and still I had yards to cover. I would never make it.

Patch stepped into the street and, using his cane as a bat, wound up and whacked the animal across the head with such force I heard bone crack. A grunting whimper followed the pealing crack and the animal fell to the ground and rolled across the dirt like a squealing tumbleweed before slumping into a twitching heap.

Patch was beside me then, one hand wrapped around my arm, running with me. His coat was open and flapping as he ran. "C'mon kid. Run!"

We burst through the doorway together. I tripped and fell, landing on my knees. Patch kept his balance, quickly turned and, using his trusty cane, pushed the door closed. It slammed shut with a rifle-shot bang that resonated through the floor boards as though an earthquake had hit. Using his cane again, he flicked across a metal bar, securing the door snuggly. An instant later, loud thuds slammed into the door followed closely by muted yelps that ebbed and flowed and mixed with a clattery of scratching that made me wonder with bated breath if the door would hold.

Patch turned to me, grinning, seemingly pleased with the outcome. "Give it a few seconds. They'll lose interest and go back into the street to eat the one I clobbered."

"Really?"

He nodded and motioned with his cane at the door. "They can't smell us in here and they have brains the size of goldfish. They'll soon forget why they were so anxious to get in here."

Sure enough, a few seconds later, silence ensued outside.

I climbed to my feet, sighing with relief. "Thank you for saving me."

Patch shrugged. "Anytime, kid."

I looked over my surroundings. The floor, walls and ceiling of the narrow hallway were made of unvarnished, unfinished wooden planks about two inches wide and two feet long. The hallway, lit by one dim bare bulb, led to a set of stairs. The stairs led to the ceiling, ending there as though the builder decided not to build a second floor. Maybe there was a hidden trapdoor at the top of the stairs I couldn't see.

"What is this place?"

"Lots of nooks and crannies in the universe," he said. "This just happens to be one of them." He smiled, his eye patch riding up slightly on his cheek. "Now I can't say whether this is a nook or a cranny, but it one or the other. And we're safe from the Crone's wolves and the Crone for that matter." He removed his gloves, stuck them in the pockets of his trench coat and stepped toward me. "My name is Gabriel."

"Like the archangel?"

"You know your Bible."

"I know Gabriel was a messenger of God. Are you…?"

"No. I was just named after him," he said.

"There's an empty grave in the cemetery marked Gabriel."

He grinned. "They're going to have to catch me first." He motioned at me with his cane. "What's your name?"

I told him and we shook hands. He had a firm hand shake, the kind of handshake you'd want the president to have.

"You have a southern accent."

"Born and raised in Goonberry Gulch, Mississippi," I said proudly, and pointed in the direction I thought the Gulch was located. "It's about a two day walk from here."

"Oh yeah," he said thoughtfully. "I thought you were from New York. I didn't think too many southern boys liked the Yankees."

"Oh, the baseball cap." I shrugged. "It was a gift from a nice family. I gave their son my Goonberry Gulch Gophers cap and they gave me the Yankee cap."

"Goonberry Gulch Gophers?"

"It's a church league baseball team I used to play for."

His one eye brightened. "Oh yeah, you play ball? What position?"

"Pitcher."

"Well, I'll be," he said, nodding in delight. "A pitcher. Isn't that something." He pointed at my head. "So what happened to the Yankee cap? That shaven gorilla take it?"

"It's in his office, I guess. Why? You partial to the Yankees?"

"Only when they're winning," he joked, and sat on the stairs, resting the cane across his knees. "How did you get away from the conductor?"

I told him the story, including my talk with the Crone and subsequent rescue by Becky.

"Huh, huh," he muttered in thought. "Who is this Becky that unlocked the door?"

"She lived across the street from me before she died."

"You came up here to see her?"

"No." And since I felt I could trust him, I told him about Ma and Pa and coming up here and about Cole forcing me to enter Limbo.

He whistled in awe once I had finished. "Wow, that's quite a story, suitable for publishing."

"Uh, Gabriel, if you don't mind me asking, what are you doing here?"

"I've been sent here to destroy this place and free my colleagues." He motioned in the general direction of the graveyard. "You saw their tombstones."

"Those are your colleagues?" I shot back. "Uh, I heard banging coming from the crypts."

"That would be them—their souls—wanting out. They came here individually over the years on the same mission I'm on now—to destroy this place. Each time the Crone won, killing them and entombing their spirits." He shook his head. "I can't imagine what it must be like to lie in the cold and dark for eternity. And that's my fate if I don't succeed."

"I see," I returned, and then rushed on and asked, "What exactly is this Limbo anyway? I mean, this place doesn't fit in with my religious views. My pastor says the place is just 'wrong' and I gotta agree with him. The place is wrong, and shouldn't be."

"With a bit of luck, it soon won't be." He leaned back and rested his elbows on the stairs behind me. "See Johnny, there is more to the universe than you can imagine. Your reality of things is only one small puzzle piece in an infinity of puzzle pieces. You know by now that your body is nothing more than a container for your spirit, and that death is not an end, but a beginning. And the battle between good and evil wages on and will always wage on. Unfortunately, you're now part of the battle. Because the only way we're going to be able to get out of here is if we beat the Crone and destroy this place."

"How do we do that?"

"Carefully. Very carefully."

(8)

For the next few minutes he told me how he planned to destroy Limbo. It sure seemed simple enough. Unfortunately, we couldn't do it from where we were standing. We had to get to the train station. And the only way to get there was to go outside, outside where the wolves were lurking.

He opened the door a crack and looked out. "We're in luck. The wolves are gone. Even the one I clobbered has vanished." He turned back to me, smiling. "I think you're lucky, Johnny."

"Lucky, huh?" I muttered. It was nice to see that he was taking all this craziness so casually. If only I felt the same.

I came up beside him and took my own look. Yep, he was right. The street was deserted, and for some reason, that bothered me.

"It sure is quiet…too quiet."

He laughed. "C'mon, let's get this over with. If things go smoothly, this can all be wrapped up in ten minutes."

I raised a brow at him. "Do you really think things will go smoothly?"

With just a hint of uncertainty, he dragged out a long pronounced, "Maaaaaaybe."

Then, a moment later, and in a brighter tone, he added, "It could."

He was right, I suppose. Things could go smoothly. They hadn't gone smoothly for me in quite sometime, but if he thought things would just sail right along without a hitch then that was his prerogative. Cuz I thought otherwise. In fact, I had a real bad feeling about what we were attempting to do.

I followed him out the door and into the street. He seemed relaxed, loose as a goose out taking a Sunday afternoon stroll. I felt as paranoid as a mouse in a room filled with hungry cats. And to think, he was the

228

one with the pre-dug grave. If I had a pre-dug grave waiting for me, I'd be plum outta my mind crazy and drooling like a baby.

We walked side by side up the street, keeping close to the buildings on our right. We barely spoke, which was fine with me, cuz frankly, I was too nervous to talk. Maybe once the place was destroyed we could spend a few minutes gabbing about the weather or baseball. But for now all I wanted was to stay quiet, take deep breaths and concentrate on keeping my panic under wraps.

We followed the same path I had taken from the train station. Within minutes we emerged from the alley near the grassy area beneath the flashing red light. We stopped at once, looking ahead in dismay.

Two wooden poles about ten feet high were struck straight up in the ground beneath the flashing red light and on the top of each pole was a severed head. Even from a block away there was no mistaking whose heads they were.

"Are those your murdering, bank robbing buddies?"

"That's them," I muttered. "But they ain't my buddies."

"I think it's safe to say that their murdering, bank robbing days are over."

I had to agree. Without legs and arms, getting around would be a might difficult.

"Couldn't have happen to a nicer bunch of guys," I commented.

Gabriel grinned at my remark, and together, we started forward.

I thought of their victims' families then. If they saw what had happened to them, they would no doubt be satisfied that justice had been served. But they would never know, cuz I would never tell. Heck, who'd believe me?

"It sure is poetic justice," I said. "A couple of days ago the two of them cut off the head of my neighbor and put it on a fence post for all to see. And now their heads have been cut off and put on display." I looked at him. "Why would the Crone do that? I can understand killing them, but why decapitate them and display them like a decoration?"

"Nothing terrorizes the population more than a bloody show," he answered. "Course it could be meant for you—something to scare you."

"But..."

"Maybe they know you've escaped," he jumped in. "And if that's the case..."

He didn't finish the thought. He didn't need to.

"We could be walking into a trap?"

"It's possible," he said glumly, and motioned for me to follow.

We hurried across the grassy infield toward the stairs where I had found 'Big Ears'. Now that I was closer to the macabre spectacle, I saw that the poles were slick with so much blood it looked like they had been dipped in red paint. I also noticed that part of their throats were still attached and curled around the pole like a snake. I wondered if the throats had been left like that so they could answer the Crone's questions.

"The wolves probably ate their bodies," Gabriel theorized, looking them over carefully. "If they're as evil as you say, their souls are most likely on the train."

Suddenly Cole's eyes flickered open, and I damn near jumped outta my skin.

"McGrath," he managed weakly, blood spilling over his lips. "Is that you?"

I said nothing at first. Then Gabriel elbowed me in the arm. "Ask him what happened?"

Cole heard Gabriel's question and the killer quickly said, "Wolves came for us. I got a couple of them but there were too many. The next thing I know some big guy is plunking my head on this pole. Then some ugly woman wanted to know about you."

I found my voice then. "What did you say?"

"Sorry. I told her the truth, Johnny. I had to."

Gabriel caught my attention and shrugged. "It makes no difference." Then to Cole he asked, "Where are they now?"

"I don't know. Honest. I don't know."

Just then Snake's eyes opened, and seeing us, he started to cry and babble incoherently. We stepped back a few feet cuz he was spitting blood on us.

"Shut up," Cole snapped, his eyes completely buried on their right edges in an effort to see his one-time partner. "Just shut up you cry baby." Amazingly enough, his order worked and Snake stopped babbling, allowing Cole to be heard. "Can you help me Johnny. C'mon Southpaw. Help me."

"Southpaw?" Gabriel questioned. "Are you a lefty, Johnny?"

Cole answered for me. "Yeah, and he's a real great pitcher."

"Why didn't you tell me? You shouldn't keep those things from your partner. You know Southpaw is a flashy nickname. You don't mind me using it, do you?"

I shrugged. "I don't care."

"And he threw a no-hitter," Cole went on, obviously trying to appease me.

"Is that right?" Gabriel said, patting me on the back. "A no-hitter. I knew you were special, but I didn't know I was in the company of such greatness."

"I ain't that great, Gabriel."

"I'd love to see you pitch one day."

"My pitching days are over."

"Still, I'd love to see it." "Well, if the opportunity ever presents itself, I'll invite you to come watch."

"Can you help me, Southpaw," Cole went on, beginning to cry. "Please."

"You're the reason I'm here, Cole," I said, an unexpected anger boiling in my belly. "Don't you remember? It's your fault we're all here. Your greed put your head on that pole."

"Yeah, I know. I'm sorry."

"I'm sure you are. And do you know something? I'm gonna forgive you. Maybe you don't want that, but you're getting it anyway. I forgive you, Cole. And I forgive you too, Snake."

"That's great, Johnny," Cole said. "Now can you help me? Can you get me down from here?"

"And do what with you?"

"There is magic in this place. If I can get my head on a body, I'll be okay. I know I will."

"You're dead," Gabriel spoke up. "You're both dead."

"We can't be. Look at us. We're talking. We're alive."

He shook his head. "Your souls are trapped in your skulls. The Crone left you both like that because souls left with the brain tend to recall more. Eventually your souls will seep out and walk Limbo. Knowing what sort of scoundrels you both were, I'd say you'll both be riding the train very soon." Gabriel then turned to me, "C'mon, let's get this over with."

"Please McGrath," Cole went on. "Please. I didn't kill you in the woods. I let you live."

"I know. And I thank you for that."

"Please…."

I walked off with Gabriel.

"Please!" Cole screamed. "You owe me McGrath."

I stopped abruptly, turned and looked up at him. He looked optimistic. Perhaps he was thinking his begging had worked. But I had something else to tell him.

"Oh, I almost forgot. I talked to 'Big Ears'. He ain't looking so good now. The train conductor beat his soul to a pulp and threw it on the train. But before all that happened, I talked to him and he told me that he buried your money in the Squirrel Flats Cemetery in a grave marked Kirby Fellows. I realize you're a bit hung up now, but if you do manage to get off that pole, you now know where your money is at." And with that said, I turned and hurried away with Gabriel.

(9)

We went up the stairs, entered through the same door 'Big Ears' had dragged me through, turned left and hurried along the platform toward Lou Purdy's office.

Like the street, the platform was deserted. The train hadn't moved an inch, though it was spewing out more steam then before, giving the place a foggy London look. Along with the sounds of our footfalls, I heard muted cries coming from inside the train cars.

"When the train steams like that it means it is ready to go," Gabriel informed, and then sighed, a troubled look on his face. "I hate the cries of anguish coming from the souls trapped on board. It's damn unnerving."

"Everything in this place is damn unnerving."

He chuckled lightly. "You know something, Southpaw? When I first saw you, I was angry because I thought you might complicate things, especially when that big oaf found you, stopping me from doing what I had to do. But now that I know you, I'm happy you're here with me."

"I wish I could say the same."

He grinned and stifled his laughter, and said nothing else until we reached Lou's office. We snuck up to the office window and stole a peek in. The room was empty. So far so good. Things were going smoothly. *Too smoothly*, I thought.

"Think there's a chance the door is unlocked?"

"He opened the door with a key," I informed.

"I guess we'll have to break in," he said, and motioned with his cane toward the pane of glass.

"Won't that make noise?"

He nodded.

"That's not good. Right?"

He nodded and pointed off along the platform to where a soul catcher stood guard. I hadn't seen the creature till now cuz it was immersed in the fog. I estimated it stood no more than twenty yards away.

"Won't that thing hear?" I whispered.

He nodded. "It'll investigate. It can't see you because your body is protecting your soul but I'm different. It'll spot me for sure and sound the alarm. And that's something we can't let happen." He made a swinging motion with his cane. "We'll have to take it out. What kind of a batter are you?"

I was a rather fair hitter, something I contributed to a better than average eye/hand coordination. Still, the thought of bashing that thing into submission sickened me with worry. What if I missed? Or what if I didn't hit it hard enough? A whole lotta things could go wrong.

"Uh, I think I'll let you do it."

"So you're going to make the guy with the one eye do everything, huh?" He flashed me a smile. "Okay, fine, suit yourself."

He went to add more, but held up abruptly, his mouth falling agape, his eyes growing wide with fright. I spun about at what he was looking at and locked eyes with Lou Purdy.

"How'd you get out?" Lou barked, and swiped at me with his bat. I easily ducked beneath the swinging pine and scurried away on my hands and knees. Then Lou caught sight of Gabriel, and if it was possible, he looked even more stunned. "Oh no—not you!"

Gabriel rammed the end of his cane into Lou's midsection with savage force. A rush of air exploded outta of Lou's open mouth, and he doubled over, dropping his bat and grabbing his stomach as if he was gonna throw up. As Lou's bat rolled away and dropped off the edge, falling between the train and the platform, Gabriel, holding his cane now with both hands, brought it down over Lou's bald dome with the force of a Babe Ruth homerun swing. The impact was so loud it rattled Lou's office window. Lou grunted out a painful moan and dropped to his knees. Gabriel bashed him another over the head. That blow sent Lou face down on the wooden platform, whimpering like a dog with a sore tooth. Gabriel, not wanting to take any chances, brought the cane down again across Lou's reddening skull. The blow sounded as nasty as all the other blows. That seemed to do the trick, for Lou lay still and quiet.

"Is he dead?"

Gabriel shrugged, and crouched beside the fallen man. "Where's his keys?"

"His pocket."

Gabriel found the key ring in seconds and stood. "We're in luck, Southpaw."

"Luck?" I scoffed. "If either of us were lucky, we wouldn't be here."

Gabriel laughed, stepped over Lou and up to the office door. "Didn't I tell you things were going to go smoothly?"

"You said it could go smoothly. And that was after a long drawn out 'maybe.'"

"Well, it looks like I'm right."

He unlocked the door and we entered the office. He closed and locked the door. He was all smiles, almost giddy.

"Nothing can stop us now."

I said nothing, afraid that saying something might jinks us.

"Where should we look for your cap?"

"Forget about it. Let's just do what we came here to do."

"No, no, no. It's important we find it"

"Well it's gone," I said, pointing at where it had landed. "Maybe he threw it out. He did say he hated the Yankees."

Gabriel quickly rifled through all the desk drawers and found only the autographed baseball. "Here." And he flipped it to me. "A small souvenir."

I shook my head. "I ain't up to stealing."

"It isn't stealing," he said. "In a few seconds that big fat tub of lard out there on the platform is going to be dust anyway. So you might as well have it. If Lou loves baseball so much, he'll want the baseball to go to a fan that will truly appreciate it."

He was right. Sides, Lou took my cap so he owed me. This would make nice compensation. I tucked the ball in my pocket as Gabriel slid the desk up to the wall beneath the clock that ran backwards, something which, in my opinion, was also damn unnerving.

"Are you sure that's the power source?" I asked. "I would have thought the power was coming from the flashing red light."

He shook his head. "Too obvious. Besides, it's out in the open. There is no way the Crone would leave something so valuable out in the open with no protection. No. It's the clock. I'm sure of it."

"And all you have to do is break it?"

"Yep. Once the power source is smashed, the barriers will come down and time will fill back in."

"That's it?"

"We'll have to take cover," he explained. "Because time fills in with the force of a hammer blow. It could get rather intense."

With that said, he climbed up on Lou's desk and, using his cane as a bat, made a few practice swings, making a whoosh sound as he swung.

"Ready?"

I shrugged. "Yeah, sure. Swing away."

He crouched into a batter's stance, took a deep breath and swung for the fences. The metal handle of the cane struck the clock dead center sending up a shower of sparks. For a second or two, it looked like the 4th of July. The crashing sound bounced about the closed up room with ear-splitting volume and the clock's glass face shattered into small jagged fragments, flying in all different directions. The interior of the clock fell apart and tiny springs and wheels and metal rods rained down like hail. It lasted only a few seconds, and when it was over, all that was left of the clock was the gray metal dish frame that was attached to the wall.

Gabriel looked at his handiwork, blinking.

"So it's over? Right? We can leave?"

"Uh oh," he muttered.

"Uh oh, what?"

"Uh oh, we have a slight problem."

"What kind of a problem?"

"This isn't the power source."

(10)

Lou was gone.

Gabriel stood in the place where Lou should have been, shaking his head in disbelief. "I can't believe it," he said. "You saw what happened, Southpaw. I cracked him pretty good across his noggin. More than once. He should still be down."

"Maybe one of those soul catchers dragged him off," I said with a shrug. "Or maybe he rolled off into the fog someplace."

Heck, for that matter, maybe he got sucked into another dimension, I thought. Not that it mattered. What mattered now was what the heck were we gonna do?

I followed Gabriel across the platform in the direction we had just come. "I don't know what to tell you, Southpaw. I guess I should have hit him harder."

This was hardly the time to play the 'blame-game'. I looked at him and shrugged. "It's no big deal. Who cares?"

"He's going to sound the alarm."

"Then we better work fast."

He nodded. "I think you're right about the flashing red light." He shook his head bitterly. "No wonder all my colleagues never made it out of here. They all must have gone after the red herrings—the mechanical things that were locked up. They all must have ignored the obvious."

"Okay. So what are we gonna do about it?"

"We have to get out of the train station and find a way to knock that light down. Once we do that—" The rest of the sentence got stuck in his throat like a turkey bone.

"Uh oh."

Again with the uh ohs. Though, like before, they were well founded.

Twenty yards ahead in the foggy steam stood a line of wolves. They licked their chops and growled.

I gulped. "Uh….any ideas?"

"This way," he barked, and ran toward the train. I followed close on his heels, stopping at the platform's edge. There was a narrow two foot gap between the platform and train. Thankfully, both of us were thin.

"The wolves may be too big to go down in that trough," he surmised.

He was probably right. But did it matter? What prevented them from simply leaning over the platform and taking a chomp of us? Still, in the short term, I suppose, it was better than staying where we were.

The steam shielded the ground so I had no idea what we were jumping onto. Most likely it was a gravel bed. But this was Limbo, remember. So maybe there wasn't any ground beneath the mist at all and we'd fall for all of eternity, which, come to think of it, was probably a better fate than being eaten alive by wolves the size of large bears.

Since we had no choice in the matter, and thinking about it only made things worse, we jumped, landing on a loose gravel bed. I stuck the landing like an Olympic gymnast; Gabriel toppled over like a drunk. I quickly helped him to his feet.

"This will buy us some time," he said, and motioned at the wolves. To my surprise, the pack had not moved. "They don't like the train."

I knew how they felt. It stunk of death and emitted an icy, funeral-like glumness that sucked the will to live right outta me. And if that wasn't bad enough, the souls trapped in the car we stood beside had heard the crunch of our footfalls on the gravel and were banging desperately on the container wall, begging to be released.

Seeing the anguish on my face, Gabriel said, "Ignore them," and led the way along the narrow passageway.

I followed behind him. "You got a plan, right?"

"Uhhhhhhhh…." He looked over his shoulder. "Not really. What about you?"

"Are there any nooks or crannies close by we can get to?"

"No. But maybe we can—"

I missed the rest of what he said cuz something banged heavily behind me. I turned, and at first, saw only steamy fog. A moment later, a pair of glowing red eyes shone through. The wolves—at least the one approaching—was no longer afraid of the train. It was also thin enough to fit in the narrow passageway.

"Uh, Gabriel," I said, and turned forward to alert him of our pending problem. All I saw was fog and my heart sunk. "Gabriel!" I shouted, listening, anxiously waiting for his reply. But I heard nothing but strong growls and the crunch of something moving across loose gravel.

Maybe he hadn't heard me. Or maybe he had abandoned me—every man for himself—though I doubted that. Or maybe he was dead, killed quickly by either Lou, a soul catcher or a wolf.

A wave of panic came over me. My legs felt as limp as overcooked spaghetti. "Gabrielllllllllllllll!!!!!"

I ran forward, tripped on something, stumbled and landed on my knees. And there, right in front of me, barely visible through the train mist, was Lou's bat. I scooped it up, scrambled to my feet, and screamed again for Gabriel. Again, I got no reply.

I looked back at the wolf. At most, it was five feet away now, advancing slowly. The steam from the train thinned then and I saw its every detail. Its dripping, wet gums were pulled back tautly in a hideous scowl, exposing snarled, razor sharp teeth. Its growl revved up like an engine. I had never seen anything more dangerous looking.

It lunged and I let out a short cry and back peddled an instant before its snapping jaws could rip off my throat. Slick saliva sprayed my face. I back peddled even faster. Then my feet got tangled up in the loose gravel and I fell flat on my backside. It lunged again, and I thought my life was over. But it hesitated, stepping over top of me, staring down at me with a satisfied, smug expression. Its breath was hot on my face as it savored its kill.

I remembered I had Lou's bat, and somehow, I found the strength to jamb it upwards. I caught the animal square in its underbelly. The bat sunk in deep and it squealed, jumping backward.

I scrambled away and climbed to my feet. The wolf recovered and came at me again. With terror-filled force, I swung the weapon like it was an axe and I was chopping wood, catching the beast square in the head with the sweet part of the bat. A loud 'crack' filled my ears and the bat splintered with explosive force. I was left holding the jagged end of the shaft.

The blow stunned the animal, but it was still on its feet, and I lunged forward and jabbed the broken bat down into its black, watery eye. The shaft sunk in deep—it had the same feel as plunging a spoon into thick pudding. My hand came away slick with blood. The wolf howled and shook his head frantically trying to dislodge the wood from its eye. As it did, I turned and ran.

But I didn't run for long, cuz a few seconds later, through the steam, I saw the glow of red eyes approaching. I was trapped without a weapon, and knew this time that I was done for. I touched my crucifix, once again resigned to my fate.

"Hey Southpaw."

I looked up and saw Gabriel atop the boxcar directly above me. He reached down with his cane. I snagged it and he hauled me up beside him.

"You bleeding?" he asked, inspecting the blood on the handle of his cane.

"It's from the wolf."

"Oh?"

"I broke Lou Purdy's bat on its head and then jabbed it in the eye."

He nodded with satisfaction. "I would have liked to have seen that."

"I wished I hadn't."

He smiled. "You okay?"

"I think so."

"Good. We're safe up here."

As the last word left his mouth, I heard Lou Purdy far off in the distant, bellow, "DEAD TIME!"

"Uh oh."

Again with the uh ohs.

The train whistle blew shrilly. A blast of steam shot up from beneath the train. The car we stood atop of shuddered and the train began to slowly roll forward, picking up speed.

"Uh oh."

"The barrier is down," I said. "So we can ride this outta Limbo?"

"Yeah, but believe me, you are not going to like where it stops."

"I don't plan to wait till it stops," I said. "We'll jump as soon as we're clear of Limbo. It's high sure, but if all I get outta this is a broken ankle I'll feel lucky."

"It'll be going too fast by the time it leaves Limbo. Besides, this thing is not going to be rattling along the Mississippi countryside. Once this thing exists Limbo, it enters a world that is far worse than the one we're in—if you can believe that."

"So what do we do?"

"We're going to have to jump—now."

I looked over the edge and gulped. I judged the distance from where we stood to the platform below to be at least twenty feet. "Uh...I don't know if I can."

"You can and you will." He pointed at the train station roof. "That's our only chance."

I hadn't thought of jumping to the roof, but now that he had brought it up, he was right—it was the best course of action. The problem was, the roof was at least six feet away. And to make it even harder, we'd have to jump up to it, not down. Also, the train was accelerating—accelerating fast. It was possible...maybe.

"When you see me jump—you jump," he instructed. "And don't get cold feet. Because if you miss this jump or wait too long..." He shook his head. "You won't like what happens."

He grabbed my wrist and stepped over to the edge of the boxcar. The train was picking up speed lickety-split, the wind stiff in our faces.

"Get ready."

The train whistle suddenly blared, jangling my already frazzled nerves.

Gabriel turned, looked me in the eye and nodded with confidence. Then he turned forward and jumped, grunting heavily, springing forward off the side of the car as though he was diving into a pool. An instant later, with Gabriel still in mid-air, my head numb with fear, I jumped.

My world seemed to go in slow motion. I could clearly see the red eyes looking up from the mist below. Then I raised my head and saw the thick, wooden cornice. I was eye-level with it, and dropping fast. I knew right then I was gonna miss the roof entirely.

"Gabrielllllllllll!"

Seemingly outta nowhere, a hand reached out and clamped around my wrist. A second later, my arm was yanked painfully. I recoiled upwards and swung back and forth like a clock's pendulum. I looked up and saw that Gabriel clung to the roof with one hand. He held my wrist in the other hand. His face was lined with stress.

"I'm going to swing you," he yelled down, and before I could question him, he swung me upwards and let go of my wrist. I sailed through the air and came down with a thud on the lip of the roof. I teetered on the edge for an instant, and then rolled toward the middle of the roof, where I lay on the warm tiles, shaking.

"Hey Southpaw—a little help, please."

I crawled to the edge and reached down. Gabriel reached up with his free hand and grabbed my hand. I pulled with all my might, inching backwards. He soon slipped over the edge and rolled onto the roof with a grunt.

We were safe...for now.

(11)

"That was close," Gabriel said, sitting up, sighing, shaking his head. "And dammit, I dropped my cane."

I figured that was the least of his problems.

"You look annoyed, Southpaw. You okay?"

I got to my feet. "No, Gabriel, I'm not okay. I'm not okay at all. And I'm not gonna be okay as long as I'm here."

He grinned. "Easy. Easy. It's okay. We're safe."

"Safe?" I shot back, angry at his caviler attitude. "We're not safe at all. As long as we're here, we're not safe."

"Ah, c'mon Southpaw," he said brightly, and climbed to his feet. "You'll look back on this one day and laugh."

"To be honest, I just hope I live long enough to look back on it at all."

He grinned tightly and muttered, "I'd settle for that, too."

With the train gone, I saw a black vastness tinged with a white mist behind the station. I had no idea what would happen if you walked off into that vastness and, fearing the answer, never posed the question to Gabriel. Sides, he looked to be too busy checking out our new surroundings to be bothered with meaningless questions.

The roof was tiled, flat and had no discernable features. No air vents, no roof drains, no chimney and, most importantly, no trapdoors, which as Gabriel soon pointed out was a mixed blessing. We couldn't get down easily, but no one could get up either. Our biggest problem, though, was that none of the four cables holding the flashing red light in place over the grassy knoll was attached to the train station roof. So destroying the Crone's power source was still, in Gabriel's words, "A bone of contention."

"So what do we do?" I asked.

"I'm not sure," he said, obviously deep in thought.

I didn't disturb him with more useless talk and looked ahead at the empty streets of Limbo. From up here I could see the stone fence surrounding the cemetery and wished I'd been near it when Lou Purdy had called 'Dead Time'. If I had, I'd be running for home this very second.

As we approached the roof's edge, the sound of voices from below drifted up to us. Then I heard the Crone's throaty cackle.

"Show yourself, Gabriel," she yelled up. "You and your apprentice."

We stepped up to the roof's edge and peered down. The Crone stood in the center of the square in front of the poles that held Cole and Snake's head. Unfortunately for them, they faced off in the other direction. Lou, holding his throbbing bald head, stood beside the Crone. They were surrounded by soul catchers all carrying fire sticks. Wolves patrolled the area in front of them, running every which way like busy ants. Behind them, a sea of spirits mingled. I couldn't make out anyone I knew but figured Becky, Mr. Zuckerman and Doc Rose were among the group. Heck, maybe even Ma.

"Johnny McGrath," the Crone said, and gestured at me. "It's a shame you've fallen in with the likes of Gabriel."

"I want him," Lou barked suddenly. "He broke my bat."

I also had his baseball but decided not to share that info with him. Why make him angrier than he already was?

He had more to say but the Crone silenced him with a raised hand. "So Gabriel, we meet again—this time on my home turf. Did you come to get your eye back?" And she gestured at the amulet around her neck.

"That's your eye?"

"Yeah, Southpaw," he muttered without looking at me. "It's a long story."

"If you both surrender," she went on. "I promise I'll give you your eye back. We can slip it right back into the socket." And she chuckled evilly.

"That's okay. You keep it. I'm used to the patch. Besides, the girls like it. Makes me look more like a rebel."

"Always with the jokes," she said, her expression hardening. "You're going to have trouble joking your way out of this one."

"Oh, I don't know. I've been in worse predicaments."

"Oh really? When?"

"You'll have to give me time to think about it."

"That's the problem, Gabriel. You don't have the time." She stepped forward, arms crossed, her eyes narrow to bitter slits. "In case you are unaware, please allow me to fill you in on your situation. You are surrounded with nowhere to go and the structure you're standing on is made of wood. I don't want to burn down my train station, but I will if I have to. So I'll make you a deal. Surrender and I will kill Johnny McGrath quickly before my cherished employee here gets his hands on him."

"You promised," Lou spoke up.

"Shut up," she snapped without turning to look at him. "So is it a deal, Gabriel? We all know how this is going to end so let's not prolong this unnecessarily."

Gabriel turned to me, looking glum. "I don't see a way out of this," he said quietly. "If you want, I can snap your neck fast. Your soul will be trapped here but at least you won't burn to death or be tortured by Purdy." He shrugged. "It's up to you."

"Gabriel, there has to be another way."

"I wish there was, Southpaw. But there isn't. There is no where to go now but up in smoke."

"Yoo hoo," the Crone yelled up at us. "Johnny McGrath, I've found someone that wants to say hello."

I looked down and saw Ma standing between Lou and the Crone. She looked terrified.

"Come down now, Johnny McGrath, or my soul catchers will turn your mother's soul black. We'll make her dance as she burns. Do you want that to happen?"

I looked at Gabriel. "I don't have a choice. I have to surrender."

"She'll do it anyway, Southpaw. Right in front of you. Then she'll hand you over to that monster."

"I don't have a choice."

Ma's voice floated up to me. "Johnny?"

I stared down at her, unable to speak.

"Tell him," the Crone urged. "Tell him to come down."

"Johnny." She looked up at the flashing red light. "Johnny, use your talent."

"Your talent?" Gabriel said. "What does she mean?"

Suddenly it all made sense to me. I took the autographed baseball from my pocket and looked at Gabriel. "Looks like you're gonna get to see me pitch sooner than you thought."

(12)

I stepped back from the edge so no one below could see me and focused ahead on the flashing red light. It looked small, real small, and I wondered, *Can I really do this?* I had my doubts—serious doubts. Course, now was hardly the time to dwell on such things.

Gabriel must have been wondering if I had the talent to pull it off as well, for he cleared his throat and politely asked, "So what do you think, Southpaw? Can you do it? Can you throw a strike?"

"It's about the same distance away as the mound to home plate," I observed. "And the target is about the same size as the inside of a catcher's mitt."

His eyes twinkled with optimism. "So that means you can do it?"

"There's no room for error," I said glumly. "And I sure wish I could warm up."

"I wish you could too," he went on briskly. "But since you've only got one ball, you've only got one pitch." He heaved a sigh. "By the way, when was the last time you pitched?"

"Yesterday. I lined up a tin can and tossed rocks at it."

"That's great," he said, perking up. "So you're not rusty."

"Well..."

"Well, what?"

"I threw real bad."

"What's your definition of real bad?"

"Let's just say if I was pitching in a real game I would have been yanked before the first inning ended."

His cheeks puckered into a frown. "Boy, I wish you hadn't of told me that."

He went to add something else, but the Crone yelled up. "What's your decision, Gabriel? Are you going to surrender or do we have to do this the hard way? I'm not opposed to burning Mrs. McGrath's soul to ash, it's the screaming I hate. But if you're willing to put up with it, then so am I."

"I've got to loosen up my arm," I said to him, slowly rotating my pitching arm. "Can you buy me some time?"

Gabriel nodded and stepped up to the roof's edge. "We're currently discussing the matter," he yelled down to her. "Weighing the pros and cons of surrender. How about giving us a few minutes?"

"Excuse me. You're hardly in a position to make demands."

"I'm not making demands. I'm asking for time." He gestured about with open arms. "Time means nothing here. So what's a few extra minutes? It's like a drop of rain in the ocean."

She was silent for a moment, then: "Are you cooking up a plan?"

"A plan?" and he laughed. "Oh c'mon. As you said, Crone, we're surrounded. So what could we possibly be cooking up?"

"I don't know. You're a sly one, Gabriel. Of all the deities I've ever encountered, you're the one I feared the most." She cackled out a short burst of laughter. "Notice how I'm now referring to you in the past tense."

"Ah yes, your command of the language is impeccable. Now, how about allowing me a couple of minutes to talk this over with my partner? Remember, eternity is such a long time."

"Alright," she said with a hint of reluctance. "I'll give you a minute to think things over. Anticipation, after all, is a fruit that should be savored."

"You surprise me, Crone. Not only are you articulate, you're also poetic." With that said, he turned to me. "I bought you a minute, Southpaw. Throw me a strike."

I kept rotating my pitching arm. It felt as stiff as a 2 X4. If only I wasn't so damn nervous. If only I could limber up with some practice throws. If only I'd listened to the Pastor and stayed away from here. If only...well, you get the idea.

"You know," I began glumly, "even if I hit it dead on, I may not break it."

"How good is your fastball?"

"It's my best pitch."

"Great," he shot back, nodding with enthusiasm. "Now remember to put as much 'umf' behind it as you can." He gestured at the roof's edge. "Where do you want to stand? As close as possible?"

I crept up to the roof's edge and went into my stance: my right hand on my bent knee, my left arm behind my back, twirling the ball around, waiting for the seams to line up perfectly with my fingers—cuz for me, that was the key to pitching.

"Gabriel, what's he doing?" the Crone asked.

And then Lou, who knew a lot about baseball, who knew what a pitcher's stance looked like, yelled, "He's gonna throw somethin'."

"Right you are," Gabriel spoke up. "My good friend here is going to use his talent and destroy your power source."

The Crone let out an ear-piercing scream, and stamped her feet like a child throwing a tantrum. As she stomped around in place, she waved her arms franticly and screamed at her soul catchers. "Burn! Burn! Burn the place! Burn it to the ground! Nowwwwww!"

They responded at once, stepping forward and pointing their fire sticks up at us. An instant later, they fired, sending huge plumes of flames toward us.

This, I thought, *was what it must be like to be attacked by dragons.*

We backed away from the edge at once as a searing wave of heat rolled by us. We watched in silence as tongues of orange flames licked and curled over the roof's edge.

Finally Gabriel turned to me. "You have to hurry, Southpaw."

"I know. I know."

"The building is on fire," he muttered bitterly as though I hadn't quite caught on to what was happening. "This place is going to go up quickly."

Thick, black clouds of noxious smoke spilled over the roof's edge and crept towards us, blocking my view of the flashing red light.

I looked at Gabriel. "I can't see the target."

Gabriel said nothing. For once, even he was too nervous to talk.

I backed further away from the smoke and went into my stance again, twirling the ball around in my hand, praying for the seams to line up and the smoke to clear enough for me to see the light.

But that didn't happen. In fact, the smoke got worse and the seams wouldn't line up.

Gabriel found his voice. "Southpaw," he sung out in a high-pitched shrill. "Things are getting real serious. The roof is on fire and getting real soft. So if you're going to do this, I suggest you do it real soon."

The Pastor had said my best line of defense was the crucifix, and all along he'd been right, so with my right hand I reached up and touched the crucifix and prayed for salvation.

"What are you doing?"

"Praying," I shot back. "Praying for the smoke to clear."

"Pray fast."

I did what he said, and as I prayed, my short fifteen-year-old life suddenly flashed before my eyes. I saw it all, snippets of memories I thought were long gone. The time when I scraped my knee and Ma kissed it better; the time when Pa taught me to throw a baseball and bait a hook; the time when I first kissed Sally; the time when I threw the last pitch to capture my no-hitter. And thankfully, it was on that memory where my mind got stuck. The memory—as vivid a memory as I'd ever had—kept repeating itself, and suddenly, I was in the proper 'state of mind' to pitch. Now if only the smoke would clear.

"C'mon Southpaw, throw."

"I still can't see the target."

"Take your best guest."

And then, miraculously, the curtain of smoke thinned enough for me to see the light; and a second after that the seams lined up perfectly in my hand.

It was game time.

I wound up, my right knee riding up toward my chin. My hips rotated forward and I threw a screaming split-finger fastball at the light.

I've thrown thousands upon thousands of pitches since then, but none, in my opinion, had ever been as perfect. It was a frozen rope of speed, a text book pitch, soaring like a comet through the smoke. It had so much zip on it I could hear it zing through the air.

An instant later, the ball struck the red flashing light dead center. A loud plunk broke over the angry hisses from the soul catchers' fire sticks. The ball bounced off the light and fell harmlessly to the ground. The light, creaking like a rusty hinge, swung back and forth from the impact, but remained in tact.

The Crone cackled jubilantly and ordered her soul catchers to lower their fire sticks. "Ho, ho, ho," she laughed. "Too bad for you, Gabriel. Looks like you lose after all." She laughed some more. "Too bad for you..." And as she went to gloat further, a small spark shot out from the bottom of the flashing red light. It fizzled out a second later, so fast in fact, that I thought, *Did that really happen? Did I really see that?*

We stepped up to the roof's edge, waving smoke away with our arms.

Gabriel said, "Did you see—"

Before he could finish the sentence, another spark shot out from the bottom with a sizzling hiss. Then another and another. And within a few seconds a large shower of sparks exploded out the bottom of the fixture.

The Crone screamed "Noooooooooooooooo!" as her power source winked off with a sizzling fizzle.

Suddenly the winded picked up.

Grinning, Gabriel turned to me. "Nice throw, Southpaw. Nice throw."

"The wind?" I asked. "What's happening?"

"Time is starting to fill back in."

"What does that mean exactly?"

"You'll see."

The buildings far off down main street near the cemetery began to creak and groan under the wind. It was as though they had come to life and were wanting to move.

"Noooooooooooooo!" the Crone screamed. "Nooooooooooo!" She danced around in a circle, stamping her feet and waving her arms above her head like some tribal warrior gone mad. "No. No. No. It can't end like this. It can't—I won't let it."

The wind grew stronger, whipping up the loose street dirt, casting the area in a brownish, spinning haze. Roof tiles and pieces of wood got caught up in the wind. They twirled, danced, and spun in the angry, out of control wind. Then buildings began to tear apart, collapsing with ear-splitting bangs and splintering apart into jagged pieces that got caught up in the crazy wind.

As the town tore apart, the spirits gathered by the town square began to disappear. One second they were there; the next second they were gone. They just winked out like a flashbulb from a camera.

The poles holding Cole and Snake's heads blew over. The impact with the ground dislodged the heads and they rolled down the street like bowling balls. With each rotation of his head, Cole cursed and screamed.

The soul catchers turned to dust with loud pops, similar to the sound a light bulb makes when it blows.

The fire consuming the train station blew out as if an invisible giant had blown out a candle.

Lou Purdy and the Crone got caught up in the twirling cloud of dust and disappeared from view.

Then—though I didn't think it was possible—the wind grew even stronger.

"Gabriel, I think we better—"

"I'm way ahead of you, Southpaw," he yelled over the wind's howl. "We have to get off this roof. We have to—"

The roof shuddered under our feet and a loud crack punctuated the wind's howl. The roof sagged and then titled. We fell like dominos and rolled toward the edge. I lost sight of Gabriel as the dirt and wind engulfed us. Then I tumbled off the roof, got tossed in the wind like a leaf, and then, miraculously, landed with a gentle thud on my back in the grass.

I couldn't believe it. I was alive. I was also unhurt.

I sat up and saw Ma standing before me. The howling wind made her soul vibrate.

She smiled, blew me a kiss, mouthed, "I love you" and then disappeared.

"I love you too," I said, then laid back down, curled up in a ball and cried.

(13)

When I was five-years-old a hurricane had blown through Goonberry Gulch. The damage to our spread was minimal—thank the good Lord—but the town was not so lucky. It took the brunt of the storm and the destruction was damn near total. What I saw now looked much similar.

Nary a building was standing. All that was left were piles of splinted sticks. If you were in the market for kindling wood, it was a gold mine.

I climbed to my feet, banging the dust off my clothes, and thought of Ma. I would never see her again and that saddened me beyond belief, but she was outta Limbo, and I suspected in a better place. So how could I not be happy?

"You okay, Southpaw," Gabriel called out suddenly, walking toward me outta the rubble. Aside from his clothes being dirty, he looked unharmed.

I nodded. "How about you?"

"I couldn't be better." He threw his arm around my shoulder and gave it a gentle squeeze. "That was a heckuva pitch," he said. "I'm damn proud of you."

He was about to say something else when he spied something moving ahead in the rubble. He walked up to it; I followed.

Lou Purdy squirmed in the dust like a dying maggot, moaning softly. He was as shriveled as a sponge left out in the sun. His skin, the color of yellow parchment, was so thin in spots you could see a roadmap of red and blue veins. His bald head was covered with age spots and open sores.

"Gee, you don't look so good, Lou," Gabriel said with an aloof disdain, raising a brow at me. "You should take better care of yourself."

Lou stared up at us with sunken, bloodshot eyes. His mouth parted slightly and he wheezed out a faint gurgle as he tried to talk. His front teeth were so loose they swayed back and forth like window shutters. He tried to push them straight with his gummy white tongue but knocked them out instead. Two teeth stuck to his upper lip; two other teeth tumbled over his cracked bottom lip and hung off his chin in a gooey strand of saliva.

"Help," he whispered. "Please help."

"Help?" Gabriel shot back as though it was the stupidest thing he'd ever heard. "How can we help? There isn't a cure for old age."

"That's all that wrong with him?" I asked.

"Limbo was keeping him young," he explained. "With Limbo gone, time has filled back in. He's now the age he's suppose to be, which is damn old by the looks of it. Not that it matters. He'll be dead in a few minutes. The shock of growing old in seconds will stop his heart. I'm actually amazed it hasn't already happened." He shrugged. "Nothing we can do for him." He motioned for me to follow. "C'mon, let's see how the Crone is doing."

A minute later we found her...well, we found what was left of her. She lay on her back about twenty yards away from Lou, partially hidden by a section of roof. She was stiff as stale bread and as old looking as an Egyptian mummy. Her mouth was frozen open in a scream.

"My, my," Gabriel muttered. "She isn't looking too good either." He laughed, crouched beside her, and with his thumb, scratched along her forearm, turning up a sawdust type cloud that he blew away with one puff. He looked up at me. "She's as dry and rough as sandpaper." He stood. "I dare say she's going to need a moisturizer."

"Is she dead?"

"Oh, she's dead alright," he replied. "In fact, she'll be completely gone in a couple of days. Even less if it rains, which it looks like it's going to do."

At the mention of that, I looked skyward. The entire sky was as gray as a battleship. I figured Gabriel was right. It was gonna rain, which was fine with me. A little rain never hurt anyone. Sides, I would rather walk in the rain then the dadgum heat.

Gabriel bent over, grabbed the amulet from around the Crone's neck and yanked on it. The necklace held firm, and with a muted puff, sliced through her neck, ripping her head clean off her body.

"Oh my," Gabriel mocked, watching as her head lolled back and forth in the dirt. "She's falling to pieces." He laughed at his wit and pocketed the amulet.

It started to spit rain then, and a gentle breeze whistled up the street, making the debris creak and groan. It spooked the heck outta me, and if Gabriel had not been with me I would have run for the woods.

We walked to the graveyard and surveyed the damage. The stone fence was littered about in a thousands pieces. The gravestones were gone; the ground torn up as though a backhoe had been at work.

"My colleagues souls have escaped," Gabriel said with satisfaction. "My job here is done. Now I can go home and get some sleep."

That sounded like a great idea, and as I went to say just that, the wind kicked up and outta nowhere my Yankee baseball cap tumbled down the street toward us. Where it had come from I couldn't say. I scooped it up and held it out to Gabriel.

"I'd like you to have it."

He raised both brows at me. "Really?"

"I can't wear it," I explained. "I'm a southern boy. People would poke fun at me."

He put the cap on his head and adjusted the bill to the proper angle. "I'll wear it often," he promised. "And when I come see you pitch, I'll wear it."

"What makes you think I'll pitch again?"

"Oh, you'll pitch again. I'm certain of it, Southpaw. You'll be in the big leagues and when you get there, I'll come and watch you pitch. I promise."

It would have been rude to doubt him, so I merely smiled.

He put his arm over my shoulders. "Do you want me to walk you home?"

"Are you going the same way?"

He shook his head. "I'm back this way." He pointed toward the vastness I had seen from the roof once the train had left. "But I'll walk you home if you like."

"Naw, I'll be okay."

"How long will it take you to get home?"

"All going well, it'll take about eight to ten hours to get to Route 9. I can hitch from there. If I'm lucky, I might make it home as early as tonight."

He nodded and stood before me, his hands buried in the pockets of his leather trench coat. "Okay Southpaw, I guess it's time for us to part company." He put a hand on my shoulder. "I don't give advice too often but I will pass along four secrets of life. Rule number one: Have faith in God; but don't wait for Him to do everything for you. Do it yourself. Which leads to rule number two: Have faith in yourself. That leads me to rule number three: Don't let your brain tell you what to do—you run your brain." He shook my hand. "Thanks for saving the day."

"You said there were four rules."

"Oh yeah, the last one is mine: only the catcher should wear his cap backwards."

I grinned. "I didn't think that was a problem."

"Trust me, Southpaw. One day it will be." With that said, he waved and started off toward what remained of the train station. I watched him for a moment, and then, just as I was about to turn and leave, he turned back to me. "Remember to look for me in the stands, Southpaw." He adjusted the brim of his new cap, waved, turned and walked away.

I thought I would never see him again.

I was wrong.

(14)

It rained on and off for the rest of the day, spiting really, as though the sky couldn't make up its mind on what it wanted to do. But that changed when I reached the spot in the path that runs outside the tree line. When I got there and could see Route 9 off in the distance, the skies opened up as if another Great Flood was happening. It came down so hard I could barely see five feet in front of me.

I was soaked to the skin in seconds, and getting a ride soaking wet, I figured, might be a problem. Who wants a wet car seat, after all? Still, I had to hope some good citizen would take pity on a teenage boy. Of course for that to happen there had to be traffic, which there wasn't. Route 9 was as deserted.

Instead of standing on the shoulder waiting for a car to come by I started walking. I soon filed past road marker 43. If no one stopped to pick me up, I had approximately a 40 mile walk ahead of me.

As I started to calculate how long that might take, a car horn honked behind me. I whirled about at once. The car looked familiar, but this was the 40's remember, and back then pretty near every car looked the same.

Rain streaked the windows so all I could see was a blurred, dark figure behind the wheel. Whoever was driving was mighty big, and that mighty big figure leaned over and rolled down the passenger's window.

Sheriff Nibbs removed the chewed up toothpick from his mouth and stared at me though narrow slits. "Need a ride, boy?" he asked sourly.

I was too tired to run. Sides, according to the Pastor he had promised to hold off taking me to the orphanage until after Ma's funeral so I figured he would just drive me to the Pastor's house, which was where I was headed anyway. I climbed in the passenger side and shut the door.

"Sure was lucky you happened by."

"Weren't no luck at all," he said gruffly. "I knew yuh be here at this time."

"Huh? How so?"

Leaving the car idling in neutral, he reached into the backseat and retrieved a thin, package wrapped in brown paper. It was the shape of a wall-hanging pitcher, approximately 18 inches by 24 inches, and an inch thick. "This is for yuh," he said, putting the package on my lap. "I found this on the windshield of my car this mornin.'"

Written in black marker across the face of the package was the following message:

Dear Sheriff Nibbs,
Please pick up Johnny 'Southpaw' McGrath, 6:00 P.M. Route 9, marker 43.Please give him this package. Fondly, Betty Zuckerman.

Beneath the message was a message for me.

Dear Southpaw,
Thanks for spending time with me yesterday. Thanks for saying 'hey' to John. Here's a little something to remember me by. Love always, Betty Zuckerman XOXO

Nibbs opened his pocket watch and showed me its face. "As yuh can see, yer right on time." He closed the watch, slipped it back in his pocket and looked me in the eye. "Do yuh care to explain?"

"I don't think I can."

"Try."

"Well..."

"Have yuh been up to that place?"

"What place?"

"Don't get cute with me, boy. I'm still sore at yuh for runnin' off on me the other day. Now yuh know what place I'm talkin' about. Have yuh been up there? Maybe lookin' for yer Ma?"

Since he was acquainted with Limbo, and would need no explanation as to what it was, I simply nodded.

"I see," he returned curtly, and stabbed a thick digit at the package. "Open it."

I did as he ordered, tearing back the brown paper to reveal an oil painting of the schoolhouse on a summer day. Though the light in the cab was dim, it was clearly a Betty Zuckerman work, for the style was exactly like her painting of the Pastor's church, which currently hung on the Pastor's office wall. Unlike the church painting, though, Betty had included people in this painting. It was clearly Ma standing at the door to schoolhouse, waving at a group of children to come inside.

I gulped and sniffled back tears.

"Get a hold of yer self, boy."

I swallowed hard, and tore off the rest of the brown paper, revealing the entire painting. Sure enough, Betty's signature was in the bottom left hand corner. Beneath her name was the date: August 3rd, 1944.

"It's a-mighty beautiful paintin'," Nibbs pointed out. "Do yuh mind explainin' how someone who is hold up in the woods is paintin' pictures? And how that someone—with no transportation might I add—was able to deliver the paintin' to me, and accurately say when yuh be walkin' outta the woods?"

"If I told you what I think, you'd say I was crazy."

"Maybe not," he shot back. "Remember boy, my family has lived in these parts since the 1800's. So I know things. I've seen things. Strange things. So I doubt there's anythin' yuh can say that will shock me much. So start a talkin'. And I want the truth."

"To be honest Sheriff, I'm not really sure how she managed to paint a picture and deliver it to you. And as for knowing when I'd make the road? Well...I didn't even know when I'd get here."

He turned off the car's engine. "The message said yuh saw Betty yesterday."

"That's right."

"Where?"

"Up the trail."

"Is she okay?"

"Uh..."

"What is it, boy?"

"Betty is dead. Cameron Mitty is dead, too. I found them both on the trail. Looks like they shot each other."

Nibbs heaved a sigh that got stuck in his throat and tears welled up in his eyes. He turned and looked out the driver's window to hide his tears from me.

I knew Nibbs was friendly with the Zuckermans, but I didn't know he was friendly enough to weep over Betty's demise.

I heard him whisper, "Damn yuh to Hell, Valentine." He sighed bitterly, dried his eyes with an old hanky, cleared his throat and turned to me. "Did yuh see it happen?"

I shook my head. "I think they had been dead for a few days."

"It says yuh spent time with her yesterday." He gestured at the picture on my lap. "The date on the picture was yesterday as well."

"As I said, if I told you, you'd think I was crazy."

"Try me."

"I think I spent time with her spirit."

"I see," he said quietly. "Go on."

"A bear was about to eat me for lunch when she came by and scared it off. She took me to her campsite. We talked. Had lunch. She showed me where she buried her husband. That's when she told me about shooting Cameron Mitty. Then she directed me toward Limbo. Told me to say 'hey' to her husband if I saw him there. A few minutes later, up the trail, I ran into their bodies. They were about thirty feet apart."

He chewed nervously on his toothpick. "The message said yuh saw John Zuckerman. He at Limbo?"

I nodded.

"Yuh saw him from the graveyard?"

I shook my head. "I went in and spoke to him."

"Oh?" he muttered. "I've been led to believe that once yuh crossover, yuh can't come back. Do yuh care to elaborate on how yuh got out?"

"I crossed over at the graveyard and came back the same way," I said truthfully, deciding not to elaborate on what went on in between.

He raised a brow at me. "How is that so?"

"I don't know."

"Yuh sure got lucky, boy."

"I don't think I'm lucky at all."

"Oh, I think yuh are," he said. "Yuh just don't know it yet."

I didn't know what he was getting at, and frankly, didn't care cuz I suddenly remembered I had a message for him. "Mr. Zuckerman wanted me to tell you that he has a safety deposit box in a Jackson bank."

"Is that right?"

I gave him the bank's address and the number of the box.

"Just what am I gonna find in there?" he asked, chewing nervously on his toothpick.

Though I knew the answer, I shrugged, playing dumb in the event Nibbs still had a strong alliance with Mayor Valentine. Knowing too much could be dangerous and I didn't want to end up in a ditch with a bullet in my head. .

"Okay," he muttered. "Since we gotta go to Jackson tomorrow anyway, I'll check it out."

"Jackson? Why there? The orphanage is in Vicksburg."

"We have to go to the train station," he said, smiling around his toothpick. "The Pastor is going too so yuh can hitch a ride with him if yuh like. Maybe yer girl will wanna go too. I can take all the Koreans in my car."

"The Yume family?"

"That's right. The Pastor is gonna put them on the train to New York."

"They made it?" I cut in, amazed. "That's good. Real good."

"They ain't the only ones that made it. See boy, after we put the Yumes on the train to New York, we have to hang around for the Norfolk train to arrive. There's someone on that train that's mighty anxious to see yuh."

"Huh?"

"Yer Pa is coming home."

I opened my mouth to talk but no sound came out.

"Yep, he made it. He got his legs shot up stormin' the beach in June. He just got back stateside yesterday. Called me up, wantin' to know about yuh and yer Ma. I had to break the news to him about yer Ma. That really threw him for a loop. I told him, I'd hunt yuh down and have yuh at the train station to meet him. He sure the heck is gonna be happy to see yuh."

I found my voice. "I can't believe it."

"He told me he's walkin' with a cane but will be good as new in a few months." He shrugged. "It's too late to save the farm, but at least yuh got yer Pa back."

"I can't believe it," I repeated, truly dumbfounded.

"Yuh know, boy, yer Pa and I go way back. If I had the money, I'd lend it to him so he could save his farm. But I ain't got that kinda money. The

Pastor does. But from what I hear he wants to expand across the street and takeover yer spread. It pains me to see him do it, but what can we do? He's the one with all the money."

"Not all of it."

Sheriff Nibbs raised a brow at me. "What are yuh talkin' about, boy?"

"Tell me Sheriff, is there a reward for the recovery of the money the Conklin Gang stole?"

"I believe there is," he returned, eyeing me suspiciously. "Do yuh know somethin' yuh shouldn't know, boy?"

"Mr. Zuckerman was not the only spirit I talked to in Limbo."

Nibbs grinned. "Like I said before, boy, it seems like yer damn lucky."

EPILOGUE—2005

Ben shifted in the armchair. "That's a heckuva story, granddad."

I motioned at the Betty Zuckerman painting propped up beside me on the sofa. "Thanks to this, the story all came back to me."

"So what happened?" he asked anxiously. "Did ya find the money in Kirby Fellows grave? And what about Mayor Valentine? Was there enough evidence in John Zuckerman's safety deposit box to bring him to justice?"

I nodded. "Nibbs had the Feds open the safety deposit box and a couple days later, the DA issued a warrant for the Mayor's arrest. Nibbs tipped him off that they were coming, though."

"Why?"

"To gloat, I figure. Remember, Nibbs took a heckuva lot of abuse from the Mayor over the years. He took it cuz he had to in order to keep his job and feed his family."

"It's a person of weak moral fiber who'll abuse a man who can't fight back."

I laughed. "Where did you learn that?"

"Grandma."

That made me laugh even harder.

"So what happened to the Mayor? He flee to Mexico?"

"Naw. He took the coward's way out. Hung himself with a bed sheet."

Ben shook his head in dismay. "I guess breaking up a gravestone and leaving the pieces in front of a fella's house is bad luck after all. Not only did the Mayor's boys die, all his misdeeds got found out and he had to do himself in."

I shrugged. "I don't think John Zuckerman's broken up gravestone had anything to do with it. Mayor Valentine had it coming—and it came. Remember Ben, the worm always turns. It's just the way life is. You get what you give—and boy, he sure got it."

"True. But he did avoid the shame of a trail. And the town's anger."

"I suppose. Taking the coward's way out saved him from that. From what I remember, his wife took the brunt of the abuse for the whole no-good family. In fact, the town refused to let her bury her two army-deserting sons and embezzling husband in the Goonberry Gulch Cemetery. She had to bury them over in the Squirrel Flats Cemetery. Their resting spots are not all that far from Kirby Fellows grave."

"Was the money there?"

"It must have been," I returned. "Cuz a few days after Pa returned home our money troubles suddenly went away. Our spread was completely paid off by an anonymous donor, something that really bothered your great great grandfather. The Pastor lived into his late nineties and went to his grave wondering who that donor was."

"Does Grandma know?"

"Word of advice, Ben, never keep anything from your better half."

"I'll try and remember that," he said, looking puzzled. "So those two ghosts I saw fighting at the cemetery—Conklin and Snake—they're fighting over money that ain't there, over money that got returned?"

"I never said the money got returned."

"Nibbs kept it?"

"Some of it, I suppose. Just to help smooth out the rough edges. The rest he divvied up, doing it cloak and dagger style so no one would know where the money was coming from. I'm happy to say he found Betty Zuckerman's gold medal. And if you ever want to see it, you can go to the Mississippi Sport's Hall Of Fame in Jackson and have a gander."

"Did Nibbs pay for John Zuckerman's tombstone, too?"

"That same anonymous donor that saved our spread did. And that same person paid for Betty's tombstone as well. They're resting beside each other up in the woods."

"If I ever hike up there I'll have a gander for myself."

"Yeah, Nibbs did okay with the money. He paid off our farm, donated some to the hospital in Ma's honor and paid for a statue of Betty

Zuckerman that's currently standing in the town's library." I shrugged. "All and all, well spent money."

"And Gabriel? What about him? Did he show up to watch ya pitch?"

""Twenty years later," I said. "The funny thing was by the time he did come to see me pitch I had pretty near forgotten about him. See, at first, when I made it to the pros, I'd search for him up in the stands every time I took the mound. But as the years went by, I thought of him less and less until he was completely outta my mind. Then, in my final year in the majors, as I took the mound for my last official start, he showed up."

"He was in Cleveland? He saw ya throw yer gem?"

"He sure picked a good time to come," I went on. "It was mid-September, and I was tired and just wanted the season to be over so I could get home with your Grandma. We had five youngins by then—your daddy a new born—and your Grandma certainly could use the help. I had a teaching job lined up at the high school in Possum Hollow and my mind was focused on that."

"Were ya still in the starting rotation?"

"Naw. My talents had been fading and though I was still good enough to be in the pros, our manager, Arty 'the fart' Ambross had delegated me to the bullpen. I'd pitch middle relief. Getting an inning or two in each week. Then came Cleveland."

"Was the team still in the hunt?" Ben asked, leaning forward in the chair, interested as a scientist watching an atom divide.

I nodded. "We had an outside chance for the playoffs. I think we were five, maybe six games off the lead with fifteen to play. So it was possible. Not likely, but possible."

"Cleveland was in it, too?"

I nodded. "They were a couple games outta first, I believe. So it was an important series for them. We lost Friday night's game. Got slaughtered from what I remember. On Saturday, it rained like the dickens and it was decided we'd play two games on Sunday. Arty 'the fart' came up to me Saturday night in the hotel and said he wanted me to start the late game so he could rest our best pitcher, Burt 'the beast' Bonhomme, for the upcoming series against Baltimore. He said if I could last five innings he'd kiss me on the lips."

Ben chuckled.

"I told him I wasn't partial to mustaches. Or men for that matter. And that if I did last five innings he could simply shake my hand and be done with it." I shrugged. "Course I didn't think I'd be able to pull off five innings. Cleveland had a helluva lotta good sluggers, and my arm was only good for a couple of innings. Three at the most."

"Guess ya didn't know yer arm so well."

"I suppose. The funny thing was, when I took the mound, I didn't even think I'd last two innings. See, I didn't sleep well that night. Never did when I was starting. And my arm felt as stiff as a 2 by 4. I was just happy it was an away game cuz at least your Grandma wouldn't be there with the youngins to see me fall flat on my face."

"Did she listen to it on the radio?"

I nodded. "And that was a damn odd thing, too. See, she normally didn't listen, cuz hey, I didn't pitch that often, and she wasn't all that interested in listening to other people play. But that Sunday, after she brought the youngins home from church, she flipped on the radio, mostly just to get the score. She told me later she damn near keeled over when she heard the announcer say I was heading out to the mound for the first inning."

"She heard history being made."

"I suppose," I said, shrugging. "A heckuva lotta people sure witnessed it. A sell-out from what I understand. It sure looked like it too. Cuz you couldn't a squeezed a fart into the stands with a mallet there were so many people. It was a beautiful day, too. Warm and sunny. Perfect for baseball."

I paused there, and Ben said, "Go on. Go on."

"We played the first game starting at noon and dropped it by half a dozen runs. At four that afternoon, I took to the mound. I don't think I'd ever been that nervous—and my pitching showed it, too. I walked the first three batters on twelve consecutive pitches. Arty 'the fart' was dying in the dugout, pacing back and forth like a dog in a round room looking for a corner to pee in. He kept yelling out to me to settle down."

"Easier said then done, right?"

"That's for sure," I agreed. "Anyway, with the bases loaded, I had their top hitter at the plate—a Cuban kid named De Castro. He was a big strapping kid with an ego to match. He stepped into the batter's box and laughed at me, daring me to throw one down the center of the plate. I was a might smarter than that of course, and pitched him outside—way outside. He let the count go to 3-0. I was about to walk in a run when I heard over the buzz of the crowd, 'Hey Southpaw, throw me a strike'. Though I hadn't heard his voice in twenty years, I knew instantly who it was."

"Could you see him in the crowd?"

"He was a couple of rows up from the Cleveland dugout, surrounded by hostile Cleveland fans. Where he got the ticket from I can't say. But there he was, cheering for us in the middle of that hostile mass of humanity. And, as promised, he was wearing the Yankee cap I'd give him."

"And…and…what did he do?"

"He stood up and waved at me. Though twenty years had passed he hadn't changed a bit. He was wearing a t-shirt and jeans this time, and of course the Yankee cap.

"What did you do? Didn't that break yer concentration?"

"I can't say I had much concentration at that point in the game anyway. I do remember breaking out in Goosebumps then, and for some reason, seeing him rejuvenated me. I felt reborn. I also felt unstoppable. I stepped up on the rubber then and threw a screamer down the center of the plate. I can still see the puzzled look on De Castro's ugly face when the ump yelled 'strike'. De Castro was a pro, mind you, and after taking a couple of practice swings, settled back in, a determined look on his face. When I struck him out on consecutive pitches I thought he was gonna cry. Then I struck out the side. From then on I owned them. No ball made it out of the infield. In fact, I got so caught up in my pitching I forgot I was throwing a no-hitter. I only realized it in the top of the eighth cuz no one would sit near me or talk to me. All the guys were crammed up at one end of the dugout as though I had the Typhoid."

"Did ya talk to Gabriel after the game?"

I shook my head. "When I struck out the last batter I was mobbed by the team. When all the backslapping was over, I looked up into the stands. He stood by the tunnel entrance, gave me the thumbs up, mouthed, 'Goodbye Southpaw' and disappeared into the crowd. I knew I'd never see him again, which, is okay, I suppose. We shared a time together. Not a fun time, of course, but as odd as this sounds, he made